MARY-CLARLE

LE

SWAN

STORY ABOUT A BETTER

AND HAPPIER LIFE

To Sue and Ken

Thank you for all
your help, support
and love.

I love you both so
much

xxxxx

1.

Once upon a time, far far away… maybe I could start my tale like this. Maybe it's just a tale… maybe it's more. What's certain is that it's about a girl, a girl who was looking for love and happiness, and found thousands of wonders along the way. But let's not rush that far. Everything in its proper time and order, since time is of crucial importance… time…

Molly Stevens was an ordinary middle-aged woman in her early thirties. As every other woman of her age, she was full of doubts and inhibitions. One would think that after a certain age we would grow out of every little phobia we have, but then we slowly realise that this is not how it is. It should be otherwise, but it still is not. Essentially everything depends on self-confidence. Some have more, some have less, but nobody doubts that they have some. Of course, there are extreme cases where one has too much or almost none… only enough for bare survival. Molly belonged to this latter group. She was a woman who liked to remain invisible; she wanted to lead a life so that nothing marked her out from others. She wanted to be a little mouse hiding in the corner, so nobody would notice her, even by accident. After a time, she honed this skill to perfection, and she virtually disappeared from the world. She was there, and yet she wasn't. Living, learning, working... existing, and with every day she awaited the end of her existence. In the mornings when she woke up, she looked up to the sky, let out a heart-breaking sigh and said the following, really quietly:

'Another day. Another miserable, godforsaken day. My Lord, why don't you let this end? Why are you still punishing me? Why do I have do continue to suffer, why don't you let me come home? Why can't it be over already?'

She wasn't religious - or at least she didn't belong to any of the religious denominations. She didn't believe in the doctrines of the churches established by people, rather she just accepted them. She knew that everybody needed some help, something to help them survive. We need faith. Everybody should believe in what they want to, what they feel to be closest to their hearts. She had faith, too... in God, Angels, but in her own silent way. She believed in love, too. She knew that true love existed, that strong feeling that conquers all, which she longed for. She knew this because she had dreamt about it once. She didn't know who the man was. She couldn't, because she had never met him... yet she knew everything about him. She was looking for that powerful, upsetting and painful feeling everywhere – but she couldn't find it.

Within her thirty years she had had her fair share of relationships, none of which had ended too happily. Now, who are we kidding? Each and every one of them was a disaster. She had always managed to find someone to whom she could apply the 'egotistic bastard' term later on. Every relationship she had had followed this pattern: someone accidentally noticed her, and started to compliment her body, her looks, her beautiful eyes, or her beautiful face. Molly always laughed at them initially: me, being beautiful and hot? Come on, I've been having weight problems since I was a little girl. Molly wasn't fat – or thin either, she was... rounded.

Her face and eyes were actually pretty, if she wanted to look pretty – but she didn't want to. She had freckles, and she hated them since she had been bullied as a kid because of them. She always wore her long, brown hair in a knot because it annoyed her – but she didn't want to have it cut short either. Her height was average. She didn't see anything special in herself, therefore she never understood why people complimented her. But those who persisted in their ideas about her beauty, and who continued unceasingly, were admitted into Molly's little closed world. Usually everything was fine in the first months. They paid attention to her, gave her flowers and gifts, she received compliments, and was taken to dinners, to the

3

cinema, or to the theatre. On each and every occasion she believed they loved her. She always believed that the current man could be the One, that she had found the man she saw in her dreams – the man she loved so much that it hurt. She did everything for her 'love'. She gave herself up again and again, doing everything she could to make her partners happy; worked, did the laundry, ironed, cooked, cleaned, did the shopping – she wanted to be the perfect partner. After 5 or 6 months, the problems came in every case. The gifts and the flowers ceased to appear, they didn't go to the movies or to the theatre anymore, and they stopped being nice to her. She became a mere maid. It became perfectly natural that she did literally everything, and then things escalated to a level that if she skipped or forgot something, suddenly she was a good-for-nothing lazy cow. She felt like a slave. She was unhappy. By then, she knew that she didn't feel the love, only wanted to. She just wanted to believe that she was loveable, and that she had found the man she was waiting for. But still, she wouldn't end the relationship. She didn't dare, because she was afraid of solitude, of what would happen if she were to be alone. When her friends and relatives begged her to leave the man who was ruining her life, she only said:

'I guess this is just what I deserve. I'm sure I did something wrong to deserve this.'

She remained in the relationship and closed out the world. She became a little mouse yet again. She endured the hits, then when no one saw her, she cried. Some beatings were so cruel that she couldn't go outside or to work for days. On these occasions, she lied that she was ill – her voice actually sounded like she was ill from all the crying. Only a few people knew the truth. They knew, but they didn't help. They didn't help, because they knew it was no good. They watched idly and helplessly as she ruined herself, saying, 'It's not your fault, believe us, you are loveable' over and over again. But she didn't believe them. Why would she, when life had proven otherwise on every occasion? Every relationship ended the same way: the man left. Usually without any message or saying goodbye, they simply walked out of the door, and Molly collapsed. She felt wretched, a nobody. She cried for days, and when she ran out of tears she returned to her empty life, and waited for the miracle to happen. She waited for the reason for her existence. To find out the reason for all this suffering. She knew that there was a reason, since everything happens for a reason. She knew, because she had read about it somewhere, and despite all the disappointments, she still believed it all the same. When she was really desperate, she stood in front of the mirror, and yelled into the face of that nobody standing there that 'EVERYTHING HAPPENS FOR A

REASON'… Then quaveringly, barely audibly, she whispered: 'Even your existence has a purpose…'

After the last breakup, Molly was completely shattered and had no idea how to move on. She felt that she couldn't handle another breakup, so she was determined that this was it: no more relationships. She had heard the saying, 'You don't have to force something that is not meant to be' quite a few times. And this was obviously not meant to be. Of course, friends and relatives came and said, 'No worries, little girl… maybe the next one will be better, not like this. He will love you and you'll see that everything's going to be fine.' And every other cliché revolving around 'next time.' But what else could they say? They couldn't just tell her, 'Just don't bother, it's not for you', 'You'll be better off alone', or even 'You should get a puppy instead.' But actually, this was the truth… or the experience, rather. She had quite a lot friends who lived like that. They had dogs, cats, parrots, snakes, frogs… yet they were lonely still.

So, there must be something wrong with all this. Some error in the system – the question was just What was it? And the other question was Who could help, and who could answer the questions? She decided that she would get to the bottom of this. She bought the best books on spirituality, read a ton of articles on the web, visited countless specialists, but still found no answer to the great questions. She learned a lot, and gained even more experiences – not necessarily positive. She sadly had to realise that desperate people like her were being fooled. They went to get help, and they were told what they wanted to hear for a good price - and of course nothing changed. The 'specialists' made them believe that their prince on a white horse would arrive, or that they would get a lot of money, or their dream job, or that they would have a football team's worth of children… depending on what each person wanted to hear. And what was all this about? Money. You can't find a single spark of the willingness to help others in many people. The whole thing is just a huge scam. Molly too had met several of these people calling themselves 'clairvoyants' or 'specialists.' She heard them out and then left disappointed. She had no idea from where and from whom she could get answers. No matter how many books, articles, con-artists or not con-artists – no answers. Of course, there were questions, more and more each day, but the answers were yet to arrive. The constant failure, and seeing people being cheated out of their money, made her even more disappointed. Relatives, friends, and colleagues all watched Molly's desperate struggle anxiously, all of them being afraid that this might end in a tragedy. When they voiced their concerns, she answered with loud laughter, -however, not with the happy, joyous kind but of that painful kind that wrenches the heart and makes one want to cry.

'Me, committing suicide? There's a lot of problems with suicide, biggest one being that it makes no sense. I'll leave when they've had their fun with me up there, and I don't think that'll happen in the foreseeable future.'

And she went on living her empty, grey life: waking up in the morning, going to work, then going home late in the evening, taking a bath and going to sleep. Next day she would do it all over again. She neglected her friends and relatives, and wasn't interested in anyone. After a while, it got to a point where she saw everything in grey. She saw and felt it if the sun was shining, but the light no longer reached her soul. Inside she was always grey skies and rain.

She could've asked for help: she could have gone to a psychologist, so that they would listen to her for a high hourly rate and maybe would prescribe some weak sedative for her. But it wouldn't have been of much use - maybe only that it would have made her addicted to the drugs. But no answer would have come.

One day, when it seemed there was no hope, she found a bar of white chocolate on her desk with a note on it with a name, a phone number, and a short message saying, 'They say that the girl knows what's what, try it out' on it. She had no idea what it might be that 'the girl' was good at. At first, she thought it was a joke, or that they had put it on the wrong desk, and it was meant for one of her nymphomaniac colleagues, not her. She even had some nasty ideas about who, with whom, what and how they could be doing it – which made her laugh loudly and whole-heartedly. For the first time in a long while. She was even surprised how good it felt, what an uplifting feeling it was… better than any medicine. But then she wondered: is this really some sort of joke – or if it wasn't even meant for her… then for whom? And why chocolate? And white, in addition – her favourite. Everyone knew that she could be coaxed to do anything with a bar of white chocolate.

She had a tremendous amount of work that day. That is why she had to go into the office earlier than usual. When every normal person was still just in the process of waking up, she was already preparing for meetings. But she didn't mind. It was peaceful and quiet. She took the note and put it in her bag. She thought that she would call the number in her lunch break. She was really curious what it was that the girl was good at, and she thought it was worth a phone call. What could she lose? Worst case scenario was that she would have another good laugh. Of course, she didn't call it in the end – she worked through her lunch break. The meeting lasted longer, then the next one began. When she was finished with everything it was late in the evening. She got home very late and very tired.

'Well, tomorrow, then,' she thought. Then she forgot to call the next day. And in the days and weeks following that too. She was so overwhelmed with work in that period that she had no time for anything, often not even to eat properly. Being always pushed, the continuous rush and the inadequate meals took their toll and she got so sick that she couldn't even get out of bed. Her doctor – who happened to be a good friend of old – ordered a whole week of rest in bed. He promised to visit his patient again a week later. When he returned, he found a zombie. He literally had to wade through piles of paper and the general mess in the room.

'What's all this?' he asked. 'I thought I told you that you needed rest.'

'I'm lying in bed. Can't you see?' said the pale character who somewhat resembled Molly – but the doctor wasn't so sure about this.

'Molly,' he began with feigned calm, 'lying in bed and resting is not the same, you should know. I told you that you have to rest.'

'I lay for a whole day, doing nothing. Just as you told me to. It was quite boring. Then my boss called. He said that he knew that I was sick but he only needed a little help. I knew you'd be angry, but... I had to. So I agreed. Five minutes later he was here with the first stack.' She pointed at her desk with a shaking hand and, continuing in a wavering voice, she said: 'An hour later he came back with the second heap you see on the ground. Tomorrow he'll bring the rest.'

'But...'

'Please, John, don't... I know perfectly well that I'm insane, you don't have to keep reminding me of it. You have to understand that even if I thought I was apart for a bit, the world and the company moved on. I have to work, since a lot of people's work and living depends on what I do. I can't rest, especially in times like these, when our competitors file for bankruptcy one after the other. These people count on me, I can't let them down. I'll write the reports, then I'll prepare the...'

'Molly, why are you scratching your chin?' John interrupted.

'I don't know, but it's not important. It'll stop, it always stops.'

'What do you mean by "always"?'

11

'John…'

'Don't John me! What's this again? How long have you experienced it, but more importantly… why the hell didn't you tell me about it?'

'John, please, don't yell at me,' said the girl, barely audibly. Her face was paler than usual, she was having difficulties with breathing, tears were running down her cheeks. She jumped out of the bed, pushed the man who was approaching her aside and opened the windows so more fresh air could get into the room. 'Crap… this usually helps,' she said gasping. 'I can't breathe… damn it! I can't breathe...' she tried to yell, but no sound came out her mouth. Her chest hurt, she felt sharp, stinging pain in her heart, and suddenly everything she ever knew ceased to exist. She felt light as a feather, she was calm and felt no pain. She breathed, existed – yet she didn't at the same time. She heard voices, but only from afar. Like someone was crying out her name, like someone was cursing – maybe it was John. But she wasn't sure about that – and it didn't matter anyway. She lay with closed eyes and rested. She enjoyed this unbelievable, completely perfect tranquillity that she had never experienced before and which embraced and rocked her. She seemed to float in nothing and in everything. It was completely familiar, yet something new at the same

12

time. She started to wonder how much time might have passed, how long she had been lying there – but it didn't really matter. It was more of a habit, an everyday practice, but she didn't feel it was important. Sometimes the voices around her grew louder, or seemed to come from more sources, but that didn't matter either. She lay and rested. She enjoyed this gift – the tranquillity she had always longed for.

'Hello, Molly.'

This voice was different from the others. It sounded closer and was familiar. She knew she had heard it often, but didn't know where. She tried to open her eyes – it was a difficult task. Everything was different, the rules of physics didn't apply here.

'Take your time,' said the familiar voice, 'we are not in a hurry.'

'That's good news,' she laughed, and she was surprised how good it felt. Similar to last time, but still different.

'Can I help you?'

'I'd appreciate that. I feel quite helpless.'

'Don't worry, that's natural. Do not "want" to move, will has no power here. At first, it's difficult, but you'll get used to it.'

'Where is "here"?' asked the girl, as her eyes slowly opened. A man was sitting by her side. He had short, blondish, wavy hair. His face and nose were nicely shaped, his full lips were smiling at her gently. The colour of his eyes was hard to determine – as though when he was born God couldn't decide that if blue or green would suit him better, so he decided on something in-between. They reminded her of the sea. His build was hard to determine. He was tall – this was obvious even with him sitting. He wore a long, white cloak, a white sweater, and white trousers. All in all, by the standard of humans, it could be said that he was perfect. But it wasn't his pleasing looks or soothing deep voice that fascinated the girl, but the unending, never before experienced kindness and tranquillity emanating from him. Nothing fake, not a sliver of hypocrisy could be felt in him.

'Who are you? Why are you so familiar to me? Especially your voice. I don't remember seeing you before… at least I'm not sure. I feel that I know you and that I don't at the same time. I'm confused.'

'I see that,' he said as he continued smiling. 'But don't worry. We will look at and discuss everything. You'll get the answers for every question. My name is Noah, I'm your guardian angel. My voice is familiar to you because I talk to you a lot – you give me reason to. Making me work quite hard, you know.'

'Understood.'

'However, before we go anywhere or do anything, there is something very important you have to know: usually you don't have to say what you feel or think. Because what you feel, I do, too. You don't have to be afraid or ashamed of this. We've been doing this for a long time. Believe me, I know some things even you don't.'

'Oh,' she said, blushing.

'I said don't be ashamed.' Noah's smile was even more gentle and understanding than before, which made Molly blush even more. 'You are starting to look similar to a lobster,' he laughed. 'I tell you, there is nothing wrong with this, you'll get used to it soon. Even if you don't, it's not a problem. The red colour of your cheeks suits you. And now, if you're ready, you should sit up. Before you do that, I'll tell you where we are so that you won't get scared. Right now, we are still in your room. You don't have to be afraid of anything. I'm here to protect you, everything is fine, even if it seems otherwise. How many times have you said that appearances can be deceiving? Now you'll learn how right you were. Now, if you are ready, let's begin. Remember, this is exactly the same as when you opened your eyes. Do not want, but feel. Your will cannot be used here, since it's not with you. You have to feel it. Anything you want to do, feel. It isn't easy at first, but I know that you can do it. You always could.'

'That is comforting,' she laughed. She was surprised by it yet again. How little she had laughed recently, even though it felt so good.

'Yes. It feels like it fills your soul with energy. Which, by the way, is exactly what happens.'

'Okay, this is funny,' she laughed again.

'I told you that you don't have to say everything out loud, only if you'd like to hear the sound of your voice. I can feel your thoughts. But now, if you feel ready, try to sit up. I know it's difficult, because we've already done this several times. Back and forth, to be honest. And I have to admit that, even though I don't really want to, it is always easier for you than me.' She pouted as a response. 'Yes, you always do that,' he said grinning. 'Let me explain something to you, it'll make it easier. Everyone receives their bodies with the "ego." Others call it the superior self, but because we don't always agree with the little bastard, we will call him simply ego, all lowercase. The ego is a necessary evil. It helps you to control your body. If you are hungry, it sends a message – or will – to your body to go and get food. If you are thirsty you drink, if you're cold you put on more clothes, if you're hot you take them off. He is responsible for the daily routines, too. You wake up, you go to work, pay your bills, go on with your business, you go home and go to sleep. You want it and your body obeys. You could say that, hey, the brain is in control. What I would say is that the brain is the headquarters of the little bastard, where he controls from. Just think about it. You take a body, put some organs in it, link it to the brain, but nothing happens. You need all the rest: the ego, the soul and the spirit. The four of them add up to a perfect whole.'

'If it is part of a perfect whole, then why are you so mad at it?' she asked as she sat up. Which she immediately regretted, and tried to lie back down quickly, but Noah didn't let her. He put an arm around her shoulders and smiled so gently and reassuringly that Molly decided to stay sitting. 'You know this is quite scary.'

'Which part is the scariest?' Noah said, still smiling.

'Every part. I'm sitting in nothing… in the air. Below me, if we can say it like this, lies my lifeless body, and John and a whole bunch of strangers trying to resuscitate me.'

'Yeah, this can be a bit difficult as a start. But try to think of it as an adventure. As a learning process. You wanted answers, you have your first. That is your body.'

'What's going to happen to it? I mean, to me? Is my time over?'

'Not yet, your body is in good hands, John will take care of it. Your ego will stay with it. Control it. You will breathe again. Your organs will start to work, too, and everything is going to be all right.'

'And then I'll have to go back?'

'No, Molly, not yet. It would be possible, but this is part of the learning process, too. You will be in coma for a while. For how long? It depends on a lot of things, but at least as long as it's needed. And no – you cannot remain here.'

'I wish I could. Everything is better here.'

'I know. Every time we talk this part is most difficult to make you understand. You need to go back, because your journey is just beginning.'

'Oh… It was quite enough for me already. I hope you are not being serious right now.' Molly let out an enormous sigh, and because she didn't want to look at Noah - instead, she studied the medical equipment, the people, her body… and John. In the end, she was only watching him. She never saw him so worried. She felt his pain, his despair. She saw the tiny teardrop rolling down his cheek. 'I didn't know he loved me so much.'

'But he did. He just never showed it.'

'But why not?'

'Because he's like that. Doesn't show his emotions. Molly, not everyone can be that sensitive and can cry as easily as you do. What would happen to the world if everyone always cried?'

'It would be cleansed.'

'Yes, you feel like that. Because when you cry, your tears clean your body and soul. But not everyone can do that. And it is not good for everyone, either. There are so many other ways to relieve stress. Some need a certain genre of music, others need nature. Some need a pet, others need sport – extreme, or simply yoga, doesn't matter, or anything in between – others need a game. A lot of people meditate – and I could go on. Every one of these is a cleansing process and the type of it depends on their personality, their temper. Everyone cries – it's only that some do it inside. John is like that. That tiny tear you saw, and that nobody else could, carried an immense amount of pain and guilt. He thinks he didn't take care of you well enough.'

'But that is not true. It is all my fault. I was a bad patient, not listening to him.'

'No, Molly. This had to happen like this. Do not forget that everything happens for a reason, and everything is connected to everything. Don't worry if you don't understand, I'll explain later. Now it is enough for you to understand that what happened to you affects not only you but others as well. Not only you will learn from it, but your environment and your loved ones, too.'

'Is this why you said that I'll be in coma until it is necessary? So that others can learn from it, not only me?'

'Exactly. While you are with me, your body doesn't matter to you. That is your earthly avatar, that you get for a single use. Even though as long as your soul is here you are visible, down there it isn't enough. This was designed like this, and there is a reason why. Molly, this is the first and most important thing that you'll have to remember:

20

everything happens for a reason. Even the smallest, seemingly most insignificant thing does.'

'I understand.'

'No, you don't, but you will,' he smiled. 'That you have heard about it is a completely different thing. If you really understood it, we wouldn't be here. We could've met 40-50 years later.'

'It's strange to see things from this perspective.'

'I know it's strange. Because everything you ever experienced, everything you knew about the world seems to be false. And I know that the reason we're still here is that you are afraid to start out.'

'This is already unbelievable, what will come next? If this is the first step, what else will I see?'

'You wanted answers. Now you'll get them.'

'I'm about to say that actually I'm not really interested in the whys. I'd rather go back and carry on with my empty life.'

'Molly, if something is new or different it isn't necessarily a bad thing. Dare to experience it.

21

Think about it as a great journey, an adventure. I'll be here to protect you, like I always have been. No matter how hard it gets I will stand by your side and hold your hand. Like I did before. You never were alone, even though you might've felt like that. And...

'I cannot go back, right?'

'Right. This is how your journey continues. Or, as I said before, how it starts. I told you that appearances might be deceiving. Now you'll see how true that is. Up until now you thought you were alive, but you were wrong. Your true self was sleeping. Sometimes it woke up to check if you or the world was ready for its awakening, and when it saw that that was not the case, it went back to sleep. To be frank, the world is ready for a change, but you aren't. This is the reason you are here: I'd like to help you so that you can finally wake up.'

'Yes, this is familiar. Sometimes it felt like I was waking from a deep slumber – but that feeling always ceased quickly. After that, I always felt that this was the end, that I'd finally gone mad.'

'I know. You needed those awakenings. You needed to feel that you were special, you had to know... or you had to at least have a vague idea of your true path. You are not one of the many. You are special, and you have a really difficult, but noble task before you.'

'I don't feel myself to be special.' Her words were quiet and sad.

'Then think about this statement once more.'

'Sure. I don't know if I want to feel special. I don't know if I could handle a difficult task, or any task for that matter. Sometimes I feel I'm special. Then I laugh at myself, or others do, or both.'

'And?'

'And what? I don't get it.'

'That's the question. And?'

'There's no "and".'

'There is. Molly, no matter how hard it is, you have to talk about what you feel and what you think. This, too, is a sort of cleansing process. It's like you are crying. It's just that this way you let out your thoughts, your good and bad feelings, your memories, and you'll let knowledge enter in their place. This is how you'll get the answers for your whys.'

'Okay,' she nodded. 'And... maybe... maybe it is true, maybe I'm special... in my own strange way. I don't know. I was avoiding this question, these situations, since I was a little kid. I could've become a leader, or belonged to the so-called elite, but I didn't want to. It was better to stay in the background, to play with people that were simple and humble. That was the case when I grew up. I was asked regularly why didn't I want more. Because with my knowledge I could be this and that, a boss or anything. Of course, I know I could be. But I don't want to. Power, success, or money don't motivate me, I don't want to rise to the top, I don't want to step on anybody – I want to just do my job. My feelings control me, they lead my way, and decide what should be my task.'

'Then why don't you listen to them?'

'I don't understand.'

'You said your feelings lead your way, but you don't do what is your task, or what you feel you should do. If you would have, we wouldn't be here.'

'This is hard.'

'I know it's hard, but it's time for you to be completely honest with yourself. Do not say what you or others think you should say, but what you really feel. You don't have to worry, here nobody will laugh at you or think you are crazy. Throw down everything that you carried, you won't need it anymore. IF you can do that, you'll be able to find yourself, the creature you really are, who you've been looking for a long time, and vice versa.'

'What do you want me to say?'

'Let's find out first what is it that locks you down. Why do you think your life went in this direction? You perfectly know that this is not okay. The fact that we're talking here is the result of a long sequence of bad decisions. You need to find the reason why. Do not think about your body or what is happening down there right now. First you have to understand what you did wrong. You need this, so we can move on, so that I can show you everything. You'll even get a little help.' As he said this, suddenly everything disappeared. They were sitting on a bench in a huge white room. Everything was white, the walls, the columns, the floor… everything.

'What is this place?' she asked.

'The thinking-corner' Noah laughed. 'Nothing can distract your attention, so you can't avoid answering questions by talking about something else.'

25

'Punishment-room,' she smiled. 'You really can think here. I feel like… my thoughts are stronger here, like I was a bit braver here.'

'Naturally. You were able to see your body, and that distracted you. You tried to focus, but you couldn't. We could've started here, but I wanted you to see that first.'

'Shock therapy?' laughed Molly again.

'Something like that. We'll need to go back, because we'll start our learning there, but first we need to talk… I mean, we need to get rid of what locks you down.'

'I don't understand what you mean. What lock? I did what life brought around. I never planned, since it was unnecessary.'

'Nothing is ever unnecessary, only what you had to do wasn't what you thought it was. Every plan you have is a step on your road towards your goal. But we are rushing forward again. Let's turn back to the original question. What do you think blocks you from doing your job, your TASK?'

'I don't know.'

'Molly, say what you feel! Here you don't have to be ashamed or adapt to other people's standards. Be honest. And not only to me, but to yourself as well.'

'Okay. I think it is you that locked me down, preventing me from doing anything. All due respect to you and who I'm going to meet, but…'

'But? Continue.'

'But you make all the lives of people on Earth so difficult. Just think about my situation. My life is just a big pile of garbage. Anything I plan, anything I ask for remains unfulfilled, even though I don't ask for anything big. I didn't dare to plan for a long time now. I realised that it is better to just go with the flow. It's better to hide in the corner, to do my job, and wait for the end to come.'

'You always say that you did your job. Which is your task. But that is not true Molly. You just think that you're doing that, because you want to believe that. But you still haven't realised what this is all for. What do you think the problem is? Let me help – it's a single word. That tiny little word is what makes your life desperate. And not only yours, but everybody else's on the planet. Think it through. You feel that you have to do something… Let's find a proper example: you feel that you should write. You even start it, but then you stop. Why?'

'Because I start wondering if anyone would care. I'm afraid that…'

'Yes! That's it!' Noah cried out.

'What?'

'Okay, think about it again. What you just said, and what was your last word.'

'That I'm afraid.'

'Yes, Molly. That is the problem. That tiny word that we've been looking for. This is the source of all problems.'

'I don't understand.'

'It's simple. We'll look at your life first, and after, if you're interested, I can show you just how much damage that one word can do… or that one feeling. You've got to know that we gave you fear along with the ego. As I said, the ego is a necessary evil, you need it. And this is the moment we have to go back. I think nothing is distracting you anymore, so I think it's time to start studying. Are you ready?'

'Yes, because I know that it will be good, even though I'm not completely sure about it. This whole thing is strange.'

'I know it's strange, but you'll understand the connections soon. But now let us start with me teaching you how to move. Just as you opened your eyes or as you sat up. You have to feel it.'

Molly thought it better to give up after a few half-hearted tries.

'That's it?' Noah asked.' You didn't try for too long.'

'Because this is harder than the others.'

'Focus. You can do it, you just have to feel it. Just like before. And you can't give up at the first sign of any difficulty. It would be cowardly to give up, and no one would say that you are a coward. So, come on! Just feel that you stand up and that you are walking. Don't look for your will, you left that with your body.'

'Okay, I'll try. I swear this is like being a little kid again who is just learning how to walk, only in intensive training,' Molly smiled.

'That smile was like when the wolf catches a rabbit and grins at it before it eats it.'

'I didn't want that to be like that,' she continued to smile. 'It's just difficult. But I'm on it, working on the solution, since apparently it is forbidden to give up.'

At first, she only moved her feet, making her toes dance, then the whole of her legs. She loved this new game, this new and wonderful feeling, and she was laughing loudly while doing it. She imagined what she wanted and it happened immediately. Noah watched the girl's attempts happily. 'Oh, how I missed this, Little Girl,' he thought to himself.

'You missed what?' she asked.

'I didn't say anything.'

'Yes, you did. You said that…'

'No, Molly, not said. Just thought it. But I see that you are getting attuned to me, which is good. However, I know that you enjoy this, as far as you can see it… and know that you can start to grasp how proud I am of you. But we should go. There are lots of things I'd like to show you.'

'Okay. Let's go.' The girl stood up and started walking.

'Nice job,' said Noah. He tried not to feel how proud he was, but he didn't really manage it. Molly was overflowing with joy. She enjoyed the pride flowing towards her. She wanted more and more. She imagined she was dancing, and it immediately happened. She was clumsy, like someone who tries to skate for the first time, but each of her movements was full of life and joy. She felt light and free.

'This is amazing,' she laughed. 'I love it!'

'Yes, I can see, but…'

'I know. We have to go… Killjoy,' she pouted.

'Are you ready?'

'No. But we can leave.'

2.

'So, we were talking about the body and the ego...' As he said it, they were back in the room.

'It's like nothing's changed,' she said.

'It changed, but not as they or you could notice. This is the main organising idea: everything is in movement, everything is changing. Despite the appearances, nothing remains the same. Something always happens; maybe it is something small and insignificant to you that completely changes the direction this world is heading in. This is why we are here: our task is to control these events, to keep them in check as the higher order demands. There is the goal, both globally and individually, that we have to head towards. Small detours are allowed, but we'll talk about that later. But now we were talking about the body and the ego. There are some who like to talk about the two as one, others don't give any importance to the body and only about the body-soul-spirit triangle – but this is incorrect, since without the body the other three wouldn't exist either. Your body is your earthly avatar that you get for a single life. Imagine it like a set of clothes.'

'This is funny.'

'Yes, it is. But maybe it makes it easier to understand. Imagine that your current life is the whole lifespan of your soul, and your body is your only set of clothes. But actually, this is not entirely true, since your soul's lifespan is much longer than that…'

'Understood. Please, continue,' she smiled.

'Sure. So, let's try again … Now, imagine that your current life is the whole lifespan of your soul, and your body is your only set of clothes. You got it because you wanted it or you had to get it, since you can't walk around naked. You use it, every day the same. You don't have another one, only this. You can buy accessories – which are the actual clothes - but when you go home you take them off and you remain with the original set… the only set. What happens to it?'

'It wears down.'

'Exactly. If you take good care of it then it will happen later; if not, then sooner. Of course, there are those who already begin with a flawed body, being born with some kind of handicap, but that is another story. Let's say that you receive a body in good condition, meaning a set of nice, flawless clothes. No matter how good care you take of them, as you said, they will wear out. You need to change them.'

33

'But why do we need more sets of clothes? More bodies? Why don't we just get one that lasts longer?'

'Because your world, your society, and the system you live in and what you live by, is not ready for that. If you take a closer look at history, you'll notice that the average age rises continuously. In the earlier years, 30 to 40 years were more than enough for you to learn what you had to. This limit gets pushed up continuously. As you usually say: "Thanks to modern medicine." Yes, sure… you could say that. But the truth is that nowadays you start your lives around the age of 30. Until then you just study, trying to gain the knowledge that your ancestors – that actually were you – experienced.'

'So, there is no point in looking for the key to immortality?'

'I see that you did not understand what I said previously.'

'Yes, I did.'

'Molly, you have the key to eternal life in your very hands. Only your bodies, your families, your circumstances change. The ego longs for immortality, since it doesn't want to accept or understand that its "contract" is only for a single life, that's all. But your soul's lifespan… compared to your current life, is eternal. Of course, this is not completely true, since everything has a beginning and an end, but it is hard to grasp, so let's say it's immortal.'

'Yes, I get this part. What I wanted to say is that a lot of people seek to make that specific one longer. Because they are afraid of dying, or it's just simply such a good life, or they achieved so much that they don't want to leave it behind. Which is understandable, to a certain degree. You struggle to achieve something in your whole life, then suddenly have to leave everything behind, so that you can start all over again in your next life. Let's be honest, this is just cruel.'

'It is cruel, but only because you decide to live it like that. And the reason this is like this is that it has to be like this. You have to learn to let go of the matter, to not get attached to objects. Now you live in a world where the object, the fortune one has, carries much more value than the person itself, than the human life. And this is where the ego comes in.'

'It was here all along,' she smiled.

'Yes, it was. I'm trying to separate things, but it's not completely possible. As I told you before, these four – the body, the ego, the soul and the spirit – make a perfect whole. They can exist together only on the Earth. It works the same way… as your breathing.'

'Which I'm not doing right now,' she interrupted.

'Yes, but you will have to soon. Look at the medical equipment, Molly. In order for you to breathe, you need your heart, and vice versa. Your lungs cannot function without your heart, and your heart cannot function without your lungs. If you'd like to describe the processes going on in your body, you cannot just simply separate them, just as you can't exclude your other organs, since they together make up a perfect whole. I can list you the muscles moving your lungs, where they are located, but if we want to discuss how they work, we need to talk about your heart, your veins, the blood, and I could go on and on. This is the same on the greater scale. You can't separate the great four, because alone they cannot exist.'

'Understood.' Molly was watching her body, John, and the nurses. She watched them fight for her life desperately. She felt John's pain. She watched his face. There was almost nothing visible of the turmoil that was going on inside him.

'Should we take a break?' Noah asked.

'What?' she started. 'I'm sorry, I didn't hear what you asked.'

'No problem,' he smiled.

'I was just watching John. I never could imagine that something could hurt him. He is always so tough and strong-willed. I often told him that he is exactly like an iceberg: cold and tough. Like he didn't care about anything or there was nothing that could anger him. I tried to see how far I could push him a few times. Mostly intentionally, but sometimes it happened for reasons beyond me... which was probably your doing. But he never yelled at me, not for anything,' she smiled, as old memories came into her mind. 'He would say when it was enough. At those times, his voice became deep and frightening, one that would make you jump to stand-to and say, "Sir, yes sir!" Now, that was scary. But he never scolded me any worse than that. I always told him that he doesn't even have any emotions, that when he was designed they removed this function from him. He always answered to this that I was wrong and that he had feelings. But I couldn't extract any more from him than that. And now I can feel that he actually has... and so much... unbelievable.'

'And you are surprised by that?'

'By how strong the emotions he has are, and how strongly he loves me? Yes.'

'Hmm. Interesting.'

'John used to say the same thing, with the exact same intonation,' she laughed, whereupon John started and quietly whispered: 'Molly, please come back to me! Please, God, give her back to me!'

'At last,' said Noah.

'What at last?'

'That's what we were waiting for.'

'For what? And what's all this about?' she asked.

'I'll explain right away, but now please go to the other side of the room, further away from your body, and stay quiet for a bit. Thank you.'

Molly couldn't say anything even if she had wanted to. As she backed to the given location, she watched curiously what was happening to her body. When she was far enough away, Noah leaned above the body and put both of his hands on her head, closing his eyes. The body and Noah were enveloped in a golden light, so bright, so amazing, and so soothing that no person had seen anything like that before. But what was strange to her was that, even though she saw what was happening to her, inside she felt nothing. Maybe a tiny tingle... maybe. But that was nothing compared to what she was expecting, since it was her body that was being cured, it was her who was receiving the love-light energy... but nothing. At that moment, Noah looked at the body of the girl, smiled, and for a second he put his hand over her heart. It might have been only for a second, but it made her collapse. All she could say was that this was wonderful, unbelievably wonderful. Molly believed that there could be no better feeling than what she had experienced after her awakening, but she had to admit that she was wrong. She thought she knew what love was, but what she had just experienced was more than anything she had ever felt. She was full of energy; it was as though she was reborn, she wanted to dance, to laugh... but she couldn't, because Noah asked her not to. Noah kept his hands on the head of the body with his eyes closed. The golden light had not dimmed a single bit, but still – nothing happened. John was more and more nervous, his pain was increasing, and he kept saying. 'Please, Lord, help! Please bring her back! I promise I'll look after her! Please, help...' As John grew more tense, Noah's smile became more and more gentle. Guided by a sudden feeling, Molly walked over to John, gently caressed his cheek, and wiped down the tiny teardrop.

'Don't worry, my dear, I'm all right. Help my body, protect her, and when the time comes we'll meet again and I'll continue to get on your nerves. Trust me!' she whispered.

John felt a strange tingling. As though someone had touched him. As though someone had told him that everything was going to be fine. And the strangest part was, he believed it. He decided that he would discuss it when Molly came back. He had never believed in this stuff, he had always looked at Molly strangely when she talked about these supernatural things. He believed in it and he didn't - mostly didn't. As a rational person he always said, 'I'll believe it when I see it.' She always responded with 'You wouldn't, even if you saw it, you Saturnian.' And she was right. He wouldn't have – these things were too abstract for him. He preferred to view his world from a more rational perspective. How things actually were. Now, that was not entirely true. He didn't like seeing the real world because he didn't like what he saw. There was no dispute in this matter between him and the girl – they both agreed that the situation was less than ideal. 'The world is heading in the wrong direction.' This sentence was uttered often by both, in complete agreement. The girl always added: 'If something doesn't change soon, or we don't change by ourselves, then fate will do the job. Which will be much more painful.'

And sadly, she was right. The evidence was right there: the natural disasters, the news about famine, revolutions, or wars. The world was moving, yes – but in the wrong direction. He often wondered who it might be that was pulling the strings. Because it had to be someone. He never liked to admit it, but he wasn't completely pagan, he believed in God. Well, not of his own accord, but because that's what he was taught. Even though he had never met him, he must exist, since so many people were stating that he did. He has to exist, because there had to be someone controlling birth, death and every other event in the world – but more importantly he had to exist because they had reached a crucial moment where, if Molly's heart wouldn't restart in a minute, he would lose her. And that was what he couldn't imagine. That could not happen. Maybe he had uttered that prayer before in complete desperation – even he didn't understand why - but if there was a God it was due time he proved his existence. Give Molly back to him.

As this thought crossed his mind, the paramedic looked at his clock:

'There is no point trying now. Time of death 8:14 p.m....'

'No!' John cried out.

'John, you know perfectly well that we did all we could. It is over. My condol…'

'No, not yet! It's not over yet! It can't be! She is much stronger than that! Let me get to her, Joseph…'

'John, please. We are both doctors. We both know that we did all we could. You and us too, but the girl's heart does not respond to anything. It is futile. Let her go.'

Being a doctor John knew that his colleague was right. He would have said the same if they happened to be in each other's shoes. They worked together often, he knew that Joseph was one of the best of his field, and he had complete faith in his abilities, since he had proven his worth dozens of times. He had brought people back from death who would have been abandoned by others. But… for some reason now he felt that he could not give up. He didn't know why, only that that he couldn't.

'Let me get to her,' he said in a frighteningly deep voice.

'John, don't,' his colleague started out.

'Don't John me, let me get to her. Now!' His voice resembled a dormant volcano about to explode. Joseph waved to the nurses, who stepped away from the body. John knelt beside the body, leaned over to her forehead, kissed it, then whispered:

'Come, Little Girl, help me,' his voice was unbelievably gentle and soft. Then he looked up to the sky and in his voice, that was deep like the ocean he said, 'It's time that you prove your existence! Please help!'

And he started the CPR. Not like the other times. This was completely different. His brain yelled at him to stop, because it was all over – but he didn't care, because his heart said, 'Don't stop!' He believed, he felt that it would help, that he could bring her back.

And then Molly's heart started beating. Not only in her body, but in her soul, too, that made her eyes swell with tears, one of them rolling down her cheek. Noah got up from her body, stepped to the girl, hugged her and wiped the tears from her face.

'Now everything's going to be fine,' he smiled.

'I don't understand.'

'I'll explain everything soon, but please, you have to rest a bit.'

'I'm fine,' she said, mostly to reassure herself. They watched the events unfold in silence.

43

Molly's body was alive again. The two doctors managed to stabilise her. It seemed that everything was going to be fine, but John found something to be strange.

'Something's not right,' he said finally.

'Yes, I think that too,' Joseph said. 'You managed to revive the body, that won't be a problem, but her soul is not with it.'

'Coma…'

'Let's say that her soul still has a job to do on the other side. John, I know you don't believe in such things. I didn't either as a rookie, but I have met a lot of similar cases during my years. I could bring back the body, but the soul stayed over there, probably because there was something that it needed to experience on the other side. Or it just needed a bit of rest and they permitted it. It could be that this is how those in heaven want those on the earth to learn something from this.'

John tried to speak, but the knot in his throat didn't make it possible. He was thinking about what might be if what Joseph said was true. And what if he was wrong. Joseph noticed John's struggle.

'You can ask me anything, if you want,' he said.

44

'There is something,' he said in a wavering, quite voice. 'Pull yourself together!' he scolded himself, then cleared his throat, and repeated: 'There is something.'

'Go ahead, then,' smiled the paramedic. At first sight, Joseph was nothing that would drive a woman crazy. Overall average build, brownish-red hair, greenish brown eyes, thin lips, straight nose… nothing that would attract a woman, but somehow, he did just that. He worked opposite to expectations. He was ordinary only until his first word. Maybe it was the calm that he radiated, or maybe his intelligence… or maybe his humour. Nobody could say for certain, but one thing was undeniable: he attracted women like a magnet. When his friends – or let's say those who envied him – mentioned this fact to him, all he said was 'Quality over quantity. And it is quality that I cannot find.'

John hesitated. He was not sure if he wanted to know all this. There was nothing material about it. But… he needed to know where Molly was now, because she wasn't here. Her organs functioned, her heart beat a steady rhythm, but for some reason that was not enough.

'John,' Joseph said finally. 'Everything is going to be fine, believe me.'

'How do you know? How do you know all this?'

'You know, I brought a lot of people back from death. Recently I started to spend my free time studying their cases, what happened to them before and after their "awakening." They told me a lot of amazing things. I think I'll even assemble a book from their reports. If you are interested, one day I'll invite you over for a beer and I'll tell you all about it. But if it would be easier to believe for you, we could even visit some of them, so that you can hear their reports first-hand. Let it be enough for now that the Little Lady is in a good place, and she is being taken care of, and when it is time, she will come back. I'm certain that she has something to do here, and I'm certain too that it is related to you, because it was you who brought her back. You together managed what I couldn't do alone. She came back because you called. Just think through what happened when you have a moment. My opinion is that it's not only her who has to learn something, but you too. You got a tough lesson from Heaven.'

'You think?'

'I think, yes. Someone just came to my mind, I'll take you to her, too. She was in a car accident and lay in a coma for quite a long time. When she woke she told me what happened to her.

46

I won't go into details now, but the main point is that when we were alone, she told me that it was not only her that had to learn from this accident, but her family, too. And that's why her coma lasted so long, because she had quite a stubborn family who would not change their opinions, their beliefs. They learned their lesson slowly. But she wasn't complaining, because she had fun over here-there.'

'What do you mean over here-there?'

'What I mean,' he continued, 'is that the world is not like how we perceive it. Especially the world beyond our bodies. Jasmin – the lady in question – told me that she just flew around in space and time with her follower like a butterfly flies from one flower to the other… without any difficulty.'

'Then how come they come back if it's so good over there? Molly didn't have a good life here. If she's happy over there what reason would she have to come back?'

'Because she has a task at hand,' Joseph said like it was obvious. 'The same reason why Jasmin came back. What it actually is she didn't tell me. She said that it's not time yet. But she promised that I'd be the first to know. But what she mentioned often, and what is important for you is that she could've come back sooner if only her

47

family learned their lesson faster. I feel I need to emphasise this in the light of recent events. I don't know what went down inside of you, because I can't see into you, and nothing can be read from your face as usual – but if you would've had nothing to learn, it would've been me who revived the girl, not you. If you want to we can talk about this, too, during that beer I mentioned. You don't have to worry that I'll tell it to anyone, I'm bounded by professional secrecy.'

The knot in John's throat grew bigger. He needed to gather all his strength to be able to talk, but it proved difficult nevertheless. All he could say was 'Thank you.'

'You have nothing to thank,' Joseph smiled. 'I like beer, I like good company, I like to help – this is one of the reasons I became a doctor. But now, if you deem it right, dear friend, I think it's time we head over to the hospital. The lady…'

'…Molly.'

'Nice name… So, Molly's condition is stable enough in my opinion that we could move her.'

'Let's try. I'll tag along, just in case you need me.' John was surprised how confident his voice was again.

'Naturally,' Joseph continued to smile.

'Are we going, too?' asked Molly.

'Would you like to?'

'I don't know. I don't know what's next. How to move on.'

'Molly, you don't have to be next to your body, there will be nothing wrong if you leave it. Everything is going to be all right now. John will protect it.'

'I know. I never would've thought that I was so important to him. He always was so distant and cold with me... just like with everybody else. He really is like an iceberg.'

'Molly, you learned astrology.'

'Yes.'

'And you even made his chart.'

'Yes.'

'Then what is it that you don't understand?'

'Everything,' she smiled.

'Fine, you failed, back to school with you,' Noah grinned. 'Then tell me, what is John's ascendant?'

'Capricorn.'

'What is a Capricorn like?'

'Tough.'

'Why do you like Capricorns?'

'Because they have posture, they are tough and confident. They don't give in to their emotions. Or if they do, they don't show it.'

'Then what is it that you don't understand?'

'Everything,' she grinned, too.

'Then everything is all right, then.'

'And now what?' she asked.

'Let's continue learning, with me explaining what exactly happened.'

'Ooooh, that feeling… It was wonderful and amazing… I can't even describe what happened to me there.'

'You got some love-energy.'

'Why couldn't I feel anything at first? And why did you wait? You said that we were waiting for something.'

'We were waiting for John to open towards us. Every person is born believing in us, but more importantly, in God. This happens for a simple reason: before their earthly births people were living with us. To be more exact, this is not faith, this is knowledge. You must've heard of parents complaining about their kid behaving strangely, that they have imaginary friends, or that they talk about their previous family or life.'

'Yes.'

'Kids are not imagining. They can see us and these things up until they are 3 or 4 years old. We are protecting them in a visible form until then. Let me correct that: visible to them. We are with them, giving them a feeling of security, we play with them, comfort and protect them.'

'And then? Why don't you stay visible? Why do we forget everything?'

'Because we have to. Your society is not ready for that yet.'

'This sounds weird. We come from you, return to you, yet we are not ready for you?'

'Yes, it's a weird situation. But it must be like this. I will tell you this a few more times, because this is the most important thing, and you should remember it all your life… or lives: EVERYTHING ALWAYS HAPPENS FOR A REASON. Even the smallest, most insignificant thing. This is all part of the learning process.'

'Wouldn't it be easier if we didn't forget everything? Or at least if we retained a great part of our memories or knowledge?'

'No. The knowledge stays in your souls. You have everything inside there that you ever experienced. It is only that by the age of 2 or 3, maximum 4, the soul withdraws and lets the ego take control. It doesn't completely go away, it whispers suggestions from the background as to what you should or shouldn't do, what would be better or the correct choice, but all in all the ego controls the body.'

'That's not what I thought…'

'I know, Molly. But think again… you had…. no, I won't tell you how many lives you had. A lot.'

'How many exactly?'

'Well… not 500.'

'Less?'

'No. A lot more,' Noah smiled. 'But let's say 500. And I would add that you have the knowledge here – which already scared you, even though there is no ego here to confuse you. The knowledge is inside you… yet you don't possess it, and it is scary. Now, let's stick to the 500. If all of your 500 lives' memories remained, your life would become chaos, you wouldn't be able to process most of the memories. You couldn't accept it and you wouldn't be able to concentrate on the task at hand. Every life is a new task, every life is the experiencing of a new perspective. If you knew what happened up until now, you might not choose the path you should go on.'

'But what would happen if I remembered only the last life I had?'

'Then you would carry on with that life. But that is not your job. If it was, then you would get everything back the same. But you wouldn't be the same person, since it is impossible to copy a life perfectly. A little divergence, and you wouldn't be the same person. A small, insignificant thing, too. You wouldn't live or experience that life the same way. I tell you: each life is a new beginning, a new task. You receive your attributes, your body, your ego, your parents, your home country, your neighbours, your friends, your school, your job, your relationships, your everything according to your task at hand. So that you will definitely learn your lesson, in the way you are supposed to learn it. But more on that later. I will show you so it will be perfectly clear. The main point is that each life is a new path, a new task, a new approach. If you remembered your previous life, then you would continue that life, and would approach the problem according to that life, and not how you actually should. This is why the ego is only for a single life - so that your conscience won't remember what was before – only your unconscious, and that too only to the degree that it is absolutely necessary.'

'Understood.'

'Don't worry if you don't,' Noah smiled.' I will show you everything in due time.'

'I actually understand this now. But not what happened a few moments ago, not that. Why and what were you waiting for? You said for John. But why?'

'John completely lost his faith recently. Now you are going to tell me "But he never had faith…" Yes, he did once. It's just that being "a man from Saturn" he didn't show it. Not this, not anything else.'

'Why are they like that?'

'Because life throws a lot of stuff at them.'

'Be clearer.'

'Okay. We throw a lot of stuff at them. They get the biggest hits from life.'

'Why is that needed?'

'It increases their endurance, gives them posture. They don't collapse, at least not in public. The can stay solid and tough even under the greatest pressure, and the most important thing is that they are honest and straight. Every great leader has something Saturnine in their personalities, meaning that they have either Capricorn or Aquarius as an ascendant. But the drawback of this toughness is that they completely hide their emotions – which they actually have, contrary to the common belief.'

'Why?'

'It's a defensive measure. No emotions, no pain.'

'So, they cannot love?' Molly asked.

'They can. Oh, how much they can. But not like you, Molly. Tough people like John love through some sort of a brain-filter. You love someone without any reason, "just because", but John cannot do that. He could list a thousand reasons why he loves you, but "just because" will never be one of them. He is your complete opposite, like if you were turned inside out. This is why you get along so well, you balance each other out – like Yin and Yang.'

'Are you certain that we need tough people like him?'

'Yes.'

'Okay, then I completely lost you. If you throw so much at them, give them such a hard life, if it is all right this way, that they can only love in this strange way, then why did this happen to us? Or to John, even?'

'It doesn't matter what one's life is like, they cannot forget their roots, where they came from. Every person has the knowledge you call faith in them. John went through a lot in his life. We needed to train him, which went so well that he completely lost his faith. He needed to see that the miracle, that he did not believe in, actually exists.'

'I don't get it. What did you have to prepare him for?'

'For you,' Noah smiled.

'For me?!' Molly's voice sounded more like a scream than a question.

'Yes, Molly, you.'

'Okay, I think I'd rather not understand this,' she pouted.

'You'll have to. But we can postpone this question, too, as we did with others. Just as a side note,' Noah smiled gently,' I love it when you pout. Your hissy-wrinkle is so pretty,' and he was openly grinning again.

'I see that you don't want to be my friend,' she snarled.' Let me tell you that you are doing well.'

'Hissy,' Noah laughed.

'Insolent,' she responded.

'Now, before we continue to compliment each other, let's go on, because we have still got a lot to do.'

'Fine. Another question, then. What was that feeling like? Why didn't I feel it at first?'

'That was Angel-light. Pure love energy. I was radiating the energy of the Universe towards you. You could do the same, too, though not to this extent – but you were glowing nevertheless. You just couldn't see it.'

'And why couldn't I feel it? Only maybe a little tingle…'

'I already told you why. You do not live in the head. The head is the home of the ego, or the conscious self. Your soul's, your unconscious' home is your heart. My job was to wake your ego. You felt the tingle because your ego and your soul are connected, even in this separated state.'

'But when you touched my heart…. it was something unbelievably wonderful.'

'Yes, I wanted you to feel it.'

'Then what happened there exactly? John restarted my heart, and you my brain?'

'Something like that. John started the engine, basically jumpstarted it, and I woke the ego up. Because even though the engine started, it still needs the ego to continue running. It needs to control circulation, breathing, the organs – including the heart - because this is its job, and has always been since your conception. And I would note here that it's not only you, John, or other people in your vicinity that must learn from what happened to you, but your ego, too. You have been together since your existence, which has become completely natural to it. Sometimes it thinks that it can take you over.'

'And you don't want that?'

'The ego is the source of a lot of problems. If he could accept that he isn't in charge, that he isn't the boss, everything would be better. His job is controlling the body. The task given to you, the reason of your birth, is not necessarily pleasant. Your soul knows your task, but your ego doesn't – it doesn't have to, because it's not its job.'

'Could it be that this is exactly its problem? That you do not allow it to see the truth?'

'Yes, probably. We are letting it in on it gradually, but it would be too much otherwise.'

'Why?'

'Because you are not ready. Even what I'm telling you right now would be too much for a lot of people. Think about it. If things didn't happen as they did and let's say I just sat down next to you somewhere, and started to talk about what I've been talking to you about – what would you do?'

'I'd think you were a lunatic.'

'Exactly. You wouldn't believe a word. And you are quite an open-minded person, because you have experienced a lot in your lifetime.'

'Because you let me.'

'That's right, Molly. We've been preparing you for this moment all your life.'

'But why?'

'So that you can transfer the knowledge.'

'And who do you think is going to believe me? They'll think I'm crazy.'

'I know. And this is the problem with the ego. It's stupid and inconsistent. It demands knowledge right know, and when it gets what he wants, it says that it isn't true.'

'Don't complain, you made it like that.'

'Well… you're right. Or half-right. We have to admit that there is an abundance of flaws in the system. But that's what we're here for – to fix it.'

'And how do you plan to do that?'

'Well, it won't be easy. We'll need a lot of persistence.'

'Isn't there an easier way? Anything that could make the process easier?

'Yes, there is, but the world doesn't want that. To be honest, we don't either. Only if there would be no other choice… but we'll talk about this later, let's stick to the more difficult road.'

'I think I know what you meant.'

'No, Molly, you have no idea. Currently your world is heading in the wrong direction. In order to change that we would need to implement drastic measures. But, as I said, we're not at that part yet. Let's hope we never will be.'

This was the first time since they met that Noah wasn't smiling. She could see in his eyes sadness and pain so deep that it scared her.

'No worries, Little Girl,' Noah said. 'We can fix this. All I ask you to watch and learn.'

'Can I ask something?'

'Sure.'

'Why me? What do you see in me? Why do you think I'm suitable for the task? Because I think you chose poorly. There are many others that are better or more up to the task than me. Who would never fail. I think you made a huge mistake with me.'

'I thought we left your ego with your body. Did it sneak after us when I woke it?'

'Ha ha.'

'It wasn't a joke, Little Girl. I was dead serious. I'm aware that this is a difficult task. And of course, I know that you never wanted a responsibility of this magnitude, no matter how people wanted to force you into it. This is why you knew this moment would come.'

'Yes, I knew. To be honest I was hoping this would be another stupid thing in my life.'

'I know it would be easier to live through your life leaning back in an armchair, resting your feet. But this is not how the world goes forward. Imagine what would be if everyone had done the same as you – you would be still squatting in caves. No, even that needed a bit of development - you would be still hanging from trees. No, Molly, that is not a viable solution. You were born with a task, and you need to do your job no matter how hard or scary it seems. And it's the ego yet again who refuses to understand this. It doesn't see the bigger picture, only that something difficult is coming again. Another task, bothering it again... And it transfers this message to your body, not what it really should do. Not the request it received from your spirit through your soul. And that's what I don't like. The path that you have to take in your earthly life is given. The same with the task that you have to complete. And it's the same with everyone, not just you. I often see that even though we keep suggesting what you should do to complete your tasks, you do anything but that. Is it difficult? Of course it is. Because things that come easy won't stay. Your conscience just skips over them, almost taking them for granted. There are things that you actually take for granted. I would add in a parenthesis that they are not granted.'

'Then why don't you make it clear to the ego what the task is? Maybe there would be no problem of this scale then, no opposition this great. I see that now you play with each other, but next to or even against each other. You say that everybody is equally important, that one cannot exist without the other. From what I see this is not completely true. You have quite a strict hierarchy in your little pets. Of course the ego doesn't like this oppression. Who would?'

'Yes…yes, you may be right. But let me use an example from your life.'

'Oh.'

'Yes, Molly… it's "Oh". How many times and how many different ways did we let you know that you should write?'

'A lot.'

'And? Is your book ready? You know what your task is, you know what should be done, but did you write?'

'Well… not really…'

'Not really? Let us rather say "Really not". Even though the message was as clear as day. Take your little laptop or a pen and paper… or anything you like, and start writing, because we have great need of your book. And what happened?'

'Nothing.'

'And why? Please, tell me…' Noah was looking at the girl who was obviously embarrassed, since she had no idea how to answer. 'Molly, this is not a torture interrogation… that part will come later,' Noah grinned, trying to ease her tension.

'Ha-ha,' she grimaced.

'Okay… there will be no torture at all. All I want is you to understand why… let's say I don't like the ego. So… why haven't you finished the book yet?'

'There are a thousand reasons…' she began. 'But really only one. I was afraid. Okay! Two. Laziness was a factor, too.'

'That's right. I like that you admit it,' Noah smiled. 'And I think it's time for us to travel a bit.'

'Where are we going?'

'I'm going to take you to a nice place, so we can speak undisturbed.'

'I thought we'd go to the hospital with them.'

'Would you like to?'

'I don't know. Would I?'

'To be honest we'd have nothing to do there. But if it makes you feel better, be it so.'

Molly watched through the window as the nurses and the two doctors put her body into the ambulance and got ready to leave. She wasn't really concerned about her body, more about John. She felt all the tension, pain, and anxiety that was raging inside the man. She felt that the helplessness was eating him up from inside.

'I don't know which is better,' she said finally 'what John does, or my way.'

'What do you mean?'

'Oh, come on, you know perfectly well what I mean,' grimaced the girl.

'I know everything. This was more like a simple rhetoric tool, to keep the conversation going. It would be quite boring if only I was talking all the time, don't you think?'

'No, because I love the sound of your voice,' she smiled again.

'And I do yours. So…what did you mean?'

'That I don't know which way is better. Completely closing out the world – which I can see now is only the surface - or what I do.'

'Crying?'

'You don't have to mock me…'

'But it's a bit fun. At least you can see that we are not the saints many believe us to be. Honestly… I don't really know which one is better. I think neither. You are two extremities. That's why you are so good together. You complete each other, you two make one perfect whole. But I think I already said this.'

'I think too. But… you say so much that I have already forgotten half of it.'

'I'll give you a notebook and a pen,' Noah laughed.

'That would be nice… So, you too banter with each other?'

'Yes, that's part of the game. Banter, pranks, but never over the top. We can't hurt others, and we don't want to…. mostly don't want to. But back to John. He always loved you. But he realises how much he loves you only now, when he thinks he's lost you. He will reassess everything inside himself after what happened to you. He will pay more attention to you and what you tell him. He will give up his principles and will consider what you and others tell him. This transformation will be hard work, because it is difficult to convince such a down-to-earth person about the real world, but it isn't impossible. The process has started, and it's all the result of the pain that losing you caused him. He always listened to what you said because he loved you... I don't say he didn't pay attention, because he always did, but only because he respected you and not because he believed a single word you said.'

'I know he didn't believe what I said. But we could have such nice conversations nevertheless. He told the real part of the stories, the facts, and I added what I felt to it. He often frowned and hemmed, but never said anything bad. And that's what I loved the most. He accepted me as what I was. Even though he never believed a word I said, he never hurt me, never wanted to change me, never called me crazy or an idiot. He accepted me being me. Often times I even believed that he wanted to discuss some matters with me. I think he was interested in my opinion about a given situation, because he knew I'd never answer the same way anyone else would. Sometimes I exceeded even his wildest expectations... We didn't talk often, but those few occasions were amazing. Not a superficial person… Never curses, never hurts anyone, never gossips. That's what I loved the most. He doesn't have the tiniest bit of malice in him. He has his opinions, but if he doesn't want to tell you then you'll never know them… His face is unreadable. This is why it was so strange to see and feel what he did. I didn't think that he could harbour this much pain… Unbelievable. If I hadn't experienced it first-hand, I would have said it's not possible. John Wolfberg is not capable of this.'

Noah just smiled as he was listening to Molly.

'This is love, Molly. Real love, not what people think when they keep repeating the word all day long.'

'But sometimes it feels good to hear it too, not just to feel it.'

'That's true.'

'Okay, I see that they are ready, and are about to leave for the hospital… with me. Funny to say it like that.'

'Do you want to go with them? To see what will happen to you?'

'Why do I feel this to be a test question rather than a genuine one?'

Noah burst out with laughter. His voice ringed like a magical bell, making the girl tremble with joy. In her embarrassment she watched the ambulance shrinking, driving away. She didn't feel the need to go. Or rather... she felt that she needed to go, but not to the hospital, not yet. She felt that she would take part in some kind of exciting adventure.

3.

'No, I don't want to go,' the girl said finally.

'Good decision' the man smiled.

'And now? What's next?'

'I'll show you a few things, and I'll try to explain some things in the meantime. Why things are the way they are and how they work.'

'You're going to show me your world?'

'Not really. Some parts, yes. Good and bad, both. But I'd rather like to show you your world, from a bit of a different perspective. I'd like you to see what the problems are and what needs to be changed.'

'Okay, then everything's all right.'

'What do you mean?'

'That if you want to show me everything that needs to be changed, by the time we finish my body will be so old that I don't even have to go back.'

Noah laughed again.

'That's not how it works, my Queen, but we'll talk about that later.'

'Your what?'

'What my what?'

'You said, "my Queen." Why?'

'Did I say that? I don't remember…'

'Sure…'

'Yes, sure.'

'Lies.'

'Yep.'

'I thought angels never lie.'

'They don't.'

'Then?'

'Then let's go.'

'Noah!'

'I wish you'd remember all my words like that. You don't have to write this down in a notebook, do you?' he smiled. 'You are my Queen, because you were and you will be. All Guardian Angels feel the same way towards their protégés.'

'I see.'

'And now, if we can get over this thing, let us continue studying.'

'Okay. And how?'

Noah looked up to the sky and said:

'Where is that notebook?'

'What did I forget?' she asked.

'Everything, Molly, everything. Now, no worries, we'll go through everything again. I told you a few moments ago that I'm going to take you to a beautiful place, where we can talk undisturbed.'

'I'm sorry, I just need to pull myself together, since I feel I fell apart a bit. It's like I'm missing a part of me.'

'Because you are. But not one, three. But before you ask, I'm not going to tell you. You are going to tell me.'

'I know the answers already. One, my body; two, my ego; three, John.'

'Nice.'

'Thanks. But… knowing these doesn't really make me feel happier.'

'I told you that your ego stuck with you.'

'No, it didn't.'

'Then what's the problem?'

'John. I saw and felt how much he loved me. Now that he's not there – so to speak, I lost him – there comes this strange feeling… missing him. And this is bad. I don't think the ego has too much to do with this. I just have so much pain from my previous relationships, that I don't want anymore. This is a rock-solid conviction of mine: I DON'T WANT ANYMORE.'

'But that's not how it works, Molly. And I think it is due time for us to travel a bit. I'm going to take you to a nice place so we can discuss this.'

'I don't think there is anything about this to discuss.'

'There is. I know what the problem is. Soon you'll calm down, but let's just go. Please, come with me. Take my hand.'

'Okay. Let's go,' Molly extended her hand, but that was not enough for Noah. He pulled the girl to himself and hugged her, not letting go.

Molly closed her eyes, but she couldn't stop the river of tears.

'Everything is going to be all right, my Queen. Now really everything is going to be fine,' he whispered. 'I'm going to protect you. Nobody's going to hurt you ever again. I promise.'

Molly just cried and cried. And she felt that she was getting cleansed. She felt lighter and had fewer burdens, and finally she calmed down.

'Do you feel any better?' Noah asked.

'Yes,' she sniffed. 'I thought there was no crying here.'

'You were wrong. Now everything is okay, this cleansed you. Too much pressure, too many burdens, too much old-new information. You let a lot of things go that you were carrying around without reason. You humans have a saying "to take something to heart." For example, because you were offended, or had a bad experience, or you screwed up, or something like that. Usually you should be able to let these things go, because they lack magnitude – they are just tiny, unimportant parts of the learning process. But for some reason you cannot. You don't have to be afraid of that, it's completely natural.'

'How nicely you describe a hissy-fit,' the girl said, sniffing.

'Now, you're making progress,' Noah smiled again. 'You make fun of your own despair. I like that.'

'I wasn't kidding.'

'Then I need to tell you that there was nothing "hissy" in this, my dear. Now, open your eyes, take a look around where I have brought you.'

Molly opened her eyes and couldn't believe them. It was as though they were in a fairy tale, like all this wasn't real, just a product of her imagination. They were standing beside a lake that was fed by a waterfall on the other side. All this was surrounded by... maybe sky-high hundred-year-old trees, as though they were there to protect this magical place. All around, mountains as far as the eye could see. They stood there like giant soldiers whose only task was to protect this tiny, fragile wonder from prying eyes. On the shore grew flowers of unimaginable beauty. The girl had never seen this many colours together, but she didn't think it was too much. They were in perfect harmony with each other, as though it was a painting. The whole place was throbbing with life, with energy. A couple of swans were swimming in the lake with their cygnets. Birds, butterflies, small bugs were flying everywhere, the lush green grass was swarming with little animals, the deep green leaves of the shrubs were being eaten by larger ones… everything was just perfect.

'This is unbelievably beautiful,' Molly said finally. 'This is an actual wonder.'

'See what a beautiful place I brought you to? I always come here to rest.'

'Nature untouched can be magical.'

'Yes, but it misses something. The something that you were given with your earthly lives, but you don't enjoy it. You almost forgot about it completely.'

'What do you mean?'

'Look around, Molly. You see this magic, you stare in awe, because it's truly amazing, but you don't sense it. And that is the most wonderful part of human life: sensing. This is what we are not given. Only the remnants of memories from our previous lives are what we have left. We partly remember what it was like. We imagine what it could be like based on those fragments, but that doesn't match the true nature of sensing. Look at the waterfall, Molly. Look how that enormous amount of water pours down. It's just amazing to look at, its sound music to your ears. Or the birds singing, the whispering of the leaves as the wind plays with them... a miracle on its own. But imagine that you could sense all this, if you were here as a human. You could sense how soothing the water is, the humidity in the air surrounding us, you could sense the wind and the sun caressing your cheeks, your body. You could swim in this sapphire water with the fishes, you could feel the water cool and caress your skin. Or you could run around in the grass, enjoying how the blades of grass tickle your feet, like some soft rug. Or... the smells. These flowers are beautiful, but what a wonderful feeling it is when you can smell them, too. Or just the smell of grass, the trees, the air itself – not only the flowers. This is the real magic you forget to enjoy. SENSES. God gave you them as presents, but you forget to enjoy them, and you don't value them.'

'You're right. But not every person is granted this sight, this experience, this... wonder. To me, neither – I have never seen anything like this before.'

'Molly, the world is full of wonders, you just don't want to enjoy it, looking at things only with tunnel-vision. You can't accept anything new, because you don't want to. I don't know why you like to view things in black and white. Mostly in black. Notice the colours, let the new, the beautiful, in. Life is not all about waking up, working, going home in the evening and going to bed. Learn to enjoy the small beauties of life. Notice that every moment is a wonder. And if you can accept these little wonders, then you'll get the bigger ones.'

'Is this really what I'm like?'

'Sadly, yes. That's why you are here with me right now. But don't worry, the situation is not that hopeless in your case – you can still be fixed. Believe me, there are people whom, if I brought them here, would only say "Mhhmm. Yes, cool. When are we heading home?"'

'Surely there's no person like that.'

'There is. Sadly. People like this have completely burnt out emotionally. Maybe because of many struggles, or for some other reason, I can't really explain that, but they are the ones who are given a wonder and who don't like it. They want more, better, always unsatisfied, while in most cases they are not willing to do anything to make their situation better. As was the case with you in a lot of ways… And I don't want to hurt you with this, but I can mention examples of this from your life.'

'This doesn't sound too good,' she said, shamefully.

'You don't have to be ashamed, enjoy the moment instead.'

'That swan couple is beautiful. How perfect and majestic they are. Of course, the small ones are not that beautiful. Maybe this is the only animal where the small ones are not cute and beautiful, but only the full-grown ones.'

'Yes. They are an example, too. Don't forget, nature is a great teacher. When the time comes, you'll understand.'

'Okay.' Molly's voice was sad. She wanted to enjoy the moment, but she couldn't. Her thoughts revolved around the few previous sentences.

'I know that I'm kind of a killjoy, and that I shouldn't attack you so quickly. Yes, maybe I should've let you enjoy the moment, maybe I ruined it all, but… I must. You are not here to rest. That will be 40 to 50 or 60 years from now. Now we need to fix all the mistakes you have made. And to do this we need to discuss what those were, because they need to change. Not only for your life to get better, but others' lives too, because as I notice… as we notice, these are typical mistakes, seven out of ten people make these – which is a huge number. Of course, not to the same extent, some more, some less, but the mistakes are quite generic.'

'Well… it's not too nice to be exposed to all this, to your mistakes, to your bad decisions – you should know this. But if you believe that it will be better for me in the long run, and more importantly for others…. so be it. Let's begin.'

'This is why you're my Queen. Because you think like this. If someone slaps you, meaning they tell you what needs to be changed and in what aspect with good intentions, you don't get offended but rather consider it.'

'But this is not true for everyone. In order for me to listen to someone's opinion, they have to work hard. First and foremost, I need to feel that they don't say it because they want to hurt me, but because they want to help me, and they want me to be happy. I completely ignore spiteful comments.'

'I know. And this is the right way. Of course, this is not the natural order for everyone. And there are a few reasons this… Oh, Molly! There are so many errors in your lives, so much to learn that I don't even know where to start.'

'What do you think about starting at the beginning?' Molly smiled.

'Maybe it wouldn't be too bad,' Noah agreed. 'Fine, let's start at the beginning. And the beginning's name is this: the ego.'

'Oh,' Molly grinned. 'that's already a bad start.'

'Why?' Noah inquired. 'There is nothing bad in it. Well, nothing good either.'

'Really?'

'No. The truth is that there is good in it. Bad, even more. Much more. I could list a hundred bad attributes and maybe, maybe I could fit one or two good ones in there. The whole curriculum will be about what is bad in your life/lives, and often its cause will be the stubbornness of the ego. Because it doesn't want to understand, to comprehend what we ask.'

'So it doesn't obey.'

'It doesn't. We don't want anything harmful, but it simply cannot understand, and because of this...

'...you don't like it very much,' the girl finished the sentence.

'You put it mildly. I couldn't have done that.'

'Sometimes you surprise me. You can react to things with such vehemence. Not really what one would expect from an…'

'An angel? You can say it.'

'Yes, from an angel.'

'It has a simple reason, Molly. I'm a guardian angel, my job is to protect and watch over your every step since the beginning of your existence. Just a sidenote: I was never short of things to do. In order for me to do my best in that, I had to experience all that you did. Good and bad both, everything. You are lucky in that aspect that you only bear the weight of a single life, but I bear all of your lives. Well… you carry it too, but your conscience has no idea of this, so you are only burdened by a single one. But I have all of them.'

'But why?'

'Oh, Molly, come on! We drifted away from the point. We should be talking about the ego, not this.'

'I know. But every time you start explaining something you end up saying "I'll show you later, I'll explain later…" I don't remember half of what you should be explaining me later on, because we have left so many things.'

'You are right. From the outside it might seem that I'm a bit disorganised, but let me tell you: I'm not. I remember exactly all that we left mid-explaining, and I'm going to explain everything as I promised you. I only didn't do so because this was the introductory period. You had to get used to me again. You had to experience quite a few things, so that you could be completely sure in everything, so that you could give all you have to learning in a way that you could embrace and open up that knowledge. Which not too easy this early on, but don't worry, you'll get your memories back gradually, since they are actually in you, they're just being blocked. My job here is to help you remove those blocks. Everything is happening as it should. We're making good progress.'

'Good, then. I'd like to help. Just tell me what I need to do.'

'Watch and learn. Later when you go back, share your experiences with others. Write. Write down everything you learned from me and yourself. The world needs to change, and the real change begins here and now. Because you became the person you are right now… who you always were, we just had to peel off everything your ego put on you. But everything is going to be all right now. If you're uncertain what to do next, I'll be here to drag you back to the correct direction, you don't have to worry about this anymore.'

'Thank you,' she smiled. She felt relieved. She felt as if she could do anything, move entire worlds. Maybe she really was meant for something special. She felt like she could fly. She felt light and relieved, which was another fantastic and wonderful feeling, more uplifting than any before.

'I thought there was nothing better than the moments after waking up.'

'That's just the beginning, Molly. We can't start at the best part. I don't think you could even handle it. And… in my experiences, you understood much easier the experienced things, if we took small steps forward. Step by step.'

'It's perfect like this. Every each of these energy surges… every experience like this releases something unbelievably beautiful in me. And I know that I said "unbelievably beautiful" several times… But I just cannot find any better way to express it, and even this doesn't get close to what I experienced.'

'Yes, Molly. This is what you've been postponing. I'm glad you're here, but you have to know that this shouldn't have been like this. If you started writing your book, you wouldn't have to be here.'

'But then I wouldn't have met you.'

'We would've... there. You could've experienced all this with me the same way. But you should've realised that you have to conquer your ego, not let it control you. Overcoming it, taking control, putting it in its place. Its job is to control the body. Nothing else. Everything else belongs to the soul and the spirit.'

'What is it that I should've done?'

'You should've had faith in God. Believe that he doesn't want anything bad to happen to you. On the contrary! He wants the best for you and everybody else. But most importantly you should've believed in yourself. That would've been the most important thing. Every mistake you made stems from you not believing in yourself. You waited for solutions from others. You wanted to hand every problem over to others, because you thought that they were too difficult. Of course. How much easier would it be if you could say "Okay, here is the task, there you go, do it instead of me. If you like, I can help... but not too much because it's difficult." No, Molly, it doesn't work like that. The task is given. Everyone's. You cannot give yours to anybody else, because it yours, not theirs. Believe me, they have enough on their plate. For example to help you, which doesn't mean that it is their job to do yours instead of you. And believe me, helping you out is sometimes even harder than your current task can be, because first they need to get you to get up and move. Because of your laziness, but mostly because of your fears. You decided that you were a nobody, and you kept repeating this stupidity to yourself for 30 years, that you are a nobody, no good for anything, you are not meant for great things...'

'Hey! I didn't tell this to myself. My environment told me this. Since my childhood.'

'You're wrong again, Molly.'

'Why? You said you've been with me since the first day of my existence. Then you should know that it was exactly like this. I have been listening to everyone telling me that I'm not good for anything, and I'm not going to be anyone important since I was a kid.'

'And?'

'What and?'

'Just this: AND?'

'I don't get it...'

'Did you show them that they were wrong?'

'No.'

'Why not?'

'Because they repeated it so many times that I believed them. I believed that I'm a nobody, that I can't make it, that I'm not good for anything, that... it doesn't matter if I exist or don't.'

'The problem with this theory, Molly, is that this wasn't what your environment told you, but what you wanted to hear to validate yourself. To feed your doubts and fears with it. Your path is set, like it or not. Of course, you don't like it, because it isn't an easy one, but that's it, there is no other choice, get used to it. You can have a thousand people around you telling you that you're a nobody, but that won't change the fact that you were born for great things. I told you a thousand times already: DO YOUR JOB, MOLLY!'

'But...'

'I swear I'm going to take your ego and put it in the trash.'

Molly was surprised by Noah's determination. She never saw him like this. She still didn't feel any anger in him. Actually, she couldn't have voiced what she felt. Maybe... Saturnal firmness. Noah noticed the girl's surprise and continued in a softer tone.

'You need to understand, Little Girl, that all that you've done up until now is your own fault. You selected the wrong information and people. All because of your fears. Remember, how many times were you complimented, how many times they told you that you were pretty and beautiful? How many times did they tell you that you can do it?'

'I can't remember.'

'Of course you don't remember these Molly, because you didn't even hear them. This information never made it to your brain, because you didn't care, because you didn't want to hear, because you didn't need this information. But believe me, they told you quite often. I know because I was there. However, if someone told you once that you were stupid and you are not good for anything or something like that... well, you never forgot that. You carried this information with you as a validation. "I was right. They see me like that, too, it's not just me who does." But in reality, nobody believed you to be like that. If someone told you anything like that it was in desperation, to make you pull yourself together, to understand that you were wrong about yourself. They just wanted to inspire you so that you might pull yourself together and show that everybody's wrong about you. But then they figured out that they only pushed you further down with this. Because you wanted this... you wanted to hear this.'

'Well... this is quite something. One moment you raise me up, making me feel I could fly, next you drag me down and stomp me in the dirt.'

'No, I'm not stomping you anywhere. I could never hurt you. I would protect you with my life. Molly! A few moments ago, you felt clearly what you didn't want to before, what you've been running from. That your existence has great significance. This lifted you up, this made you fly.'

'No... Not just that. There was something else.'

'Tell me.'

'That I felt safe. I knew I could fly because you are here. You said, "If you are uncertain what to do next, I'll be here to drag you back to the correct direction, you don't have to worry about this anymore." And the best part is that I felt that these were not empty words, but you really meant them. This is what gives me wings. Safety. That I know that if I fail, you'll be there to pick me up.

That I know if it will be difficult, you'll be there with a reassuring hug. And you saying, "I'm here, I'll protect you, no harm can come to you. Or if it does, we'll fight it together" is enough. This is what I've been looking for in my entire life. Safety.'

'But Molly, you had this since you existed. I'm here to watch over your every move. You can't see me, but you've always felt my presence. You can't say you couldn't. Why isn't the safety that I… we… provide to you enough? Because you can't see? And? What then? Don't long for seeing, that's the habit of the ego. Don't want to see everything! Sense! Sense and believe! You can't expect another person give you what you want. No one can grant you that safety you need, because no one has it. Not even John. I'll let you know that everybody's looking for what they are, but no one can find it, because you should look for it inside of yourselves. Many relationships end because of this. They get scared by the responsibility, by giving something to the other that they don't have themselves. Or the other option, that they are so disappointed in their partners because they didn't receive what they hoped for. Everything could be so simple, you'd only have to have faith in yourselves and in God… the True One. The true True One, who doesn't fit the description of earthly churches sometimes. You can often hear "I'm a God-fearing person." Who invented this colossal stupidity, that you should be afraid of God? You don't have to be. You should trust and believe instead, believe that he knows what he's doing, and follow his instructions and requests. But the ego cannot do this, because it cannot see him. And this is what I don't get. Why should it be able to see everything? Why should it understand everything? It answers: because I have a right to do so. But then what? If it gains the knowledge it wants, then comes the "seeing is believing" part. But we cannot show everything. Or even if we show it, doesn't believe us. Just like John. And we end up running around in circles, not getting anywhere. Oh, Molly! There is so much to change, because the world is heading in the wrong direction. I know that I told you already but I'm going to tell you many more times while you're here. Imagine your world as an express train without brakes, rushing towards a wall, where it all ends. There are still a few junctions, opportunities to turn into a new direction, but not too many. If you reach the wall, it's going to hurt a lot of people. This is what we're trying to avoid. This is why you're here. This is why I'm trying to get rid of your biggest fear: that you're alone. You aren't. A lot of people who help you and protect you surround you. Do you know what the problem is, Molly? That you are looking for what you are giving in others, too. But others don't have what you do. You give an enormous burden to others, because others cannot handle what you are capable of. You were born with a pure heart, you lack every form of selfishness. You can be selfish only for love. If there is someone that can love you in the way you need it, then you encroach upon them and don't let them go.'

'Because I need charging. I just give and give, and receive nothing in return. I'm drained, and can't handle it anymore. And this is what no one can understand. It's not solving stuff instead of what I need… well, that happens, too, I admit, but in the end I always realise that I can't do that. I just need someone who is there for me. If I want to give up, or just feel like I can't do it anymore, he only needs to say: "Don't give up, you can do it. I can believe in you." There is no responsibility… I think.'

'Believe me already that there is. Loving you is an enormous responsibility.'

'But why?'

'Because you are extremely sensitive. That's why. Because you need to be handled carefully, to be protected. Not from others, because you can handle that alone. It's himself who loves you you have to protect yourself from. So he doesn't hurt you or exploit you even by accident. This is the greatest burden, this is what people cannot handle, those to whom you show your real self to.'

'Then I'm never going to show it to anyone again.'

'You don't understand…'

'Yes, I do. It means that I'm going to be alone.'

'You are never going to be alone. You never were. I'm here for you among many others. But yes… you'll be without a significant other for a while.'

'That's good,' she pouted.

'I know that it isn't good. I know that this is not what you wanted, but please, understand that there is no one who can bear the weight that you put on them. But if you'd like to, we could try again… try and find you someone new.'

'No. Won't work. We tried already. Just leave it. Do our job.'

'Molly. You have to decide now. This is the crossroads of your life. I can still send you back. We'll find someone to be there for you.'

'For how long? 2 years, tops. No one can stand me for longer. And I'll be more broken after that. No point, even I see that now. Forget it. Let's do what needs to be done. I'll do it alone.'

'But I already told you that you are not alone!!! There were and will be loads of people who will stand by you and help you, these are the people who love you. And one of them will love you more than anyone anytime – except me.'

'John?'

'Yes. He is still afraid. He wanted to run away ever since he knew you. But he cannot. He wants to let you go, but clutches on to you in the last moment. Give him time. When you go back, too. Give him time, so he might familiarise himself with the idea. What is waiting for him.'

'Why? What's waiting for him? Nothing. He doesn't have to love me.'

'He doesn't love you because he has to. You saw and felt it.'

'I'm never going to force anything on him, especially myself. I have so much to thank him for… he gave me back my life – I could never hurt him. His friendship is one of the biggest treasures in my life. I'd rather let him go if that's what is needed for him to be happy.'

'Molly! Give him time, don't force anything. Believe me, everything will slide into place, they just need time. Especially him.'

'I don't get it then. You say that there is no one that could stand as my significant other with me, then you say that John could… Which one is it, then?'

'He is not your significant other, he is your partner. There is a difference, you see.'

'Of course I don't.'

'He would be your significant other if you would wake together, live together. He is just your playing partner. You wake and live separately, yet together. We will talk about the topic of relationships a lot, because there are a lot of problems with that one, too. Actually, after the ego relationships, the institution of marriage is the second biggest problem group in my opinion, because you don't do it properly.'

'That doesn't sound too good.'

'It doesn't. How about we start our little journey? I'll show you everything, and then we'll come back here to talk a bit before I let you back.'

'Not a good idea. I don't want to go back.'

'I know, Molly. But you have to, we talked about this. You know you have to, there is no other way, no matter how hard it is. But don't think about this just yet. We'll discuss it when its time

95

comes. By that time you might even get bored with me.'

'Maybe,' she smiled.

'Ha-ha. Now… what do you think? Are you ready? Can we go already?'

'Can't we stay a bit longer? This place is so beautiful…'

'Molly! We waited long enough. We need to go.'

'I know. I just don't know if I want to.'

'Now, this is what I told you a few minutes ago! That it is harder to get you going than your own task. We leave. Now.'

'Sir, yes, sir!'

'Now, that I like. You being such an obedient little gal. This is how I have to treat you then, firm and strong,' Noah grinned.

'Don't you dare!' the girl snarled.

'If I'm nice to you, patronise you, treat you with love, you get emotional and grow uncertain. If I'm firm with you, you do your job.'

'This is something that we'll change really quickly, then. I love it much more when you love me.'

'I like that better, too, but I'll see how it will be. But now, no matter how long you wanted to stay, we are leaving.'

'Okay, okay… we're leaving. But where?'

'Up.'

'Where?'

'Up. Hold my hand and close your eyes.'

The girl knew she had no other choice, so she obeyed. She was certain that she didn't want to either know or see all this, but she knew that she didn't have any other choice. She felt that no matter how painful it was going to be it was better to get it over with, since this was her fate and it was inevitable. Like the fact that she must go back. She knew she had no other choice. This was her lot.

'We're here. You can open your eyes now,' Noah said.

'I just closed them, should I open them already? How come?'

'On this level it's just like that. Open your eyes, there is nothing scary here.'

There really wasn't anything special there. They were sitting atop a bridge in a huge, noisy, dirty, smoggy city. Beneath them flowed a so-called river; a stream of dirty water, littered with garbage, dead vegetation, and animal and human carcasses. It was disgusting as far as the eye could see.

'This is horrible. Where did you bring me? From one extremity to the other?' grimaced the girl. 'Which city is this?'

'Welcome to one of the cities of the ego.'

'This is disgusting.'

'I know. The perfect location for us to start learning about the ego.'

'Going to be a nice story, I expect.'

'I'm not going to show you pleasant things. I've got to admit that this is only the beginning. But I promise we'll take breaks and see nicer places. I'll show you the counter-examples, even though those are rarer.'

'Fine. Let's begin.'

'Finally, we got here. Before we do anything, you should know that I'm really proud of you.'

'Why is that?'

'Because you made it this far. I know how hard it is for you. I know it was not easy to digest all you've seen up till now. What comes later will be even more difficult, but I believe and know that together we can solve anything. I told you already, and I'm going to tell you many more times: I'm here, to help, to protect you. If you are ready then we can begin. So:

4.

The ego:

As I told you before, the ego is one of the great four. Along with the body, the soul and the spirit, the ego is of equal importance during your earthly lives. On Earth there is no existence of one without the other, they connect, they intertwine, and by forming a perfect whole they create something wonderful – what we call human life. They help and control each other along the often difficult and barrier-filled road towards the perfect order.'

'Nice definition. I'm going to write this into my book, and when I'm really famous, so famous that my – actually your – theories will be taught at universities, the students are going to hate me for having to learn it by heart,' Molly grinned.

'Molly, stop fooling around,' Noah grinned with her. 'How can I be serious, how can I teach you, if you make a joke about all of it? And by the way... when we get into the university, we'll need to incorporate it somehow that this is my theory, too... Or my truth, too, not just yours. Let's call it the "Molly-Noah Ego Theory."'

'Fine, let it be so. But let's continue. It's starting to get interesting. Our theories being taught at universities... My vanity would like that... I'm paying attention. Please, go on.'

'I love you when you're like this, you crazy chick.'

'Why only now? I'm always adorable. Even when I'm hysterical. I'm lovely when I'm hissy.'

'Well...'

'Hey! Don't you dare telling me that I'm not!'

'I wouldn't dare to say something like that, even if it's true,' Noah continued smiling.

'I think it's better if we continue. So we were at an intertwining, perfect whole, perfect order.'

'Exactly. So you do pay attention. At least a bit.'

'I usually do.'

'Then, if we were at theories, here's the next one. I told you once, you'll get it back exactly as I said before: the ego is a necessary evil. It helps you to control your body. If you are hungry, it sends a message – or will – to your body to go and get food. If you are thirsty you drink, if you're cold you

101

put on more clothes, if you're hot you take them off. He is responsible for the daily routines, too. You wake up, you go to work, pay your bills, go on with your business, you go home and go to sleep. You want it and your body obeys.'

'Just a sidenote, the previous one was better. This won't make us famous.'

'Molly, pay attention. Seriously, you act like a little kid. Watch, and learn.'

'Sir, yes, sir!' Molly jumped into a stand-to.

'Good… that's what I like. So, we were at… Where were we?... Oh, yes, I wanted to tell you, before you belittled my truth, that just like you experienced before, the ego lives in your brain. There is where it controls from. That would be its only job, to control the body. But somehow that's not enough for it.'

'Yes, we talked about this before. I told you then that you might have to revise the roles. Maybe you should be more honest with the ego, give it some greater role, trust it or believe in it more. After all, it is one of the great four.'

'Yes, we thought about that before. Look around Molly, this was the result.'

'I don't like to. What is here is horrible and painful.'

'I know it's horrible, but you have to face reality.'

'And what about you handling this situation differently? Maybe making it understand the situation in a different way... Not like this.'

'Molly. Believe me, this is the hardest part. And not simply difficult, it is difficult made even more difficult.'

'I don't get it again.'

'Then I'll explain to you and show it to you. Let's start from far away, so it is easy to understand. Earth is not the first stop, and currently not the only one. It is foolish to believe that the Earth is the only habitable planet in the universe. You believe that because it makes the ego feel safe. Banging on its chest, me-me-me... Well, no. There are plenty of habitable and inhabited planets, with plenty of lifeforms, with different levels of development. Not every planet has the evolutionary descendants of apes as the dominant species. If you don't mind I'm not going to show you these. There are enough movies about these "strange creatures." Quotation marks, because for them you are those. You have this as natural, they have something else.'

'Yes, we discussed this with John before. We both think that they/you are preparing us with these movies for encounters. Cartoons, movies, the aliens are everywhere. What we believed to be impossible is becoming more and more natural.'

'You are right. The encounters are a must for your continued development. Humanity has yet again reached the limit of the technological advancement that you could achieve without help. There's only downhill from here. Take a look at your world, at this city. If you don't change, this will be the fate of the whole world. And this is because you don't know how to proceed further. You don't see where you could develop further. You'll need help for that… again.'

'You said "again" a couple of times, why?'

'Because it's not the first time you received help. A small nudge that helped you to get out of the nadir. This is what'll happen now… what should happen… if you can embrace it. Or this is the end, which is not possible.'

'Why?'

'Because Earth is too valuable to let it be destroyed by your wastage. You even got a deterrent example, but of course you misinterpreted it.'

'I don't know what you are talking about.'

'Dinosaurs. Millions of years back they were the dominant ones on this planet, the apex predators of Earth. Everyone knows the end of the story, a huge meteorite came and killed every living thing. The reason was was that they reached that point of no return. They couldn't develop further, and the end came. And it was not Earth that got destroyed, only the creatures living on it. Of course not every one of them, because we didn't want to render this beautiful planet uninhabitable, but to create something new. Something better, more perfect. And this is where the third basic rule comes in, which I want you to remember, because it is really important: every end is the beginning of something new. You have to let go of the old if it isn't good for you anymore, so that you can embrace the new.'

'It's often hard.'

'I know it's hard. Because no matter how bad the old thing is, you cling to it, because it is certainty. Certainly bad, because you suffer from it, but you still cannot let go. Even though letting go is a really important thing. If you can do it in time, you can get the good, the better, the different, sooner.'

'Understood.'

'We'll see, Molly, if you understand or don't, because currently understanding now what I say is not enough. What matters is that you can use all you learn from me in practice. Now, I drifted off again… You know what? Come, grab my hand, let us go on a little trip.'

'Where are we going?'

'To see dinosaurs.' As Noah said this, Molly found herself in a new, wonderful landscape.

'How do you do this? And why didn't I have to close my eyes this time?'

'You didn't have to close them before, either, I just thought it would be a bigger shock if you opened them when we were already there.'

'But how?'

'There is no space or time on this level. That was designed for Earth, so we could keep the events in check, but I'll explain that, too. Let's not rush forward. Take a look around what a nice place I brought you to.'

'Yes, it's amazing. Where are we?'

106

'The same place we were before, only a few million years earlier. Tell me what you see.'

'Thriving, throbbing nature. I'd like to run around in the grass, play with those dinos having their lunch over there. Or to climb into the crystal-clear waters of this stream. I see the fish swimming, frogs jumping, mosquitoes flying. Everything is so perfect and in harmony, it's enchanting.'

'What keeps you?'

'We are talking... I mean, learning. I can't leave because I have to pay attention.'

'Who said that?'

'No one.'

'Then go. Enjoy it, if you are so enthusiastic about it,' Noah smiled.

And Molly went. Ran. Enjoyed the untouched nature, the closeness of the animals. She was happy and free. Nothing to cause her discomfort, nothing to hurt her, she just ran and ran. Rolled around on the ground, in the water. It's true she didn't feel the cool of the water, the smell or the touch of the grass, or the caress of the sunlight, but she imagined them, so everything felt perfect. She was happy and started to feel lighter, as though she had dropped some sort of a great burden. Finishing playing, she sat down next to an animal resting in the grass, touching it gently. Molly didn't feel the warmth of its skin… or cold, or the touch, or the smell. She tried to imagine. She started to get what Noah meant: you can imagine the feel of touching something, but it isn't the same. She had never valued it before, taking it for granted, an unimportant aspect. She had had it and she hadn't cared about it, hadn't realised its value. It was then that she finally grasped what it really meant - that we don't know how much something or someone means to us until we lose them. This is true. And sadly, we cannot realise their value until the trouble happens.

'But let's look at the bright side. How many people can say that they petted a dino?' she asked the animal lying on the ground. 'Do you agree, little guy?'

'The animal raised its head a bit, then put it back down instantly. It seemed as though it gave her a tiny nod. Molly just smiled. She felt everything to be perfect. She became one with the landscape, with nature, she became a part of it. She didn't feel as though she were a visitor now. Quiet, peace, calm and safety. Harmony made manifest.

'Feels good, doesn't it?'

'Why don't you come and play with me?' she asked.

'I can't now. And it would be better if you'd joined me.'

Molly didn't understand what was going to happen, but she saw that Noah's face grew solemn – and that couldn't mean anything good. She stood up, walked to the man, who extended his hand towards her. When the girl took it he pulled her close, and whispered: 'Everything is going to be all right.' Suddenly, three predators appeared out of nowhere, disrupting the previous peace. They struck at the herd, murdering them. Molly felt the unimaginable hate and contempt emanating from them. They didn't look at anything, only wanted to kill. They ravaged and tore up their victims, without paying attention to age or sex. The girl felt that they didn't do it out of hunger, only for the sake of murder. No motivation except the lust for destruction in them.

'Do something, this is horrible,' she whispered.

'I can't,' Noah answered, then hugged the girl even stronger. They watched helplessly as the panicked animals tried to defend themselves, to fight for their lives, but it didn't matter. The three killers were stronger and more cunning. Screams and death throes filled the landscape. Molly felt the fear of the animals, their begging for help, for someone to help them, or for this to be over already. Maybe their attackers felt this too, because they slowed down. The previous quick, remorseless attacks bringing quick deaths were replaced by playful murders. They let their victims to lie in pain for longer, they didn't kill instantly. Chased and shoved the animals around. Those who tried to escape were further ravaged, those who gave up and didn't move were left on the ground to die.

Molly tried to get out of Noah's arms. She couldn't watch the animals suffering passively any longer, but the man didn't let her go.

'This is how it has to be. You cannot do anything,' he said in a calm voice. 'I know that it's terrible to watch, but you have to see this.'

Tears were streaming from her eyes. She was powerless. The animal she was resting with so peacefully just a minute ago was lying in the ground, dead, its blood soaking the ground. The land slowly grew quiet. The predators had finished, no one had survived from the herd, so they left contentedly. As they were walking away, one of them turned around and there was some sort of a wicked grin on its face. He felt unbelievably strong and cunning. He was perfectly content with their 'work.'

'They didn't eat,' she said after a long time.

'What?'

'You saw that they didn't eat, right? They killed, but didn't eat.'

'They didn't kill because they were hungry. Just because they liked it. Because they could do it, because they had the strength and the skills to do so.'

'I thought that animals only killed for two reasons: because of hunger or in protecting their territory, their packs or herds.'

'Yes, that is the original design. Called the circle of life. This was meant to be a sort of give-take game. But here, for some reason, some of the more advanced species thought that they could exterminate herds, species, just for fun. This wouldn't be too much of a problem, because nature was designed in a way so it could cope with losses like this. Look, Little Girl. Here comes a whole lot of smaller and bigger scavenger animals, who will make use of the fallen animals. This is just the start of a whole chain of events. Give me your hand, I'll show you.'

111

'Okay.'

'I know that this is not a pretty sight. I know that no one would watch this happily, but you had to see it. If it weren't so, you wouldn't be here. If everything was okay on Earth then we shouldn't worry about this, only about fixing your life. But it's not like that. Now, let's go.'

'Where?'

'Here again.'

Molly only saw a flash, like someone flashed a camera into her eye, which blurred her vision a bit. When she regained her sight, she was shocked. They really were at the same place. The clearing, the trees, the stream… everything was the same, yet somehow they weren't. The grass wasn't so full of life. Everything was overgrown, grass reaching higher than before. No mosquitoes, no frogs hopping around, and not a sight of herds of dinosaurs anywhere. The whole scene had a sad and lonely feel to it.

'What happened?' she asked. 'Were we really here before?'

'Yes, we just jumped a few hundred years into the future. I told you that the massacre before was only the beginning.'

'Yes.'

'Nature can cope with a massacre like that. Of course, every life lost is painful, but still, they can be replaced. But what happened back then became unstoppable by now.'

'But what happened exactly?'

'Every plant and animal has a role to play in the circle of life. The food chain is known to you, I don't have to explain that. You know too that species going extinct upsets the balance. If somehow that still happens, nature is so wonderful that it can correct that, so there is usually not much of a problem. But here the situation got so bad that it couldn't be fixed. A few species rose from the others – which wouldn't be much of a problem, but things didn't go the way they were supposed to. The species that started evolving did not use the gift that they received properly. They didn't use it to make better circumstances for their less-developed fellows, but they wanted to show dominance. I think they misunderstood their position. Or maybe we chose... we chose a too aggressive species... I don't know. But one thing's for sure: that massacre was the first step towards the extinction of dinosaurs.'

'I'm not an expert in this, I couldn't name any of the previous dinosaurs, but even I know that

113

it was a meteorite that meant the end for the dinosaurs, that rendered the planet uninhabitable for a while. Or am I wrong?'

'You are not. But that was just the end. The result. The meteorite came, because it had to. Because Earth needed to be cleansed completely.'

'That sounds scary.'

'Come, I'll show you.'

He didn't even have to ask, Molly gave her hand. Noah grabbed it and in that instant, they were suddenly in space. She was speechless.

'How do you do this?'

'I told you already that there is no space or time here. That was designed for Earth to control, but more importantly to keep the flow of events in check. Imagine it as when you were learning to walk. You have to feel where you want to be, and you'll find yourself there, no problem.'

'I could've used this skill before, so many times…' she laughed.

'Well… yeah. I could never get you to leave in time. You were always late. But never mind, it was good like that.'

'And… why are we here?'

114

'Look at your world, Little Girl. What do you see and feel?'

'That this is "the" wonder.'

'Exactly. And how much time do you think it took to create such a wonder? So that everything is perfect, as it should be. So it would have temperature suitable for the development of life, so it would have enough food, water, air, and light. Let me tell you, it wasn't easy.'

'I guessed that much.'

'No, you have no idea. And nobody else does either. I know that it is hard to believe, but everyone, even people without faith, know that the solar system didn't come to be as it is on its own. Nothing like a complete system popped out of nowhere. Every planet is where and how it should be, the position, size and shape of every one is based on complex calculations. The smallest distortion would disturb everything. The balance would fracture, because of which the Earth would not be habitable. Every part has its own function, how they affect each other, and are in connection with each other – but we'll talk more about this later. What is important now and why we are here is for you to understand what actually happened. The wonder known as the solar system came to being. With planets, asteroids, different minerals, etc. Earth came to be, too. And on Earth: life.'

'So, the Earth was not intentionally designed for humans?'

'Not really, no. We started an experiment on how that species you called dinosaurs could evolve, how they would get along with their lives if they were provided a bigger space. We knew there could be troubles, since we knew the attributes of the species, their properties, but it was worth a try.'

'And they failed.'

'That's right. In order for us to restart the whole thing we had to do a complete cleansing. We had two options:

1. We destroy Earth.

2. We keep Earth, and we just do away with life on its surface... doing a clean sweep, to put it bluntly.'

'That didn't sound nice, you're right.'

'Yes, I know.'

'I guess you didn't like the first option, you didn't want that.'

'You are right. Look around, Molly. Earth itself is a wonder. Look at this huge blue and green planet… Often times I just come out here and look at it in awe, how perfect we made it. And once you are full of the sight, and you look around… Isn't it just fantastic? To destroy this because of the folly of a single species? No one could expect that from us. So, no matter how hard decision was…'

'Clean sweep.'

'Yes. We sent a huge asteroid that cleansed the world. Raised the temperature on Earth so high that all life died on it. Look. This was it.'

Molly saw an enormous of rock approaching the planet at immense speed. It sped forwards unstoppably, and crashed into the blue planet.

'Is it a problem if I don't want to watch this from any closer?' she asked on the verge of crying.

'You can see everything you need to from here. We won't go closer.'

And she saw. As the meteorite crashed into the surface of Earth everything got destroyed. That beautiful blue and green planet, which was throbbing with life even from this distance, ceased to exist. Everything became parched, dry, and empty.

'What happened to the animals?'

'Do you want to see?'

'It's enough for you to tell me.'

'Come, let's take a look.'

'I wouldn't like to go back there. It's bad enough a sight even from this distance. I wouldn't like to go any closer.'

'Please,' Noah said softly.

'Okay,' she said quietly.

They were on Earth again. It was even more painful from up close. There was only ash where plants grew. Rivers, streams evaporated at an observable rate. The animals that had not died in the crash were in horrible pain. The composition of the air changed, their bodies were not used to it. They hyperventilated, then slowly asphyxiated. Horrible suffering and destruction everywhere. She was powerless. She just stood there and watched. The sight burned into her soul – she might never erase it from there. Maybe she wouldn't have to. She was beginning to understand why she had to see all this.

'This is what you told me about?' she whispered, fighting with her tears. 'Not long ago you told me that there is a way, an easier, but more painful way towards change, that neither the world nor you want. Is this it?'

'Do not think about that.'

'Noah, please answer! Is this the possibility you want to avoid? Is this why we are here right now, why I had to see all this? Please, be honest.'

'Yes.'

'And now? What next?'

'I'll tell you what happened next. Nothing for a several million of years. Earth needed to regenerate. It needed to prepare for the development of new life, which is neither easy nor a quick process. We selected a new species that could be the leading species. Less aggressive, fewer problems. On other planets we succeeded with similar species, so we thought that there couldn't be too much trouble with them. Of course, we learnt from our mistakes, we needed to be careful. I'm not talking about only the dinosaurs... And I wanted to avoid this discussion for a while, because this is the hardest to grasp and digest.'

'What do you mean?'

'Molly, as I told you, everything happens for a reason. The planets coming to being, different

119

lifeforms on them – neither are a coincidence. Because there is no such thing as coincidence. Especially not one of this magnitude… Whoa, Little Girl, I have no idea how to explain this to you so you would understand.'

'Try being honest maybe?'

'Sure. The planets and species developed… putting it bluntly: they were created for a goal of crucial importance: to gather information. As I told you before. we created various lifeforms with various bodies and attributes on various planets. The circumstances differed, too, so not every species lived on the surface. We solved this problem by putting these planets far away from each other, so they wouldn't interfere with each other's basic development.'

'What do you mean by basic development?'

'It means that every species has a level of development they have to reach. Then it is decided what's next.'

'I see. Then I guess what we saw a few moments ago was the nothing next.'

'Yes. They reached that level of development that they had to, so we could decide if it was worth showing and giving them more or not. It wasn't. Believe me, Molly, a decision like this hurts for us, too. A lot of our work went into controlling and maintaining a planet this big. And in addition… it was us who created this lifeform. It is extremely hard to destroy your own creation. A lot of discussion and dispute precedes a decision like this. Oftentimes, we give them one last chance, then another, and another, so that they might change. Sometimes the species realise what they did wrong. But this is not always the case.'

'Then comes the destruction.'

'Sadly, yes. But only the species', not the planet's. It is seldom that we have to destroy a whole planet. It only happens if the habitant species deal so much damage to it that it becomes irreparable.'

'Why do you let that happen?'

'Molly, even we cannot know everything, cannot foresee everything.'

'Understood.'

'Good. Where was I? Oh, yes. Development, evolution. I told you that the path is set both globally and individually. The individual path has three goals:

1. Development of soul

2. Collecting and transferring information

3. Karma

I'm going to try to explain it so it is easy to understand. Before your birth you receive one or more tasks that you must to complete in your life. You get a body, an ego, you get a life with a certain environment, meaning a family, schools, friends, loves, relatives, associates, profession, jobs, and I could go on. The point is, that everything that happens to you during your life does so so that you can complete your task. There are things and people who help you in this; others pull you back, sometimes completely halt your progress. Help, I think is obvious: so it helps you, nudges you towards your goal when you are about to give up. And setbacks are for testing your strength, so that you become even stronger, even tougher, even more persistent. And all this for the reasons I mentioned before. The point is, that everything that happens in your life – both good and bad – does so to help you towards completing your task, which is the development, the growth of the soul. Next is the information, which could be discussed together with the first one because they are the same thing, but let's take it in two.'

'Sure.'

'Thank you,' Noah smiled. 'So… information. You storing information acquired throughout your lives is not only important to you, but to us as well. You get a given situation, and we see how you react to it with the background we gave you. That situation, in the meantime, will be given to other people, with different backgrounds, different attributes. This is all information to us. We compare and analyse which one is better. We gather experience about how should we do our business in the future. It's beneficial both for you and us. The same is the situation in the bigger scale. Whereas individual development doesn't have too much time, only about 70 years now on Earth, the global development has a bit more time, since the question is not about a single person but about a whole group, nation, nationality, planet, etc. Bigger the group, longer the time it needs. But! The foundation of everything is the individual's development, since there is no society without individuals. In order for you to understand: now you feel that the life on Earth and the Earth itself are something really old. Let me tell you, that they aren't. This is one of the youngest of the inhabited planets, and one of the least developed ones. Just think about it… 2 to 300 years ago you were still riding around on horseback, and trains were marvels. You cannot call this an advanced society. Sure, your rate of development has drastically increased in the last 50 years, but it's still evanescent, almost nothing, still. You are nowhere near what the peoples of other planets have already achieved a long time ago. Remember. When you were a kid, where were mobile phones? It's a common item today, but it wasn't 20 years ago. If you look at it this way, you can easily grasp that the population of Earth believes itself to be immensely developed, but they are not, not by a long shot. Of course, compared to the other species you know you are… but believe me, their number is extremely low. And the biggest mistake of the humans is that you don't want to embrace the new, you don't want to let it in. Look at the many discoveries, the multitudes of new and wonderful things in your lives. Inventors dish out newer and newer, more and more amazing ideas and what happens? Nothing. You don't need it. War for oil continues, still hundreds, thousands die for it, but this question shouldn't cause any problems in anyone's lives for a long time now. There are so many ways to deal with this issue, but no, humanity doesn't need that, because it's new. But let's not rush so far ahead. They say, "Back when I was a kid, it was like this and that." Yes. It was like that because it had to be back then, but then is not now. And yet they don't care about this. They hold back the kids, almost chain them so they cannot fly. Or… just take a look at institutionalised education. What is going on there? They are living in the past. Kids today still have to read stories and poems from 100 to 150 years ago, filled with words no longer used in common speech. They make the kids read text that they don't even understand. Of course they're going to hate it. Even though reading is crucial in the development of the brain, but the "wise old" people cannot understand this, so the hellish circle forms again. They hurt the kids - they are like this and that because they don't read. This makes them feel bad, so they try again, but they just simply don't understand, so they just stop. With this continuous repetition they get to a point that they don't even want to pick up a book. They listen to how stupid and worthless they are, they say, "Okay, fine, I am," and they leave it at that. The brain and the imagination stops developing, the kids become shallow, and by the time they are 18 they won't care about anything... they will be tired... like one of the undead.'

'Like me...'

'Yes, Little Girl.... Like you. And I think we just got back to the ego.'

'I guess we're travelling again.'

'We can stay if you'd like, but I see no point in that.'

'You didn't finish explaining what you wanted to show me with this.'

'You finish it. You know perfectly well.'

'I think I know. But I'm not sure I want to know.'

'That's it! That's what I was talking about, Molly. Does it hurt? Is it difficult? Of course it hurts, and of course it is difficult. But at least you'd have to make a move, to actually do something, which you cannot do. Pull yourself together!'

'Okay. Sorry.'

'Don't apologise; rather do your job. I told you already. So… what did you learn?'

'That the bones of the dinosaurs and the evidences of their lifestyles were left for us by you not for us to bring them back, acting as God, but to learn from their mistakes.'

'This is the benefit of history. Not bringing it back, but learning from the mistakes of the past. But… no. All you want to do is go backwards. Because it was like this back then and how well it worked. Yes, it was, and yes, it worked, because it was back then. Now it isn't back then, now is now. This is the problem with the world controlled by the ego: uncomprehending and slavish.'

'So, I guess this is the cue, back to the mud we go.'

'No. I'm going to take you somewhere before that.'

'It only can be better than this.'

5.

It wasn't. Molly found herself at the crucifixion of Christ. The crucified, beaten, tortured, blood-soaked man was alive, but only barely. She heard the cursing of people, she felt their hate and their spite. She saw that contented smile in their eyes: yes, we've got this one, too. The saddest thing was that a lot of them had no idea why this was actually happening. They just saw that the person next to them, or their neighbour, relative, or friend did it and, just so that they wouldn't be marked out from the crowd, they did as they saw others do. They had no idea who this man was or what he did or didn't do. They just followed each other like mindless sheep, without thinking.

'I'd like to go back,' Molly whispered.

'We won't stay long. I just showed you this so you'd see the man who could've brought a change to your lives and so that you could see what happened to him. I'd like you to feel the people. They had a great spiritual leader in their hands whose fate was to make your world a better place, to start it on its road of development, but they - you, as a species - didn't want any of that. The ego won and your people got stuck almost at the same

128

level for 1,700 years. Okay, this was it, we won't stay here any longer. Come, let's leave.'

'Where to? Please, let it not be worse than this.'

But it was. No aspect of it was better than the prior situation. Each situation was the same, only with different people, in a different age.

'Witch-hunt,' she mumbled.

'Believe me, we made several attempts in the following 1,700 years to make your world into a better place, so that you could start out on the road you should have, but all our attempts ended the same way. Murder. The greatest explorers risked their lives to push the world forwards in great secrecy, but often they didn't survive their attempts of doing so. We sent healers to stop the outbreaks, the destruction, but they met early demises as well. It was a sad 1,700 years for everyone. But progress cannot be stopped. You can slow it down, but you cannot stop it.'

'Do we have to watch how that woman gets burnt and tortured? Do we have to watch, but, more importantly, feel how those people around her abuse her, again? This is horrible.'

'This is the ego, Molly. Maybe you are starting to understand why I don't like it. In every person there was the whisper of soul and the spirit to "go and help," but most of them couldn't even hear it with the ego screaming. They felt some kind of a bad feeling, but they didn't pay attention. They just shrugged, and thought that there is nothing wrong with this, that she must've deserved it, done something wrong. Their loved ones and relatives turned away from these people, or they were the ones that hurt them the most. It was a hard period, Molly. For humanity and us both. But we made it through.'

'But I still don't understand. Why don't you do something?'

'We cannot interfere by force, that couldn't work. As I told you, 1,700 years is a long time for you, but not for us. We thought it could serve you as a lesson… as a deterrent example.'

'1,700 years?!' she said, her voice rather a scream than one of shock.

'Yes, sadly you have difficulties comprehending anything. We rarely met a people like yours: slow, lazy, and backward.'

'You forgot "living-in-the-past."'

'No, I didn't, I just thought I had said it enough times already. Acceptance is a huge problem of yours. You quite often say that "This is my share," and you even endure something bad for years believing that "This is your share." And I'm not talking only about your screwed-up relationships, but about everyone's lives altogether. They believe they cannot do anything, so they live in a bad situation for years. They don't want or don't dare to change, rather just endure, sink into apathy, accept, then grow tired of it and everything remains in the bad position. And I'm not talking only about relationships, but about everything that isn't good. Workplace, family relations, neighbours... anything that you can imagine. Anything can be bad. And all of these could be good, or even fantastic, too; you'd just have to transform your lives a bit, your way of thinking, letting the bad go, embracing the good, only you can't do this for some reason. Can I show you another thing?'

'Do it,' muttered Molly, accepting. 'I'm not even going to ask if we could do something to help the poor woman. This whole thing is horrible to see. Look... a lot of them even enjoy this. How can people be so stupid? Seriously... at times like this I really wonder if we even should do something for them. Why? For whom? For these people?'

'I believe you'll utter these questions quite several times, and my answer always will be, "Yes, it's worth it." I'll show you why. You cannot save that woman, just like you cannot save the others. You know perfectly well that she wasn't the only one. Believe me, even though it is horrible to watch and endure this, the people who fell victim got their just rewards in their next lives. God is not ungrateful, especially not with innocent victims. This is what we call karma. But we'll talk about this, too. Now come, we need to go.'

'I guess next stop is the First World War.'

'Yes. The reason for the First World War was dissatisfaction. Or rather, let's say the arrogance that grew out of that dissatisfaction. What they had wasn't enough, everyone wanted more and more. More power, more territories. Enter the mentality, "I'm stronger than you, and I'm going to prove it." And they wanted to prove it by expanding their authority, by gaining more territories at the expense of others. Of course not everyone liked this. There were countries who only wanted to protect their colonies, but there were those who grew overconfident and wanted even more, saying, "If they can, then I can do that too." This mentality caused the deaths of 15 million people over the course of four years. Was it worth it?'

'No.'

'Of course not. Yes, sure, you can hide behind the Industrial Revolution and the need for resources and new markets... yes, they were needed. But I doubt that this price should have been paid for it. A little rational thinking and all this could've been avoided.'

'Or if you'd have intervened.'

'We did.'

'When? In the fourth year?'

'Molly, you need deterrent examples. We let tons of people die, yes. But we believed that this would be one great lesson for you and you'd learn from this, not doing anything like that again.'

'You were wrong.'

'Surprisingly, yes. Other species never continued destroying themselves this long – they always found solutions to the problems. But we saw that this doesn't work with you. I'm afraid that the war would still be raging if we hadn't said after 4 years that okay, this was enough. We hadn't worked that hard so you could mutually destroy each other, so the peace negotiations began. And what did we see then? Not even close to what we expected. We thought that the sheer number of victims, of the dead - who fell basically for nothing, since neither country achieved anything worthwhile – would calm you and force you to view the world from a new perspective… Of course nothing like this happened. 21 years after the first one ended, you started the Second World War. We couldn't believe.'

'This is why the second was so devastating?'

'Yes, because you needed to understand… you needed to learn that this is not the correct way, because war leads nowhere. You paid an enormous price, a lot of people died in horrifying ways. We empowered some of the generals' lust for power. If you want this, then so be it. The six years of bloodshed, which claimed the lives of tens of millions of people.'

'Yes, I read about this, around 50 million.'

'That number isn't exact either, but that is not the point. The point is that it is the multitude of the previous death toll, and the second one was much more cruel and bloody. Various, horrible methods of torture, and in the end the nuclear bomb… These left a huge impression in people and you finally said that it was enough, and you still believe this today. Of course there are still smaller conflicts, but nobody dares to wage a full-scale war because that would assure the destruction of humanity, which would be good for no one.'

'There is something I don't understand. If the situation is really that bad as it seems, as you show me, then why even bother saving it?'

'Oh, Little Girl! The fact that right now we are concentrating on the bad things doesn't mean that the human species cannot be saved and needs to be exterminated, or that we should let them destroy themselves. We are only discussing this dark side so you could see what the ego does, what it's capable of if given power.'

'I thought you had forgotten... again, the topic is the ego,' she laughed.

'Of course I didn't forgot. I already told you, I might seem disorganised, but I know why we're following this order.'

'Good. I don't always get it. Like where we are currently. You said you'd show war, but you aren't.'

'I don't see the reason why. We are currently in the nothing... in the emptiness between two worlds. This is what we're gliding through if we are travelling between times. Now we have stopped.'

'You can do this?'

135

'Of course I can. How many times have you said, "Everything is possible, you just have to want it." You have no idea how true that is. Yes, you are often obstructed in your earthly lives by the body and the ego, but let me tell you: nothing is impossible there either. You just have to want it, work towards it, and do your job.'

'What are these flashes? This all could be so harmonic. These colours are so calming and beautiful. Just like the flowers by the waterfall. But these flashes ruin the harmony.'

'Those flashes are travellers,' Noah smiled. 'We'd be just like that if we hadn't stopped.'

'I don't see anybody else here. Why?'

'Because this is not a place where travellers usually stop to rest. Every guardian angel who gets their protégé for a short time has their own favourite places for stopping to rest, but to be honest with you, I like to stop here, too.'

'I like it here as well. Doesn't matter where, I just don't want to see all the evil for a while.'

'Would you like to rest?'

'We're doing that right now,' she smiled sweetly. 'This is good.'

'Now… come.'

'Where to?'

'Back to the waterfall. You'll recharge. There's nobody there.'

'No… it's all right here. Let's stay now.'

'Would you like to take a look at John and you?'

'No.'

'I thought you might miss him.'

'Sometimes. But I hide it well.'

'Not from me.'

'Shame. Whatever. I don't want to go back. You told me that we shouldn't live in the past, that we should look forward. I say let's go on.'

'Now… come.'

'Where to?'

Molly found herself at the waterfalls again.

'Rest. Close your eyes and recharge. You are completely drained, we cannot continue like this.'

'But…'

'No "but…", Lie down in the grass for a bit and rest. You saw a lot of horrible things, you're exhausted.'

'I'm fine.'

'Of course you're fine. That's why you keep asking what's the point in saving your world.'

'You saw what I did. You told me that we need to learn from history. There are so many negative examples, but you saw the world, the people, we haven't learned anything from the mistakes of the past. And…'

'And now you go and lie down in the grass and rest.'

'But you don't get that…'

'No, it's you who don't understand what I'm saying. Molly, please, do as I say. It is necessary right now. Please,' Noah's voice was gentle, but firm. The girl rarely saw her guardian like this, no wonder his behaviour surprised her.

'All right.' Molly lay down, closed her eyes, but couldn't rest. Her feelings kept her going, she tried to process the information she had been given. She could sort out much of it, but there were still some things that she couldn't fit anywhere. She decided she wanted to lie no longer and sat up, but she couldn't. Her power left her and she fell into a deep sleep.

Noah just sat by the girl and watched her.

'Sweet dreams, my Queen,' he whispered, kissing her forehead gently.

'Noah, this is overwhelming for her,' said a familiar voice behind him. Noah didn't even turn around – he wasn't surprised by his friend's arrival.

'I know. I have no idea how long she'll last.'

'Do you need help?'

'Not yet. We would just confuse her. Thanks nevertheless, Peter.'

'Do you think she suspects I'm here?'

'No. I've known for a while that you were here, but she hasn't noticed you yet. Say what you want.'

Peter sat down by Noah. The two men looked completely different. While Noah was tall, had blondish hair and blue eyes, Peter was much shorter, and had brown hair and brown eyes. Straight nose, sharp lips, proportionate build. He too wore white trousers and a T-shirt, and a white cape on his back like his friend.

They sat for a long time above the girl in silence, watching her rest. Peter knew how important that girl was for Noah. He knew Noah wished he would leave and leave him alone with the girl. He knew that if he left, Noah would do something he was not allowed to: send back Molly to Earth. So he stayed. They sat next to each other in silence. Listening to the song of the birds, to the music composed by the leaves and the wind, the rumble of water, all the while watching Molly. Noah intermittently touched the girl when she was turning in her sleep restlessly. He gave her some energy that calmed her.

'You can't do that,' Peter said finally.

'I know,' Noah answered. 'But that would be the best choice. She is much too fragile, I'm not sure she'll make it.'

'You know that she can handle anything. Much more than this.'

'Not now. In this life, she has collected too much junk on her. I'm hardly making any progress cleaning it from her.'

'I know, but… Sometimes it feels like it would be better if I sent her back to John. They could live happily, have children, and we could figure out some other way to solve this problem.'

'Sure, easier, but not better for anyone in their world, and that includes her. What do you think, how could she look in your eyes, or how could you sleep if you'd hurt her and the world? Because that will happen if we don't finish this. What would she feel when she saw millions suffering or dying? Could she say, "Yeah, Noah, you've made the right decision sending me back, at least I'm happy"? You know this wouldn't be the case. I know it's still a bit difficult for her - okay, very difficult - but I have watched her, and it becomes easier for her day by day. Of course, she asks the question whether this world or species is worth saving or not, but honestly, my friend, tell me: don't you ask the same question from time to time?'

'It has occurred to me.'

'Then what's the problem, Noah? Keep going, she'll manage. Think about your strategy. Maybe you should show her something nice besides all the wrong... something that raises her spirits. Not only the bad stuff, because it's too much. Not just for her, but for everyone.'

'Okay. Thanks, Pete.'

'That's what friends are for. But now I've got to go, I have work to do.'

'How's he holding up?'

'It's difficult for him. But he keeps going. You know John, he's complicated.'

'Yeah, polar opposites.'

'I can't always decide which one of us has a harder job, you or me.'

'Me,' whispered Noah almost inaudibly.

'Maybe…Well, I really need to go. Take care of this woman and don't give up. You can do it. We will help you with anything you need.'

'Thank you,' said Noah smiling.

Peter disappeared as suddenly as he arrived. Noah was finally alone with the girl. He did nothing, just watched her. Her long brown hair, her lightly freckled nose, her beautiful, big, kissable lips, her perfect curves. He saw in his mind her playfully smiling face, her pouting face, he saw her dancing, laughing, crying.

'Oh, you woman! You have no idea what a treasure you are,' Noah whispered.

Pete was right. It had occurred to him for a moment to send Molly back to Earth, but he had to realise that it would be bad for her in the long run. She would be happy for one year, maybe two. John would protect her, he'd never hurt her, but they'd both feel that this was not the path they should be treading on, that this was not right – and it would ruin their happiness. No matter how hard it is, no one can avoid fate. The task is given – everybody accepted it before their birth. Like it or not, there is no backing out now.

'Good morning,' said Molly smiling.

'Rest some more,' responded Noah.

'I can't. Just as not too long ago I could barely move – even though I wanted to – now I cannot rest any longer – even though I find the idea really appealing. What I feel now is that I must keep going.'

'Molly, you don't have to. Believe me, you can rest some more.'

'And you believe me that I don't want to. We can go, if you want.'

'So be it.' Noah stood up, bowed, then offered his hand to the girl. 'Let me help you up, Your Highness,' he said, grinning.

'Why are you calling me that?'

'Because you are a Queen to me, that's why.'

The girl reached for the offered hand with grace, then let the man help her up.

'Thank you, my Knight!' she said, mimicking a queen. 'Now, tell me my duties for the day.'

'Your Royal Majesty must accompany me on another trip into the filth. If you think you're ready. If not, we can rest a bit longer.'

'I require no more rest, we can go. Thank you,' she said with a queen's voice, before she started laughing. 'This was funny.'

'Why is that?'

'Because I like these kinds of games. Shame that I am not a member of royalty in reality.'

'Why not? It's just a question of attitude. If you behave like a queen, you will become one. If like a nobody, then you will become a nobody. It's always you who decides who you really are, who you show yourself to be. You have decided a very long time ago that you want to be a nobody – this is why people often treated you like you weren't even there. You wanted this, and allowed others to treat you so. Remember: everybody goes only as far as you let them go, never further. Of course, they try, they push your limits, but it's you who decide where those limits are. In this regard, too, you should've strived to achieve balance – but you didn't. Instead, you let them stomp on you. This is a basic trait of any species: the weak is defeated – in nature, this means their deaths. And I know what you are thinking – that we are not born with the same traits and qualities. Some are born rich and some are born poor, some with strong and others with weak will, some are beautiful, others are ugly… But believe me, everything is constantly changing. Beautiful can become ugly, the ugly can turn beautiful. Weak can become strong, and the strong can become weak. What you always have to keep in mind is that it's the attitude that counts, how you decide to handle the given task or situation that fate gives you. Believe me, there's always a way to steer your life in another direction. To be honest, every day is a new opportunity to change. When you say, "Oh, it happened again" or "Every day is the same" – that's repetition. If repetition does not satisfy you, or gives you a bad feeling, then you probably gave the wrong answer to the question. If this happens, it might be a good idea to think about what it could be that you're doing wrong and what it could be worth changing in order to remove the bad or unpleasant situation from your life. You just have to make a different decision.'

'That isn't easy. Often we don't even realise what we did wrong.'

'Yes, I know. But pay attention to yourself, to your everyday life, your tasks, the answers to those tasks – and you'll see what needs to be changed. First you should try it by yourself, but if you don't succeed, ask for help. Believe me, you'll always get the answer. The correct path can reveal itself through a friend, or you might see it in a movie or read it in an article. Help always comes – you only need to dare to ask for it.'

'Sometimes I'm afraid to ask for help. In some cases when I did ask, I instantly regretted it.'

'Yes, it's so often that you say, "Oh God, help me!", and when the help arrives, you wish you hadn't asked for it. What you don't understand is that help doesn't necessarily mean that you get something nice and pleasant. Of course, in the end you will get that, but first you have to start out on your path. What God helps you with is in finding what's yours. And yes, maybe the first steps will be difficult and frightening, but if you don't back down – it will be wonderful. You'll be happy. But everything has a price – you have to let go of some things in your life. These are usually things that you cling to but you shouldn't, because they don't serve your development. This can be work, objects, apartments, or even one or more people. And letting go or getting rid of something hurts. This is when you say that, "I shouldn't have asked for help." Or, some people even threaten God that they won't speak to him after their deaths because of all the bad things that have happened to them.'

'I don't know who could say such a thing,' said Molly grinning.

'Of course not you… right?'

'Me? Saying that? Never… well, sometimes. And I rarely mean it. And only for a few days.'

'Indeed, because after a few days you realise that what happened to you is a new task that leads you in a good direction. We know that this is hard. Especially that you do not see where the road leads, or what the purpose of it all is. This is when faith becomes important. You must have faith that in the end everything is going to be all right, and that you're not alone. When you get a new task, don't panic, just ask for help – and we'll help in solving it, too. This is why I'm with you. To support you, always and everywhere.'

'Thank you.'

'The problem is, Molly, that this "Thank you" was out of courtesy, not out of gratitude and honesty. But believe me, what I say is true. I believe I've told you already that the pain that you feel hurts me much more. It is so horrible to see you cry. I feel your pain just as you do. I always try to suggest that this isn't right, and should be changed – but you never listen. We both know that you're heading in the wrong direction – you because you feel it, and I because I know where we should be going. But sometimes you can be so uncomprehending. And other times stubborn.'

'Why? Just because I often say that, "Yes, this is bad, but this is what I got, so I must deserve it"?'

'You know this sentence of yours drives me up the wall. If you deserved it, then it would make you happy, but you're not even close to happy. Sometimes temporarily you are – so that you might learn from it. Or because you were clinging to something or someone you shouldn't have, so by getting it you might understand how bad that clinging was. Molly, the problem is that you're asking for things that are not for you. You get them, so you can be sure that they're not for you, and what do you do? You stay in those situations for years, because those situations were what you were given. This is the stupidest thing in the world – you should've realised this by yourself. Often create problems for yourself that hinder your development. I wish I knew why, though.'

'I don't know either,' said Molly, shamefacedly.

'No, not this! Rather think it through and change the situation. You'll get every help you need to do so – you just need to ask.'

'And how do I know what is good for me and what is bad?'

'This is what feelings are for. If something is good, it makes you glad, your heart and soul fills with happiness. If something is bad, you feel it as such. But if you don't believe your feelings, just look in the mirror, at yourself. They say that the eyes are the window to the soul – this is true. If you're happy – meaning that you're on the right path – your eyes are shining; if not, they are empty and dim. Always pay attention to your feelings. If you don't believe them, then pay attention to the smallest details. For example, if your voice cracks, stop talking. If your leg hurts, stop walking. And I could go on. Everything gives signals, leading or trying to lead you in the right direction. If only you'd let them.'

'I see. So, all I have to do is to pay attention to my feelings. I guess if something is wrong, my only task is to change it. But how do I know in which direction or how I should start? Or how do I know that a thing really needs changing? Is it bad only so that I can learn from it? How do I know what I need to learn?'

'I already told you: ask, and the answer will come in some way. This could be an intuition, an article, a friend's advice, anything. If something is bad you have to change it. The "how" will be evident. Giving up everything and leaving it behind might not be the proper solution. If there are things or people in your life who don't serve your development, you must leave them behind or let them go, no matter how painful the goodbye is. But there are things, situations, and people who you shouldn't let go, bearing with them instead.'

'But how do I know which is which? How do I know who I should keep and who I should let go?'

'Who stays, stays. Even if you try to get away from them, they'll still stay with you. Those who want to go are going to do so no matter what you do.'

'And how do I know what's the right answer?'

'Feelings…' said Noah smiling. 'Still, the feelings. And the repetition. Pay special attention to these two.'

'I don't pay enough attention, right?'

'No problem. I'll keep saying it until it sticks in that small head of yours. Feelings, repetition, feelings, repetition, feelings, repetition…'

'Echo,' said Molly grinning.

'A beautiful place like this has that too.'

'Yes… You know, even though you said that we are leaving…'

'We are still here. I like it here. Believe me, I FEEL better when I see this and not the other.'

'I know: feeling, repetition, and echo.'

'Clever. Even if you are joking around.'

'It's easier to remember this way.'

'Then joke away. No matter how you do it, just remember them, because these two things are crucial.'

'Yeah, I realised that. It's just that I thought that we don't always understand these things.'

'What do you mean?'

'I mean we don't even realise that something is repeating itself. In some cases, repetition has to go on for a very long time until we finally realise what we should realise. We repeat hundreds of times the sentences "Oh, it happened again" or "It's always the same." We only say it, but we don't pay attention to what we say. There's no problem with the small-scale stuff, they follow each other rapidly, and we realise our mistakes quickly, that we're doing something really wrong, and this might be a condition. But when the heavy things - like relationship problems - come around, it's much harder. We don't change our partners every day, so a repeating problem like this could take away years or decades from our lives. I've seen people who suffered living with someone throughout their lives.'

'That was his job,' said Noah, barely audible.

'I don't understand.'

'I know. This is the part when you go nuts – this is why I don't want you to understand.'

'I won't go nuts.'

'Yes, you will. Look! The landscape is beautiful at this time. So unbelievably calming.'

'Yes,' said Molly, only looking at the man, not caring a bit about the landscape. She was getting more and more tense.

'Fine, let's leave this place. I don't like to argue with you here. This is where we come to rest. Come, take my hand.'

The girl knew that Noah was right – they shouldn't discuss anything further about this in this magical place. It might leave a bad feeling in them and the wonder that they could only find there would change, would be contaminated by a negative memory – and that would not be good for either of them. She looked around once more, because she didn't know whether she could ever see or feel the beauty, harmony, and tranquillity that she found there again or not.

'Let's go,' she said with a deep sigh – a sigh that sent away every bad feeling she was clouded with - reaching for Noah's hand.

'We will come back, don't worry, but come, we have to go now,' smiled the angel.

Just as he said this, they were in the thinking room again. There was a table in it with paper and pen waiting for Molly.

'What's this?' she laughed.

'Take notes. We have a lot to do and a lot to learn.'

'Are you serious?'

'No. I was just pulling your leg, hoping you'd smile again. But you can sit down nevertheless, I'll explain some things to you.'

'Okay, Professor!' said Molly smiling, and she sat down on the chair. 'I guess we are going to discuss the ego again.'

'That's correct. It's about time we started actually learning something.'

'We were learning already. A lot of things have changed in me since I came here.'

'I know. But this was only the introduction.'

'Okay, let me guess what comes now: the ego is one of the Great Four, there's no life without it on the physical plane. It is a necessary evil, that you do need, but sometimes it would be better if it didn't exist since it creates too many problems. Also, side note: you don't like it.'

'I see that you sometimes you do pay attention.'

'I do… sometimes… rarely,' said the girl, grinning.

'That's not enough, you understand?'

'I don't understand.'

'I thought that you'd tell me our great Molly-Noah Theory by heart. Then I would've been very proud of you. This isn't bad either, I'm still proud, don't worry.'

'You mean this? "The ego is one of the Great Four. Just as the body, the soul, and the spirit, the ego is necessary during your earthly lives. None of these can be present without the others – these connect to each other, essentially intertwine, making a perfect whole in order to create something wonderful we call a human life. They help and lead each other through the often difficult, obstacle-filled, bumpy road leading to perfect order. The ego is a necessary evil. It helps controlling the body. If you're hungry, it sends a message – in other words, an order – to your body to go and get some food. If you're thirsty you drink, if you're cold you get dressed, if you're hot you take off your clothes. It is also responsible for your daily routines. You wake up, go to work, pay your bills, handle your affairs, then you go home and go to sleep. You just want it, and your body will follow the orders." Oh! I left out something, but I can't recite it by heart: the ego lives in the brain. It's there where it controls from. This would be its only job: to control the body – not less, not more. It wants more, but you'd like to give it less, if it was possible.'

'Yes, this is what I meant,' said Noah with a satisfied smile. 'So, you are paying attention.'

'I told you. But you never believe me. This theory's especially important, this'll be our way to immortality, I cannot allow myself to forget it. But jokes aside, what now, Professor?'

'Put the feelings next to the ego.'

'Why?'

'Because they're important. That's what I've been talking about all along. Didn't you pay attention to that?'

'Of course I did. I just didn't think you'd put them together with the ego, rather with the soul or with the spirit.'

'Well… you're half right. This is quite a mixed thing. I already told you that they cannot be entirely separated. Now you can see how true that is. Well… are you ready?'

'Yes. Let's do this.'

'Good. Let's see:

6.

The feelings:

We differentiate three different types of feelings:

1. good feelings;

2. neutral feelings;

3. bad feelings.'

'Neutral?'

'Yes, we'll talk about that, too. I put the good feelings in the first place because it felt good.'

'Hahaha,' said the girl, smiling.

'Yes, I did it for this mocking grin – it's worth everything. So, in first place I mentioned the good feelings, but since we are learning about the ego, let's start with the bad ones. So: bad feelings. There are plenty of these. You can't even imagine how many. Let's take only a few for example, without being exhaustive: anxiety, anger, fury, hatred, despair, fear, jealousy, vindictiveness, vainglory, greed, envy, selfishness, malice, mercilessness, gloat, guilt, pain, grief, weakness, lack of confidence, being unsatisfied… and I could go on. Bad feelings can be recognised by the simple fact that they make you feel bad. It could be this easy, but it isn't. These feelings, too, are generated in you by the ego.'

'And why don't you do something against them?'

'Because it wasn't us who created them.'

'I don't understand.'

'I could tell you that it's simple, but I would be lying. I already mentioned that Earth and the other habitable planets are all part of the learning process. Every species has a different task, which we call global development – there is the individual development, too. Both serve the purpose of gaining and providing information.'

'Yes, I know that. What I don't understand is how bad feelings come into the picture.'

'Bad feelings are another type of necessary evil. You need them in order to fulfil some of your tasks. Got it?'

'Of course not.'

'Oh, Little Girl! How can I explain so you will understand?'

'I have no clue. Can't help with that.'

'I would pass on this question, too, if it was possible, but it isn't,' Noah said, scratching his head, fidgeting with his hair, pacing back and forth in front of Molly. The girl started to get dizzy. Long minutes passed in complete silence. You could hear the buzz of the flies in the room if there had been any on this plane. The girl didn't say a word, she didn't want to push or disturb her teacher. She thought they had time, and that they were not in a hurry. She definitely wasn't. This place was much better than being down there. She wasn't hungry, cold, or hot, she didn't have to work or worry about everyday problems. True, the time spent here wasn't a bed of roses, it had its hard moments and she knew it would have a lot more, but all in all, being here was much better than being on Earth. Especially considering she could be with Noah. They had such a deep and emotional connection between them that she had never experienced before. It was above any of the earthly emotions. It was wonderful, uplifting, yet painful at the same time. She wondered about their upcoming departure, when she would have to go back...

'Now... let's try it this way,' Noah said suddenly, startling Molly.

'Excuse me?'

'I figured out how to explain it to you. Just a sidenote: now it isn't the time to think about goodbyes. That won't be anytime soon.'

'Heey!' she said. 'Stop peeking into my thoughts!'

'But it's my job. Now... let's continue. We were discussing the bad feelings.'

'I bet that you knew all the while how to explain it to me, and this break served only for suspense.'

'Something like that... but now listen. As I said before, bad feelings are a necessary evil in your life, just like the ego: a crucial part of the learning process and the gathering and providing information. These feelings are those you have to overcome. Many believe that we don't have them. But they are everywhere. Let me tell you an example: pain. If something hurts you, I, your guardian angel, feel it tenfold.'

'Are you angry with me those times?'

'Sometimes. But this anger is not like with others. I don't store it either, like you, because we know that there is no point in it.   This   happens to me in a moment, and it takes you one day at maximum, but with others this could last a week, a month, a year... sadly, I have seen examples when it lasted a lifetime. The duration depends on the personality and spiritual development of the given person, among other circumstances. I'll show you examples, but before we drift any further away, let's stick to our current topic. So: bad feelings have two types. One is for motivating the ego, the other is to keep it in check. Just think about it: anger, rage, jealousy, grief. In a bad way these are motivators. Opposite to this there are those emotions that keep the ego in check, often completely blocking it: fear, weakness, lack of confidence, guilt or sloth. I'll show you examples of this. Come, let's travel for a bit.' Noah grabbed her hand and they found themselves on the courtyard of a house.

'Where are we?'

'At a family's home. The man's name is Colum, the woman's is Jessica. There are three kids, too: Kiam, Lena, and Bobby.'

'Got it.'

'Come, I'll show you why we came here.' Noah took her hand and guided her towards the house. The small courtyard had an enormous tree in the middle. Clothes were hanging to dry on the line stretching between the house and one of the branches. The ground was littered with toys. This could have been a usual sight at the home of three

161

kids, if only they hadn't been surrounded by trash. Everything was dirty and untidy.

'This doesn't bode well,' she whispered.

'You don't have to whisper, no one can hear us. But I'd like to ask you to not judge a book by its cover. And keep this mentality for our later lessons, too. As I told you before, everything happens for a reason.'

'Okay.'

They entered the house. Molly instantly retracted her previous sentence: the courtyard was neat and tidy… compared to the house.

'Oh…' she whispered.

'I told you, don't judge at first sight… nor at the second.'

The house was horribly dirty and untidy. Clothes, toys and rubbish littered the whole place. The kitchen was full of dirty dishes, the table and its surroundings were filled with garbage and scraps of food. The kids kicked these all around, playing carefree, like this was the most natural thing in the world. Their dirty little hands and faces revealed that they hadn't bathed for some days now, but that didn't bother them either. They ran around, played, and laughed, not paying attention to what surrounded them.

'Where are the parents?' Molly asked.

'In the bedroom. Come, let's take a look at them.'

'Do I want to see that?'

'Come'.

Molly was shocked by the sight that was revealed to her. The bedroom was tidy compared to the rest of the house. An extremely thin woman in her forties sat on the edge of the bed and cried quietly. A huge man paced back and forth in front of her. Sometimes he stopped, just to start again.

'I'm waiting,' he said finally. His eyes were burning with flames, his mind wasn't clear. His voice was chilling and frightening. 'Who is it?'

The woman couldn't answer, she just continued crying. Molly felt the woman's fear, pain, and helplessness. She heard the faint begging for a miracle, for someone to help because she was so weak and defenceless, unable to protect herself from this insane man.

'I asked who is it?' the man yelled, inarticulately.

'Nobody. There is no one!' came the quiet answer.

'Don't lie to me, you dirty bitch! I know that you have someone. Every woman is a cheap whore! You are no exception. Tell me who your lover is, you hoe. If you don't tell me I'm going to bash in not only his but your head too. I'm going to tear you to pieces... making fish food out of you... nobody's going to recognise you.'

'They wouldn't even now,' came the quiet answer.

Molly felt the man's hatred. She knew that he meant what he said. He had been planning how to kill his wife and her lover for a long time, planning every detail, knowing when he would do and say what. Only problem was that he had never managed to catch her with anyone. He had even hired a private eye, but to no avail. He had paid a ton of money, and what had he got? Nothing. The woman had been said to be morally immaculate. Worked, raised kids, led the household. But he didn't believe anyone! Every woman was a bitch! He knew because all of his lovers had been. Of course he hadn't told them this, only thought so. He had been nice to them, had pampered them, and when they couldn't give anything new to him he had just thrown them away. But the wife was different. He couldn't throw her away, since back then he had sworn 'Till death do us part' before a priest. At least he should keep this one promise, since he had broken all others, usually. So there was no solution but 'Death do us part': the woman needed to be killed. All he needed was a motivation. Cheating would suffice, if only he had found something at long last. But no matter how hard he had looked he hadn't found anything, and it was infuriating. He thought about what would happen if he were to get stuck with the three kids after she had gone. But he realised that there was no problem here either: they could go to the mother-in-law. And he would finally get back his long-lost freedom, to live his life freely. He even thought about divorcing, but where's the fun in that?

'Okay, Noah, how long do we have to watch this?' Molly asked.

'I think you see the point.'

'This man is insane.'

'Yes, I know. This relationship is an extreme, the situation is not as bad as it is here, but there are more instances like this. We will return to them several times during our lessons.'

'Will someone help her?'

'You'll see. Let's not rush forward. Let's focus on why we're here now. As I said, bad feelings can be divided into two groups. Those that motivate the ego and those that hinder it. The case of Colum and Jessica is an excellent example of this: Colum's jealousy, anger and fury motivate him, and Jessica's fear blocks her.'

'But why doesn't she do anything?'

'That's funny coming from you.'

'Nothing happened to me that was anywhere near as serious as this.'

'It could've been. Only you were luckier. You have better karma than her.'

'I can't argue with that. I can feel and see her desperation. I never felt anything like this. It hurts her so much. What do you think, will she get any help?'

'You always get help, you just need to ask for it, Molly.'

'And when?'

'When you're ready. Help always comes when you're ready, not later, not sooner. Exactly in time. A lot of people are impatient, they want to rush time forward, and are often angry, desperate, or disappointed that the awaited good did not come. You should understand that it all depends on you. You shouldn't rush time, but accept your task, stand up bravely and proudly and complete it, no matter what fate brings. You shouldn't criticise; instead, you should do your job. I know it's hard, but believe me, it's worth it, because the reward comes sooner this way than any other.'

'You do something, but you have no idea whether it's good or just leads you to your doom.'

'I told you already that you should listen to your feelings. Here we have the story of Jessica. What do you think, how old is she?'

'Forty. Maybe a bit older.'

'She's thirty.'

'What?!' Molly's question sounded more like a scream.

'To be more exact, she is going to be thirty next month. What's your opinion?'

'Shocking.'

'Do you think she's on the right path? Is this her task?'

'No.'

'You're wrong. Currently, it is this. This is what you didn't understand last time. No matter how painful it is to admit, currently this is her task; her life is a lesson for you, so you could learn what bad feelings are exactly.'

'This is cruel.'

'Yes, it is. Molly, you should understand already that there's always a way out. We give you all the help you need, but we cannot act instead of you. That is your job, not ours. Ours is only providing help, if you ask for it… or if it's truly necessary. Yes, I understand that it's difficult. Especially if you don't see the connections, and if you don't realise why things happen the way they do and where you should head next. I can only answer the same thing to this: help always comes. A sign from somewhere. You only have to notice it and not doubt or criticise it, but bravely face what's to come. Because the ending will be happy. I know what you think: it's easy for me since I can understand more easily why something is the way it is, what should be achieved, and that I exactly know what's the end of the road. But believe me that it's not easy for me either. You often give us a hard time with hesitation, doubt, and little detours. I know what the path is – just a sidenote: you know it just as well – it's just extremely hard to keep you on it. Sometimes you make detours so big that they leave me scratching my head about how I should steer you back. But now back to Jessica. She was a beautiful woman when she was younger. Every man wanted her. She met Colum, fell in love with him, and married him really soon, and the kids came. In truth, she had no idea about who this man was. She saw the small signs that something was off, but she didn't care because she was in love.'

'Or because she believed in you,' Molly added quietly.

'Yes, I thought this would be your reply. Believe me, we didn't want to hurt her. Their marriage is a task. She needed a mate like this in order to realise how valuable a person she is.'

'But women don't marry and give birth for some task, but because they want to be happy. Okay, I know that every relationship is a difficult task, since you have to adapt to each other, changing personal needs and desires so that they fit both people... but this is over the top. And you said her life serves as a teaching example for me. Now, I want to scream because of this. I don't think you could tell me anything more disgusting.'

'I know. But like it or not, it is like this. Everything has a purpose and a reason. You need to understand this. I told you that she has a chance to change things. She got, and will get, countless opportunities to change, but we cannot act instead of her. We straighten, handle her life, but we cannot help her if she fully resists us. Then this life of hers will serve as a counter or a teaching example for others by showing what shouldn't be done. She'll get the same task in her next life, because she needs to learn her lesson. Everything repeats until you give the correct answer to the question. And before you completely freak out, let's discuss this topic more slowly and more thoroughly. I'll explain everything in detail so you understand why things are the way they are. Because we are jumping around again, which never ends well. So, we were at the point where they got married and the kids came. Jess always lacked confidence. She didn't have a happy childhood, she didn't receive the spiritual support from her parents that is needed for a healthy level of confidence. Of course, this has a reason why, too. I don't want to go into previous lives if you don't mind, only to a necessary extent. The point is that in her previous life Jessica received every help to believe that she is capable of great things. But she couldn't do it. She got the same task this life, but we made it more difficult. If she doesn't learn again, she'll get the same task in her next life, but that one will be a tough lesson. You again could say that this is cruelty. No. No, it isn't. It is necessary for spiritual development. You cannot advance to a higher level if you do not have the basics. The house isn't stable either without its foundation. The time period you witness now is the laying of the foundations. I believe it's understood that the man is a scamp. Changes his workplace twice a year, because he isn't satisfied with anything. He wastes his salary, on other women, alcohol, and tobacco. He never helps his wife, only if you count rarely being at home, since he always tries to find a job far away from his family. He comes back once in a month or two, and then only for a few days to make the life of his wife and his kids' lives miserable. When he's home the script is always the same: he pits the kids against their mother, he often even helps them throwing the toys around, showing them what to do and how to make their mother suffer. Meanwhile, he follows his wife around, bullying her, saying that he is a bad mother, and how disgusting a woman she is, that no man would touch her because she's ugly, untidy, dirty, smelly, and lazy, and I could go on. This goes on for a few days and when he gets bored of being home he takes all of the family's money and disappears without a trace. Then she cleans up both the house and herself. She prayed for help quite often earlier; nowadays it's getting rarer.'

'And why don't you help her?'

'We do. We have given her countless opportunities to leave this husband. Family members, friends, neighbours have tried to help, even official bodies, but to no avail. There have been some occasions where they got close to divorce, but Colum always begged himself back into her graces. He always knew what to do and how, so that she would accept him. Those times he promised anything, he was nice and understanding, paid attention to her and their kids, helped them with money, all so that he could stay. When Jessica decided to give him another chance, everything started all over again.'

'I don't know what to say to this. Maybe that I cannot condemn her. It is easy being smart from outside, but for those who are stuck inside these situations it's hard to get out of them or to change them. Because here too there are the three kids. It is hard even when you're alone, just look at my example, but with kids… I don't envy her.'

'Because none of you trust yourselves, or your abilities in solving situations. All in all, Jessica is doing everything alone. She needs to feed the children, to work and pay the bills…'

'You don't understand. They often say that humans are social creatures. We were created in such a way that we need someone we can rely on. Even those who say otherwise. I often said that I'm fine alone that I don't need anyone, but it's not true. This is why we stay in hellish relationships like this, because even this is better than nothing, the solitude… Okay, this is not… This relationship we see here… well, I can't imagine anything worse than this. I think if help came right now Jessica would never accept this husband again. There is a point when you cannot endure any longer.'

'Molly, you still have to learn to trust in yourselves. You need to believe that you are not destined for such a life. Yes, this is your share right now. But not for life. This should be only a small period; the bad things do not last for life. Or at least they are not supposed to, but how fast you learn your lessons depends only on you.'

'I say again… it sounds good as a theory. Everybody's smart from the outside. Believe me, after it happens I know what I should've done before. I often bang my head on the wall – sometimes literally – because the solution was so obvious and simple, and I struggled with the given problem for years. So, even I know what needs to be done if it's not my life we're discussing. But if you're in it everything's different. There is a huge problem in those cases. Fear. They say that fear binds – well, it often does.'

'Yes, that's the point I wanted to get to with you. Fear is a necessary evil that is essential with the ego. If it wasn't there, there would be nothing holding it back, and it would be doing what it wants, and the world would end up in chaos. But this way, we can say that you have a vague appearance of order. If something doesn't work properly, all we have to do is increase the fear and the ego instantly slows down, and doesn't allow more stupidity for itself. The same situation with guilt. Essentially there is no such thing, only for the ego. These are the forces for holding back. It's just that the ego often makes bad decisions alluding to fear. I mean that it usurps for itself the power of fear, even when there is no need for it, keeping the person in a bad situation for years, whereas it shouldn't. And this is the better possibility. There are occasions when a whole group or country is stuck in a situation they shouldn't be in. I know you always freak out, but these are excellent counter-examples. The people suffer from the poor decisions or fears of their leaders, but their situation serves as a deterrent for other leaders and people: "Yes, this is not an example we should follow, we don't want this." I know that you don't find this just, but if you don't see things like this you can commit the same mistake easily. Other, more developed planets are luckier in this aspect. They don't have to learn from their own mistakes, because they got to a stage where they can study other planets' peoples. This makes it a bit easier, but not too much. Often it is hard for them to refrain from intervening, from giving others the knowledge they already possess. But every advanced people has the rule of "observe, don't interfere."'

'I understand, but this whole deterrent example thing still sounds cruel.'

'I know. I already told you that the path is given, both globally, both individually. This is their task. Believe me, they'll get their rewards in their next lives, because taking up something like this and completing it with a head held high and without breaking is a huge sacrifice – even we know that. But now let's get back to the original topic, the hindering, the "holding-back" bad feelings.'

'I think I understand them. They are needed so there is not an even bigger chaos.'

'There is no chaos on Earth. You should've seen the planet where the feeling of fear was absent. It was only created as an experiment, and then compared to the average time we give for development we terminated it quite quickly. Now, that was chaos. You don't want to hear about it. On Earth only the direction is wrong, but we'll fix that.'

'I get it. But I have no idea how we could change all this. Jessica, for example. She was so afraid of solitude that she got stuck in an abusive marriage. And she's not the only one. I know a lot of people who suffer from their relationships, but don't dare change; want to do something, but cannot make a move. And I'm not talking about only women. Men and women are both suffering and neither can see the way out. And if we are talking about counter-examples, there are quite a lot of counter-examples proving that changing is not worth it, because the next one will be no better. I saw a lot of examples of this, too. You know what I'm thinking? That it's interesting that we're talking about relationships with regards to bad feelings. I thought that it would come at the good, or maybe at the neutral feelings, but at the bad feelings? I didn't expect that.'

'It's you who keeps bringing it up. I'm trying to lead the conversation, but somehow, we keep turning back to here. Let's finish discussing the bad feelings already, and after we can discuss relationships, too, if you want. I'll explain then and there why you're wrong. But now before you say or ask anything, please let's focus on the original topic. I promise we'll discuss it and make everything clear.'

'Okay.'

'Thank you. So... we were at... that you need to know that the bad feelings are present in every part of our lives. I showed you the relationship of Jessica and Colum because the main point was quite obvious in their case and it helped you understand the differences. But bad feelings are everywhere. Come, let's walk for a while, leave them alone.'

'What will happen to them?' she asked.

'Everything will happen as it's supposed to.'

'Well... that sentence of yours is the most worrisome.'

'You'll understand later that it's not. But we need to go now. Come, we'll walk and I'll explain in the meantime.'

Molly couldn't move. She stared at the woman sitting on the bed, crying silently, almost inside. She felt her anxiety, her pain... and maybe something else.

A vague feeling, a decision, growing stronger by the moment. They both were surprised by that, maybe Jessica more so than her. But Noah just kept on smiling.

'See? I told you everything will be as it's supposed to. You can see for yourself that everything is going to be fine.'

'Why do I feel as though the woman fulfilled her task, by being a teaching example for me, and that from now on…? No, no way… this is stupid. No way, I'm imagining things again.'

'If you say so… Now, come, let's move.' Noah took her hand and they finally departed. They exited the house, finding themselves on a road in a suburb. It was a hot summer day. Little children were playing carefree in the shades. The older ones sat on the grass some distance away, discussing the great questions of life. The adults were doing the same. Cars rarely passed by there, only the residents used this street, so the traffic was almost non-existent. Everybody seemed happy.

'Everything is nice here. How are you going to explain me what I already understand, the point in bad feelings? Good feelings would suit this place much more.'

'I just wanted to show you that you don't have to view the world through horrifying events. You say that "Every cloud has a silver lining." And this is how it is exactly. But… what is true too is that the best thing is if you can find the reasons for bad things, and if you can understand that they were the best things that could have happened to you. If you got those two down and if you learned them, you are already one step closer to your ultimate goal.'

'I understand. But what I don't understand is how you want to teach me here? Everything is peaceful and harmonic. People seem happy. Yes, I feel that everyone has their problems, but altogether we can say that everything's fine.'

'Oh, Molly… You shouldn't keep overcomplicating things. When the ego came to existence we didn't want it to take too many liberties. We knew there would be a lot of problems with it, because it was created for a single life so it could serve its purpose better. Because we knew that sooner or later it would want to break out of its boundaries – which cannot be allowed under any circumstances – we gave it the bad feelings. I told you what we could see a few moments ago were the empowered versions - in their natural state they are supposed to be completely harmless. Look at the kids, how they play. Since they are smaller, the ego in them has more control, but even they know that even though they'd like to they cannot pull the hair of Katie, the neighbour, because mom or maybe Katie's mom would be angry. Or… how fun would it be to race out from the gates to the streets, but they can't because a car might come and run them over, because mom keeps telling them that, and cars do actually come intermittently. When you're older… well, you actually have these feelings in your whole life because you need them, it's just that later on you don't do stuff because mom or dad told you so, but because it's you who bear the consequences. I think you know perfectly well, but I'll tell you nevertheless that the ego likes to push its limits, even when it knows that its deeds might lead to serious consequences. This is a natural human trait, which is essential for development.'

'Hey… I don't understand this. It's allowed and it isn't?'

'Yes,' Noah grinned.

'Would you care to explain? Please…'

'Sure. You say that "Rules are rules." However, there are always loopholes. If you followed every rule by the letter, humanity would not advance.'

'You know that this completely goes against all you said before?'

'No, it doesn't, it just complements it.'

'Okay. Usually I get what you mean, but now somehow I'm not able to.'

'But it's so simply complicated,' Noah grinned. 'Molly, everyone knows that the system is flawed. We tried what it would be like if a race got a free hand, meaning not getting feelings along with the ego. Neither good nor bad. They did their tasks like machines. We decided back then that feelings are needed, even though the result is not good in all instances. Just think about it: as I said, you don't do things for two reasons. Either someone told you that you can't, or it's your own experience that holds you back. The wise learn from the mistakes from others, the less wise learn from their own, but explorers learn from neither.'

'You know that this becomes less and less understandable?'

'Look, it'll all make sense soon. Or at least I'm trying to clear it up for you. You know too that there are rules that need to be followed. Whether you like it or not. For example, you have to go to school and later you have to work. If you want to cross the road you have to look both ways, after buying things in a shop you have to pay, you cannot simply walk out. But I'll say something even more simple: you have to get dressed, keep yourself clean, keep your home and your environment clean, etc. These are basic rules, otherwise known as norms. If you don't follow them you'll have to face consequences. You can often hear people say that "I'm afraid that..." Everyone knows, or at least suspects that going against these have their consequences. This fear helps you to actually do what you have to, what

181

your parents, your environment, and society waits for from you. But pushing limits is a natural human trait. You can observe it even in babies, during the so-called "terrible twos". It's simply that the little ones try to see how far they can go without punishment. They perfectly know what they do is improper according to their environment, but they push the limits instinctively. If they see that there are no repercussions for their actions, then they incorporate them into their social norms, and they might push their luck even further next time. Wise parents stop them in time, less wise ones let their offsprings do what they want, even though they know that their kids' behaviour doesn't fit the common practice.'

'I hope you don't want to tell me that these kids become explorers.'

'No. Usually these kids become the counter-examples. Of course not always, because there are cases where, if not the parents, the education system or the environment can fix the mistakes of the parents, but – and I think you too saw many examples for this – only with great pain and at great cost.'

'Then where are the counter-examples?'

'They come right now, don't be impatient! We talked about those 1,700 years that were the "I don't like it" period in humanity's history. A long and painful period, it was, for everyone, so hopefully common knowledge will hold it for a long time.'

'Counter-example?'

'Yes. This, too, shows what enormous stupidities the ego might commit. Afraid of the new, of the change, because it doesn't see the whys, the reasons. Too much fear can create such a strong control-system that on one hand it is impossible to follow, and on the other hand it makes no sense, since it doesn't serve development.'

'Intimidation by the higher power, often based on religious reasons.'

'Yes. Back then it wasn't mom and dad or the neighbour who said that you can't, but the current leaders. But don't think this big. Come, let's sit down on this bench and I'll show you it in a smaller scale. There is that kid.' Noah pointed at a boy, aged about 5-6. Short brown hair, average build. Nothing special at first sight, maybe only that, even though many kids of his age lived in the street, he was still alone. 'He's David. A very special kid. The parents of course aren't satisfied with his quirks, they wanted a normal child.'

'What's special about him?'

'He sees things differently compared to others. He received a gift that few others do: he doesn't forget anything that has happened to him before his birth. He knows and sees everything that is part of the true reality. He knows and sees why things happen the way they do, and what people are really like.'

'Lucky.'

'No, he isn't. Just think about it, this is a huge burden for him. Firstly, his parents and environment expect him to be 'normal.' The only problem with this is that he is completely normal; it is the environment and the parents that aren't. And when he tries to explain this to them, the parents freak out, rushing him from one doctor to the other, because "he is mentally ill." They make up non-existent illnesses to match his mental state, giving him medication, thinking that that will make him "normal". And David lets them do that, because he knows that it has a reason why.'

'He is a counter-example, too?

'No, he will be an example worth following when he grows up, given that he doesn't break down mentally until then.'

'Isn't there anyone to help him?'

'There will be. It's just not time yet. The kid knows this perfectly well, because he sees everything and knows everything. About everyone and everything. He is the man that you can't fool. Nobody can.'

'It must be hard for him. For the parents, too.'

'Yes, it is. Think about it, he sees a person on the street and knows exactly what their personality and karma is like, what tasks await them in their lives. He even knows how people's souls become distorted, how much they have to work, what will happen to them, or what they'll do later. This alone is a huge burden, but without help, going up the hill is even harder. What do his parents and teachers tell him? That he shouldn't, that what he sees and feels is not there, that he's just imagining. And that is the better case. Because often the parents' patience runs out, and then come the fights, the yelling, the freak-outs. But there are the kids same age as David. If he lets anyone behind his defences, they will laugh at him, make fun of him, or call him crazy. That's why kids like him usually live their lives alone, or with a very few friends, to whom they often don't reveal who they really are. Because they can't. During the years they learn that these things are better kept secret, because that way they avoid a lot of pain, suffering, and disappointments. So, they strive to live a normal life, effacing everything else, trying their best to ignore it. I know that this, too, is a harsh example, but maybe you'll understand from it what I want to tell you.'

'Not really, to be honest.'

'Because you are being impatient,' Noah smiled. 'All I wanted to tell you is that what they tell you is not always the best course. You don't have to always accept what your environment wants to force upon you.'

'So, let me get this straight: we have to obey, but at the same time not?'

'Something like that. This is the hardest part in the world controlled by the ego. Continuing on your path despite the wind that blows you backwards and the storm raging around you. You often say that God gives the most difficult tasks to his strongest and greatest of his soldiers. This is true. The reason for this is that they carry the world forward, and this requires great strength, bravery and perseverance, which often can be achieved only by great slaps. But in most cases these people know… or they believe and feel that they were destined for great things.'

'So, there are those who don't obey, who don't do what the environment or society expects from them?'

'Yes. But in complete secrecy in most of the cases. They seemingly mingle with the crowd, leading a normal life so that they don't cause any problems or pain to others or to themselves. But in the background, in complete secrecy they do their tasks. Because if they don't, they can't be completely happy, they'll always miss something. You didn't write, you couldn't find your place.'

'Yes, you're right.'

'Because your true task is writing. Others have something else. But what you have in common is that you move the world forward, making life better or more special. Yes, I know that it is a huge burden, and the ego especially likes to protest. Oftentimes it hinders you instead of helping, burdening itself with imaginary problems, because it doesn't believe that the task it was born for is good and needed. It wants an ordinary life, but it cannot have it, since fate always knocks it away from the ordinary. This wish cannot be fulfilled, or maybe after all of the tasks are done.'

'And I guess that never happens.'

'Well… not really, no. Special people have so much to do that often one life is not enough to complete all of them. Especially if we count the little detours.'

'I have no idea what you're talking about,' grinned Molly.

'Yes, I thought so.'

'Okay, okay. I had quite enough, I know. But if I were as lucky as David, knowing who I am and why I came here, then…'

'Then you wouldn't be you. These detours were needed, but there will be none from now on. When you go back, you have to dive in to work. You'll get all the necessary information, and after that there'll be no more slacking.'

'There is none in work. If it's work, I do it. If it's only fun or passing time, then I don't.'

'I know. I know you. But let's get back to our original topic. I hope now you can understand why I said that great explorers do not learn from either their own or others' mistakes. They follow their own lead, no matter whether they are told that they can't, that it's impossible, it cannot be done, etc. They know perfectly well that it can be done. Sadly, in earlier times they paid with their lives for their stubbornness, but luckily, or as you say 'Thank God' – and you have no idea how true that is -, in this day and age these special people are only looked upon sideways.'

'I'd like to add that not by everybody and not everywhere. There are countries where these people are supported. Of course not in every instance and not always towards a good goal, but overall we can say that the situation got better.'

'It will be even better, believe me, you just have to work a bit for it. But I need to add that it's not like that they always go against the flow, not listening to anyone or not keeping any rules, because that's not true. They get dressed too, since they can't walk around naked. They go to school – well, they usually do it enjoying it or urged by lust for knowledge, and not because it's obligatory. They work and pay their bills, too, because it's crucial for their everyday lives. They are in perfect knowledge of this, it's just that... there are things they are passionate about, a task that they need to accomplish, that leaves them no rest, motivating them, even if everybody else says that it's impossible.'

'Lucky are those who receive support in everything.'

'Let's say instead that they have better karma. Those who receive all the support for their endeavours have nothing else to worry about but what they were born for. They learned all that they had to in their previous lives. In truth, these people are born down to move the world forward, to help. They lived in a world in their previous lives where that invention that is presently being worked on was common practice. They know that their invention will work because it was not just tested, but was in everyday use. True, they have no idea when and where that was, but that is not important for them.'

'I must say that these are interesting things.'

'Molly, you need to understand that the time and space you know does not exist in reality. It was invented for the physical plane. Imagine, what would happen if you would get things as they truly are, that you could jump around? Chaos. That's why no matter how every species wants time travel, they cannot have it. Even the most advanced ones. Think about it, they would make a mistake or do something wrong, they would instantly go back to fix it. That wouldn't be a problem, because they would learn from their mistakes and fix them, and therefore they would now know the right way. But from a single person's mistake only a single person can learn. And I'm not saying this properly. It doesn't have to be a mistake, it can be both a good or a bad thing.

Anything - and if it happened, it wouldn't just affect the life of a single person. I don't know how clear this sounds. Maybe this is still unbelievable to you, but I'm going to show you examples later for this, too. And before you ask why not now: because it is more complicated than it would seem at first. Yes, I know that it's still clear, but in order for you to understand the whys, I still have a lot to explain. And… again I don't know where we were.'

'Time and time-travel.'

'So you are listening,' Noah grinned.

At times like this Molly secretly admired the man. His beautiful sea-blue eyes, his full, rounded, kissable, and biteable lips, his well-built, manly, but nevertheless soft and gentle features. It was impossible not to notice that he was a perfect man. But it wasn't mostly because of the looks, but because when she was with Noah she felt that everything was perfectly complete. Since they had been together, everything had fallen into place, or what hadn't yet was in the process of doing so. She didn't feel huge flames, or emotions overwhelming everything, only simple tranquillity and peace.

Actually, she didn't dare to even think about what she felt: she didn't want to think about these things because she knew that the angel felt everything that she did. This made her blush. Noah of course didn't mention it. He acted as though he didn't even notice it. He let her fight those battles inside, because it was needed for her to get closer to a great realisation.

'So, time and time travel,' the angel continued. 'These two terms are like the secret to eternal life. Every human could have it, could learn how to use it, could enjoy the possibilities granted by it if they were ready – but of course not on the physical plane. You go there to learn. You could enjoy freedom back home, but of course only if the time has come and if the soul has earned the rights.'

'What does that mean?'

'You get rewards only for a job done. Half-done work, half the reward.'

'Sounds good.'

'I know it doesn't, but you have to understand: important people have tasks that cannot be just left mid-progress. They have to complete it, by hook or crook. No excuses.'

'I don't think we should go deeper into this reward system, because I don't agree with you. Just leave it.'

'Sure, because you're still sulking.'

'I'm not sulking, I just don't like it. That's all. But I think this topic is completely unimportant.'

'You're wrong. Put your discontent aside, and let's discuss it. Believe me, it is of crucial importance.'

'If you insist, so be it. But don't be surprised if I interrupt you. I have tons of negative experience regarding this topic. I asked often for things that were very important to me, and I didn't receive them, or not in the shape I was expecting them.'

'Yes, there's the problem. I told you to put your discontent aside, because otherwise you won't be able to embrace what I'm about to tell you. Well, then:

7.

The reward system and karma:

You all labour under a great delusion. Many of you believe that the reward, the longed-for good, the wanted object or person will just magically appear in your lives. Sadly, this is not how it works. Rarely it does happen, but for that you had to work really hard in one of your previous lives, you had to complete something that would have been impossible for most people. But as I told you, souls don't get these for free, only because they worked for them; it's just that maybe in that life there was no time, opportunity, or way to enjoy them. And here let's add karma quickly, too. We could give overcomplicated definitions of karma – a lot of people do exactly that - but we'll refrain from that. So: karma is the response to your actions.'

'That's all? The ego definition was much better.'

'Yes, and you already forgot that. But you can remember this.'

'Nice of you,' she grimaced.

'Just frank,' Noah replied.

194

'Not, it isn't. Do you want me to recite it?'

'Not necessary. I know that you know,' he grinned. Molly gave him a look that contained nothing like her previous one. In this one, there was no kindness at all. Noah burst out laughing.

'Oh, Little Girl! I just wanted to shake you up a bit. You take learning so seriously, we needed something extra.'

'This was something less, more like,' she pouted.

'I love when you sulk. Those times that little hissy-wrinkle appears next to your shapely, freckled nose. I like it very much.'

She hid her nose with her hand, but by now she was laughing, too.

'I'm never looking at you again.'

'Shame. You have a pretty face, I like to look at it.'

'Are you wooing me?' Molly looked at the angel, shocked. She even forgot to keep her hands in front of her face.

'No. This was but just a remark. And now that the distraction went so well, we can continue with our original topic – karma and rewards. But if you're too tired we can rest a bit, too.'

'No, thanks. Let come what may, I'm ready.'

'Molly, you need to know something really important. We don't have to progress in such haste. We can take our time, since, as you know, there is no time here. You can rest anytime you want.'

'Thanks, but no. Let's proceed, I'm fine.'

'Sure. Let's make a better karma-definition then. Even though I think there was nothing wrong with the previous one. It had everything it needed, succinctly.'

'Right. I get it now. It's not me who needs these detours, but you. So you can have time to think about what to say.'

'I admit, yes. But I'll deny everything later. Now... The definition of karma, second edition: Karma is the response to past actions. Its quality corresponds to the quality of the given action, the time of its emergence/occurrence is undefined, but unavoidable, detours or exceptions not allowed.'

'Nice.'

'Glad you like it. And now I'll explain what this means, but there are two things you need to know. Firstly, this whole thing isn't as simple as it might seem. Secondly, karma and fate are two different things. Yes, they connect, but you can't mix or combine the two. And now to the actual explanation. Karma is nothing else but cause and effect, the result of actions. Many believe that only bad deeds have any effect, any result, but that isn't true. Good ones have, too, that's what we call a reward. But this whole rewards system works differently than what you imagine or how you'd like it. The truth is that this whole thing is just as complicated as it seems to be and as difficult to explain. And in addition, you don't make it any easier, either. On the contrary, sometimes you can twist originally simple things into such complicated matters that it leaves us scratching our heads about what to do to get you out of those situations.'

'I guess you are talking about me,' she grinned.

'You might find it funny, it's not always the case with me. Of course, you don't laugh when you get what you deserve.'

'I usually growl then.'

'Yes. I wish I knew why. It was you who earned it, but after that you cry about how miserable you are and you are angry at us. You should be angry at yourself. Or, what would be even better, you should be grateful, draw the conclusions, and proceed into the direction you should be heading.' The seriousness of Noah surprised her. 'Molly, I don't want to hurt you, all I want is you to understand how grave this matter is. A few moments ago you said that it is of no importance, don't even talk about it. But this is one of the most important things in the lives of humans. Oftentimes, it is your anger towards the reward system, or your disappointment in it, that hinders your progress, your faith. Sometimes it's worse than fear, and that is unbelievable.'

'Yes, I know that. What I usually have a problem with is just that I complete something that I feel to be a great feat, but the good thing doesn't come, the so-called reward. Then I say okay, maybe this wasn't enough, and I complete another, then another, and another. Of course, I see that what a change I went through, how good all those steps and lessons did me, but the reason why I did it, what motivated me, still doesn't come. I can be deeply disappointed at those times, that's when I freak out and give up.'

'Isn't change enough reward in itself?'

'No.'

'Why not?'

'Because I don't do something because I want to change. It's only you who want change, It's only good for you, for me it doesn't matter. Of course, if we view things globally, there must be some use. But for me, as an individual, it's all the same.'

'I don't like when you're like this.'

'Don't worry, me neither.'

'Do you feel good in this state?'

'No.'

'So, do you think this is the correct way?'

'Certainly not.'

'Then why do you do it? The other thing: you say that you do it for a reward. I guess for an object or for a person, since you want to get them. But what if you don't have to get that object or that person? You can cling to a person/object so hard that it is unbelievable. It is possible that you shouldn't even do anything like that, since something/someone much better could be waiting for you. You should just let go of the old, so the new might come. Or, sometimes it would be enough if you'd let go of this fixated desire… this feeling of "I want that, no matter what," and you might receive the reward immediately.'

'Objects are not hard to let go, people are.'

'I know. This is something you have to learn in this life. Letting go. This is what was never easy for you, and I think it'll never be. What I mean is that you won't ever be able to completely let go, since inside you'll always be attached to everyone you ever loved. But hey, at least you don't show it, which is progress.'

'No, this is cruelty. But I learned that it hurts less if I do it myself rather than if you take them from me.'

'Molly…' Noah ran his hand through his hair to ease his tension. Not his tension, rather hers. He felt as though painful memories surfaced, and he lived through all of them. Molly's eyes were welling up, she had to gather all her strength so she wouldn't cry. They sat next to each other silently for a long time. None of them dared to say anything. Finally, the angel broke the silence. 'I know that you think we want to hurt you with this, but believe that that's not true. This is what was needed for your development.'

'Okay.' The first tear ran down on her cheeks, then the second, followed by many others.

'Please don't cry,' Noah whispered.

'I'm not crying. Let's continue. We were at karma, fate, letting go.'

'Yes, I know, but let's talk first. You need to calm down, and you need to let go of this pain.'

'Not important, let's go on.'

'It is important, very much so.'

'But what? That I don't dare to love? That I rather harden my heart so I won't feel anything? That if I get to love someone all I can think about is how and when I'm going to lose them? That because of this I often act sternly, that I'm often spiteful or rude just so they grow to hate me and leave me sooner, because I think that way it'll hurt less, but in all honesty, I die inside every time? Pushing them away, whilst all I want to do is run back? The problem is that you give, then take away, give and take away, give and take away… and the truth is that now even though you give, I don't want it. This way I won't be disappointed, it surely won't hurt. So, as you see, this is of no importance, there's nothing to talk about. Let's move on.'

'But this is not good this way.'

'Yes, it is. Perfect, if you ask me. Please, let's move on. Or continue the previous discussion.'

'Okay, but you should know that we'll have to return to this topic, because relationship problems, letting go, and fear of solitude are common problems. It's not only you who's affected, but millions worldwide. Sadly.'

'And you think we're going to find a solution to this? I doubt it. Different problems for each people, and different experiences for each of them. You can't… we can't help every one of them. And this is what I say "Sadly" to.'

'You're right. But if we point out the causes, the problems, we can start them out in the right direction. After that it's everyone's own task to find out how to proceed. Some will manage, some won't. It will be the choice of every individual.'

'I think dealing with this topic is a huge responsibility.'

'And I think not dealing with this topic would be a huge irresponsibility. But we shouldn't argue about this, let's turn back to the original topic, since that is the basis of everything. We don't start building the house with the roof, either.'

'I think you already said that.'

'I think, too.'

'Why did you cry, Princess?' came a voice from behind. Noah smiled, but Molly was really surprised.

'Hello, David. Come, sit with us,' he said.

'I can never surprise you,' the little guy said. 'Hey, Noah. Nice to see you again. And of course, you too, Your Majesty.' David bowed a little towards her; she blushed because of his action. 'So she doesn't know yet.'

'No.'

'Did I come at a wrong time?'

'No. The perfect time, actually,' Noah smiled. 'Tell me, what's up? Is everything all right in your current life?'

'I don't complain. But this not-forgetting-anything proves to be a bit harder than I imagined. However, seeing where you're at – or aren't – makes me say that my share is not too bad. Of course, there are drawbacks. My parents, for example. No matter how I explain to them they refuse to understand what is completely clear and obvious to me. They take me from one doctor to another, treating me like an idiot, because I must be mentally ill. Sometimes even I believe that I have gone nuts.'

'You know you didn't.'

'Luckily, Paul's here.'

'Oh, Paul,' Noah grinned.

'Oh, come on. I didn't want a woman in this life, so she wouldn't distract me, being in front of me all the time.'

'This is funny,' Molly said finally.

'What is?' David asked, then turned to Noah. 'Where are you at? Is it this bad? I thought you wouldn't screw up this big this time.'

'You have no idea how much we managed to screw up.'

'Well… if you're sitting together, alone, and if she's staring at you with this much love in her eyes, then very much.'

'I don't look at him with love,' Molly said.

'Should I bring a mirror? All due respect, my liege, but you should've grown out of this "belonging to someone" weakness of yours.'

'Oh. Strange being hurled this by a 5-year-old.'

'Well, Noah! Good luck. I think our liege is an amnesiac.'

'Not an amnesiac, she just has a lot of trash on her. But the purge is in progress. Everything will be fine, but yes, the situation is not the brightest. But I have to add that it's not hopeless either.'

'Sure. You only say this because she's here. Noah! Be more honest with her. I'll rephrase. Be more honest with her about herself. Don't keep her identity and task a secret. You and I both know that we have to accomplish great things. Lot of work, short time. I know you protect her, guarding her from everything, but you shouldn't. That's not why she's on Earth right now.'

'This is harsh. I understand now why we have to forget everything after birth. Parents would kick out their kids quite quickly if their kids spoke like this at the age of five.'

'Six. But you're right. Believe me, I have to have a great deal of patience to deal with them, too. Often I play stupid so they calm down. Sometimes I wipe my face involuntarily, because I feel like I'm drooling. Not an easy job, this.'

'What do you think, who has it harder? You or them?' Noah asked. 'And put your self-pity aside.'

'Ha-ha. My Lady, you need to know, everybody has their weaknesses, and this is mine. But if I wish to be honest… neither of us has it easy. I don't think either that our relationship will be a fruitful and long one. I'll carefully persuade them to put me into a school for geniuses as soon as possible, and that will be it, thank you very much. I'm going to look for one that is as far away as possible, so we don't have to meet often. And before you freak out, it's not that I don't love them. I do. Mother had her share of trouble at my birth, they love me, try to raise me, control me, they worry about me, guard and protect me. This is why I forgive them the countless doctors, poking, and examinations, because I know that they do it for me… because they love me. It's a shame that they don't understand what I tell them. That this is normal, not the way they're living. So, in a nutshell, I love and respect them, but I know that I can't stay for long, because that would not end well.'

'I'm sorry,' Molly said.

'You shouldn't be. This is my task. And before you tell me that these are harsh words from a 6-year-old, let me remind you that it is only this body that's six years old. Since I perfectly remember several of my previous incarnations, I possess more knowledge now than an average 90-year-old person on Earth at this exact moment.'

'Isn't it hard like that?'

'No. This is what's natural. I don't know what it feels to be average, so I don't feel the task to be difficult. When you're born you get a new conscience, with which you can complete new tasks with a clean sheet. Your spirit remembers everything, but only shares that much – only opens so much of the soul's little containers for you – that is absolutely necessary in your current position in your progress of development. I became not a new person, but the same one I was before. My ego is of course new, you can't revive the old one, that's how it was designed and that's how it is perfect. The only difference between me and other humans is that my conscience has access to all the information that happened to me in my previous few incarnations.'

'Molly, you need to know that this is an exceptional case, you need a completely pure soul for it, which is extremely rare,' Noah said.

'Yes. I got harder tasks before than anyone could imagine. What you got before and said that you can't bear because you felt it to be impossible to bear was a walk in the park compared to mine.

207

But I always knew that this was my task, that I'm doing good and I'm helping, moving the world forward, helping the development. Believe me, personal interest is not what carries the most importance, but the interest of the whole. Of course, the individual is important, too, since that lays the foundations. You have to feel good, in order to be able to do what's needed. But when you feel good depends only on you. There are some who, even though living in the greatest wealth, having the most expensive houses or cars, are still unhappy. And there are those who live in a half-collapsed hovel and still feel themselves the happiest people in existence. Only a question of attitude. If you do your job, you're happy, because that is your path, that is your task. If not, change.'

'And what about if what you saw here angers you, and then you use it improperly, therefore you head in the wrong direction, not where you're supposed to?'

'That is not possible,' Noah said. 'Paul is only one of the guardian angels that are tasked with assisting David.'

'And the other thing is… that I consider to be most important thing, that there is no wrong direction in my opinion. Especially with me. You might see it as wrong, but it might be exactly what's the best course. What is your opinion about the world wars?'

'Nothing positive.'

'Yes. As a conclusion, you could say that humanity has suffered because of it. But I wouldn't necessarily call it bad. Don't look at me like that, rather think a bit... but most importantly, start waking up, please. Being a dumb bitch doesn't suit you. I'm sure Noah already told you that both of them were necessary. Originally the first one would've been enough, but humanity didn't learn from it, so came the second one. You can hate, you can be angry at those who started the second one, but the world should be angry at itself because it didn't learn what it should've from the first one. Look at it now... Those bombs with such destructive capabilities caused such a shock to humanity that they don't allow even the possibility of a third one. Not even the most wicked of the leaders, since everyone knows that it would mean the extinction of humanity, and who would that be good for? No one. Not the Boss, not the leaders down here. You need to learn how to resolve conflicts peacefully, this is what the leaders of the world need to understand. Selfish interests do not matter. We are thinking with countries, after all. However, you can observe groups even now where there is no complete assimilation, everyone keeps their sovereignty, but they still can work together. I must add that this is still in its infancy, but it will slowly develop and will work, we just have know how to do it right. Good news is that they will; we will know, because we'll have no other choice. Because - and here I would like to continue my previous train of thought - because we'll soon understand that we'll have to think in planets, not countries. We shouldn't represent our countries, but our planet.'

'David!'

'No, don't "David" me. Enough of sparing her. She needs to know the truth. No more babbling. You treat her like a little baby. If I have to know this at the age of six, then she has to as well, because she has a more important role in the machine than me. Of course, I get it, you need to discuss the basics, the whys, the faults, but you need to grow up, Your Majesty, because we have little time. You should understand already that these are serious topics, much more important than "will you have someone who will love you until the end of your life or even more or not." By the way, you have. Not will have, but you already do. You just can't see the wood for the trees. The other thing is, if you accept advice from a midget, don't look at love like you do currently. A bit differently. Love is… is attachment, rather than what you imagine it to be right now. And it's not for what you think, but I believe Noah will show you this as well. But where was I? Yes, I know. You and everyone can see that the direction is wrong. War cannot change it because that would mean the end. We need to change the world and unite it in a peaceful, but firm way – which none of the leaders are able to do right now. I'd just like to add that they don't have to, soon it will come…. what needs to come. Our task is to prepare the world, to move the world forward with our deeds in the correct direction, meaning showing the way… and now if you'll excuse me, I think I need to go. The door is opening, my mother is coming. If she sees that I'm talking to myself again she's gonna freak out, and I don't need that.'

David stood up from the bench and bowed. 'It was a pleasure, My Lady. I hope I didn't confuse you too much. I wish you good luck in the following, have fun studying, and we'll meet soon. Oh, quickly, another piece of advice before I leave: don't fight, don't resist your fate, your task, because it was determined prior to your birth. Do it, because there is great need for it, even though you might not see it like that. Believe me, those who sent you knew why it was you, why it was there they sent you, why in that certain way, and why at that time when they did so. And I would like to add that they chose wisely. It was my pleasure having the pleasure. See ya.' David jumped up on his bike and cycled away towards their house. The door opened, and a blonde, shapely woman around thirty stepped out. She looked around, looking for her son, and when she saw him she tapped her imaginary clock that it's time, they should leave. David left his bike in the middle of the lawn and ran towards the door, but his mother's angry look and the knocking of her shoes made him turn back, pick the bike up and put it in its place. He then ran to the door again, hugged his mother, kissed her hand, trying to ease the tension, and turned back for a split second, smiled and winked at the two sitting on the bench before the door closed behind them.

'Wow,' she said finally. 'That was something.'

'Yes, I know. Not your average guy, never was. This is why he got what he did.'

'You didn't answer a question completely. What happens if they don't do what they are supposed to?'

'What happens to everybody else. At first smaller, then bigger and bigger warnings. If they still don't get it, if they still don't come back to the path which was destined for them, there is the most drastic solution. This is why we use it so rarely.'

'Death?'

'Let us say "restart" instead. But there is no possibility of that with David, since he has vision of not only his current and previous lives, but the whole system. Therefore, he knows that there would be not much point in going on private adventures, since he knows what he would cause with them. He has an opinion, he is listened to, and sometimes his ideas are even applied, because everyone knows that he is aware that he can progress further if he plays as a part of the team rather than trying to do the impossible alone.'

'Can I ask something?'

'Sure.'

'Who am I?'

'You'll realise it on your own when it's time.'

'It would be easier if you'd just tell me.'

'Yes. But I won't.'

'Why am I a princess, queen, liege, lady, majesty, etc?'

'Later. Not now.'

'But… you aren't expecting me to lead anyone, are you?'

'No. Our task is learning, then later teaching. You need to share what you have experienced with the world, meaning that you have to write. This will launch a process that can move your lives forward.'

'You think this is possible?'

'I know it. But now, if it's possible, let's move on. Before David's interruption, we were at fate, karma, reward system. I told you what karma is.'

'Yes. The result of our actions.'

'Yes. Why I told you that we shouldn't overcomplicate it is because it's that simple. If you do others good, you'll receive good in return. If you do others bad, then that. This is the whole thing, simply put. I also told you that you cannot know when you'll get your reward, but you can be certain that nothing remains without consequences. So, if you do something bad to someone, you'll get your punishment, there's no escaping it. Lucky are those who receive it in their current lives, because they can start the next one with a clean slate. Unpleasant things happen to you quite often, and you have no idea why, since you have done nothing wrong… The problem is that you did, it's just that you can't remember it; you didn't do it in your current life, but you have to endure its effects nevertheless…What should be done when this happens is enduring it with a head held high. It'll be much worse if you resist or get angry, because you'll cause another problem for yourself. Then you'll be dealing with not one, but two or more tasks, which have more effects. Believe me, it's not worth it, because in the end only the causes will fill your life instead of you walking your path. If you do good, you'll get good in return. Again, when that will happen cannot be predicted, but it will arrive no matter what. I often see people wondering after doing a good deed why they didn't get it back instantly, or not from the direction they expected it to come from. No, wait. I'll rephrase. Take two people. One does good to the other, helps them in trouble. However, when they need help it is not necessarily that the other person helps them. This is when you say that they are ungrateful, since you were there when they needed you, but just look at them now… What needs to be understood is that it is not necessarily they from whom you should expect the help, because maybe they're unfit for that task. Help will arrive, and in most cases from a source you wouldn't even suspect. Some grumble about this, that they help while the others don't even lift a finger. Of course. Because some of you need to help

215

and others don't. One starts a process that the others have nothing to do with. And if we're discussing individuals, I'm going to tell you a bit about karmic relationships. Here too we can distinguish good and bad relationships. I believe it's completely obvious which is which, and that there is no need for explanation.'

'I think a lot of people think that karma is only a negative thing.'

'But it isn't. You often feel with a person that you've met them before, you know them, have talked to them. You also feel that with them you feel good and safe. Now, you got them because of your karma. They are those with whom you were together through multiple lives, loving and protecting each other. You can distinguish them by the fact that you don't have any intensive feeling towards them, only that everything is in order, that you feel at home with them, safe and sound.'

'Like John.'

'Yes, exactly like John. You love and protect each other, even if it often causes a lot of trouble. These are the strongest karmic bonds. And this doesn't necessarily mean relationships. Both of you have your own lives, tasks, or remaining debts towards others, but you are there for each other, making everything a perfect whole. When you're together you feel like home. John came into your mind now, but there are and were others.'

'My grandma.'

'She was a really important person in your life. She wasn't with you every minute; she couldn't be, because you and your mother had to deal with what work you had left and what you brought with yourself, but you always knew you could count on her. And she could always count on your love, since that was what she needed.'

'I miss her.'

'I know. But she had to go, because she had given all the knowledge and information you needed, so she didn't need to stay any longer. You need to know that she still loves you much, and she still protects you – only not from Earth.'

'Some other people came into my mind.'

'Yes, besides your grandma and John there are and will be some important people in your life. You'll always know who they are, because you'll feel that special feeling that we discussed a moment ago. Well… I think that's quite enough about good relationships, let's discuss the bad ones. These are the ones that can give you a hard time. You fight with someone or against something, they drive you crazy, you have no clue what to do about them or the whole situation. Nothing works, whatever you try. You often think about letting go or running away, but you know you can't do that, because there is something that drags you back every time. In most cases it is your family members that cause you the greatest trouble, because you either can't get them out of your life, or only with much difficulty and pain. This is like this because you have the most to do with them in your life, learning from them, or paying your debts to them… or vice versa. And now let's put fate here, too. *Fate* is what you undertook for your life.'

'Some say that we can choose from different tasks before our birth. They usually add that we should imagine how bad the others could've been, if we chose this, because who would be as stupid enough to choose the worst option.'

'The soul,' Noah grinned. 'The soul and the spirit are those stupid ones, always choosing the worst one, because they know that if they learn what needs to be learned they become more, and they will be able to experience the good more fully, with more experience. They know where they're headed. Just think about it – the mountain climber doesn't start from the peak either, but from the bottom, takes a step upwards, then a second, and a third, and so on. This is the same in life. Both in the earthly and in the soul's life. Step by step, to the

218

top. Of course… there are obstacles, and there are dangerous missteps, but those can teach you what is right, where you should go or where it's worth to head so you'll reach your goal in the end. I have told you so many times: you fate, your path, your task is given. Before your birth you chose the most suitable with your helper or helpers, so that it might serve as your next step. You added the consequences/debts that you still had to work off from your previous lives, and based on that you chose the best location and people for you, those that you will need to complete what you have to with. If everything was ready, all details discussed – by this I mean the allowed detours in your life, and that what can have and how big an effect -, then…'

'Wait… so, you say that before my life I know how many big mistakes I'll make and what the consequences are going to be?'

'It's often you who chooses them.'

'Wow.'

'I know that it's hard to believe, but it's true. In that moment you can see your path from the beginning to the end, you know and see what you need to do in order to get out of the circle, so yes… it's often you who decides what and how you receive things, in the case of you detouring from your fate.'

'I am so strict with myself.'

'You can't even imagine. We often made easier what you chose for yourself. You need to know that these memories are lost to the souls, they don't remember what happened before their births, not even after returning home, since they are not needed. To be honest they are so hard that it's enough to live through them only once.'

'Well… if I imposed such a punishment on myself, I can imagine.'

'No, you cannot, but don't argue about this, I'll rather continue explaining. Where was I? Oh… yes! So: if you've discussed everything thoroughly – what and how you need to do, what will be the task, who will be the punishment and/or the reward, what circumstances you'll have, and most importantly where you need to get to – you start out on your journey, hand in hand with your ego. This is the moment of conception. In the foetal state the soul has time to prepare the hardships awaiting it, can make friends with the ego, distributing the tasks between them. When they have discussed and distributed everything comes the birth. After this your helper is visible for you until you're 1 to 1 and a half years old – in this case, me. This is to

220

prevent you from feeling lonely and to give you strength to complete your task. We do everything together during that time. Then we gradually disappear, thus giving room for you to develop.'

'I have a question.'

'Go ahead.'

'I often saw that little babies move their mouths like they were speaking. Also saw that these times the grown-ups around them babble to them, and the babies just raise their eyebrows.'

'Yes. This is when they say, "Tell me what you want," or "Look, it's like he/she's talking." You have no idea what goes on inside the little ones at that time. Often times it is better that you don't,' Noah grinned. 'Infancy is not different from any other period. The best examples of this are the ones you experienced through your development. You can say that with every experience you become wiser, but what is deep inside you doesn't change too much. Of course, you show that it does on the outside, because the outside circumstances demand this from you, but you remain the same person during your whole life. You could remain that mischievous little child you were, if only society would accept this. And since we can think forward, we can go backwards, too: no matter how hard it is to believe, the same is the situation with the little ones as well. They talk, yes – or they would, but their bodies don't allow them, since they are not developed enough to make them able to express themselves. The part of their brain responsible for speech is not developed enough. Language with which they could make themselves understood is unknown to them, they literally have to learn it by heart. And not to mention that your soul has to wrestle with an ego that is just as underdeveloped, one that has only the basic instructions in itself. Of course, the soul has done this before, nothing new, but it still is, because every ego is different. And it doesn't remember a lot of things, how to do them, since it was so long ago, and it isn't really its task to remember all this, even though a portion of it was stored in the soul. And now as a side note, we need to mention that not every piece of information is stored by the soul. The ego has its own storage compartments: there goes the junk that we don't need too much – but the ego stores it, since it believes it'll make its life better, making it remember a certain event in the past. But this is wrong, because it doesn't do that, instead just it eats away at it. This is dangerous because if it eats away for two long, it might even devour the ego completely. The ego needs to understand that things happen for us to learn from. We need to draw conclusions, then move on. You often waste yourselves on things that you really shouldn't, on things that carry no significance in your lives, yet you still cling to them. Side note over.'

'At these detours you always forget where you were,' she smiled.

'Usually, yes, but not now. So... the soul has quite a hard job, since it cannot express itself, it cannot make notes of every important piece of information, even though it would like to. This is when it usually urges the conscience. We need to get stronger: sit, stand, walk, speak, so that we will have time for the most important notes. Only by the time they get to when they're able to do that, they forget everything, and we, the guardians, retract from their lives too. Thus everything is forgotten.'

'I'm not going to ask if is this the better way since I met David.'

'Yes. Even though I did not intend him to be a teaching example. Or not just that. To be honest, it's better and it isn't at the same time. If everyone would come down to Earth with all their knowledge it would be different from what it is now. Everyone would come as an adult, thinking responsibly, and life would be joyless. No play, happiness, or joy. You wouldn't care about anything but your tasks, completely forgetting to enjoy what was given. We need to strive for balance in all areas of life. This doesn't mean that you should be neutral, though. No. It means that your base state should be that you feel happy, that you wake up every morning thinking that yes, life is beautiful. That it's nice to be here. If you get that, if you can thank your existence, your life, that you feel, then everything would be fine, since your base mindset would be happiness and gratitude.'

'Yes, even I know this. It is easier to endure negative detours from this mindset, not even talking about the positive ones.'

'Nice. David! Our Princess is starting to wake up!' Noah shouted. The curtain moved, David looked out the window, a satisfied grin spreading on his face. All this in a single moment, but Molly was surprised nevertheless.

'This is how goes,' Noah said with a big smile. 'And we can continue. We should get to the end of the reward system finally.'

'We are building, Noah. We're building.'

'I know. Now, we were saying that by the time the body gets developed enough to be able to record the knowledge it believes is needed for it, its family, or its environment in its current life to make working together smoother, the ego gets so strong that it doesn't allow the soul to do that. And this is when development comes. You learn or repeat what your predecessors bequeathed you. This is the period of kindergarten and school. During this you learn the norms of the given society and the world, meaning the rules that apply for your current life, what are those things which you can and cannot do, what is accepted and what is not. Of course, you don't have to store every bit of information. Only those bits you really need. Next step is the period of love and having kids.'

'Well, now... this isn't like this.'

'This is the original order; your bodies are coded like this. I know that this period has been pushed further away, since a lot of you only have kids after their thirtieth birthday now. I don't want to label this, because I don't know whether it's good or not, since we are yet to gather enough information.'

'Are we being tested?'

'You could say that. Back then, the standard was that after school you get married, you have kids, then only after that you pursue your career. Now the kids come right in the middle of the career, oftentimes just as a sideline to the family. In my humble opinion, the age of 25 to 26 would be the ideal for everyone. But this is also only a guess, because you can't draw exact conclusions that apply for everyone. This is quite complicated, since a lot of factors need to work together. I mean that it's not only a single person's karma and fate that needs to be taken into consideration, since a kid's birth affects not only the parents lives, but many others' too, from their birth to their later ages. You can't even imagine how much work and attention this system needs to function without a fault - meaning as it should work, since a single movement, a minuscule change can change the course of the whole process. Think about it: you've written stories before. You started writing, you had a great time, but for some reason you had to stop for a moment or a day. The next time you sat down you were already a different person than before. Different mood. You were more, since you experienced or could have experienced something that would change the whole direction of the story. This is the same with your lives. It's only that if something changes with a person, not going as it supposed to, then everything else changes, since everything is connected, intertwined. This might not be easy to understand now, but it's okay. We'll talk about this more later, but this is really important.'

'You were at starting a family.'

'Yes. I explained to you not long ago that the learning process is about 30 years long. You develop, work off your debts – the largest ones, for example, that you owe to your parents or siblings, are usually done by this age, one way or the other, so it won't distract you in your later developments. I would add as a side note that you usually create new ones for your older years nevertheless. And if all of your serious debts have been "paid," and you have learned what you had to, your real task can come. The task you were born to do.'

'Fulfilling our fate.'

'Yes. I have to add that this is theory. In practice things rarely go this smoothly.'

'Don't look at me like that, Noah,' she said shamefully.

'Then whom should I look at?'

'Look at the bright side. At least I'm here with you.'

'But this is not the place you should be right now, Little Girl. I have to tell you that some have called my attention to the fact that we have both done this on purpose – you unconsciously, I consciously - so that we could spend some time together in the middle. I don't think that…'

'I guess this wasn't the first time.'

'No, Molly, it wasn't. But, now we finally got to the reward system, we have the bases covered. We learned what karma is, what fate is, you know that you shouldn't mix or put the two together, but they complete each other, connecting.'

'Sorry for interrupting, but I'd like to add something. I often hear from people that there is no such thing as fate, that predestined tasks don't exist, and that everyone can decide freely what they want to achieve in their lives.'

'Yes, I know. And it's good like that.'

'But why?'

'Because there are people who don't like the idea of being controlled. There are those who say, "I'll decide what I want." This is free will.'

'Why is this any good?'

'Because they actually want to do their true tasks. What is it that you do freely, by your own intentions? You do what makes you feel good, what brings joy, happiness and satisfaction to your life. And what is it that can give all this goodness? When can one be truly happy?'

'If they walk their set paths, doing their jobs.'

'Exactly. And do you see why this is good, why this is perfect this way?'

'Because the task is the result of free will, meaning it is not forced upon them.'

'Exactly. They do it, because they enjoy it, causing them happiness, and not for the sake of a reward they're expecting in return. Of course, what's due is due, they just don't expect it, and this makes it wonderful.'

'Why do I feel that I'm going to get punished?'

'You aren't. Maybe only a little. As I told you, in standard circumstances every person's learning process – which includes starting a family and paying off the greatest of karmic debts - ends at about the age of thirty. This is the period you have in which to complete these tasks. Only there are special cases, a lot more recently, when people don't do what they're supposed to, not even close. There are a lot of reasons for this: most common are solitude, laziness, fear, not caring about anything, or a complete lack of faith. And here comes what you think I might scold you for. The problem is that I cannot tell you that "Hey, you did good, nice job, that's how it's done", because I would be lying. If you'd done it properly, we wouldn't be here and not this way, so don't take it as scolding or punishment, but learn from it, and do it better next time. Because what happens nowadays? You're stalling, as though you had to do that. And if you start out in a direction that's not even close to your supposed path. You can make detours so great that we have no idea how to fix those, how to lead you back towards your correct direction.'

'But it's not that simple.'

'It is perfectly simple. The path is set, like it or not. Since you got the gift of free will, you can decide freely how great a detour you want to take to reach your destination. True, the fastest road is the hardest and most painful, but detours create lots of karma, meaning in the end you create more problems for yourselves than you need, and for a long time, too. Imagine this, Molly: there are two cities. Simply put, call them "A" and "B." You can get from A to B quite simply, following the straight line, but you can also get there by travelling around the globe in any direction.'

'And what if someone doesn't want to go anywhere?'

'There is no such option. You can take a detour that lasts through one or two lives, but that only hurts you. Ego says that it's okay, that won't be me anyway. True. It won't be that one, but the soul, your most important part, your substance and being, will be the same. Why would you want to cause trouble for yourself? You have to know that the first task you get is always not too hard, to be honest. Not always pleasant, but it can be endured.'

'I think otherwise.'

'Molly, good and bad things rarely stay. You often think about them as integral parts of your lives. You miss them when they're not there. Easiest example for this is air. You often say that the most honest and purest love is the one like breathing: natural. However, you can now see that breathing is not natural, only you take it as such. It is there and that's good. You use it, pollute it, because you think about it as a given. But it's not. It's so not. But if you have to fight for something, or something hurts you, it leaves a stronger impression on you. Nobody comes to have a vacation. Thinking that the ones with material wealth do is a misconception. They, too, have to learn. They have, or should, learn mostly humanity and empathy.'

'Materially wealthy?'

'Yes, there are those with material wealth, meaning they have a lot of money. They can do a lot of things others cannot. And there are those who are wealthy in an emotional way. They might not have huge houses or expensive objects, they might not travel around, but they have everything they need: they're happy. Often these people are happier than those we mentioned before.'

'Possibly.'

'Surely. This is the reason why the given path is filled with difficulties. Learn, because it's worth it. There are countless examples of that.'

'I don't know that.'

'Of course you don't. How many stories have you seen in which they did what they had to do, and in the end, they received everything they longed for, even things they could never imagine. You usually react to this with "Because they were lucky," or "Because they could do it, I can't," or "It's easy for them," or "How good for them," and I could go on. But you're wrong. They don't have it easy, it's not good for them, they didn't have luck, etc. They just did what they had to do, their jobs. They followed their feelings. While others slept, rested, idled, travelled, or had fun, they worked hard. If you'd ask these people how they got to where they are now, you'd be surprised. Most of them would say with faith, persistence, and hard work. They are the people you should look up to, those that could serve you as an idol, because they did what they had to do, without detours, but in a straight line.'

'How can we know that we all could have this?'

'You've got to have faith. Faith even in the invisible. And this is the biggest problem nowadays. The depressingly wide spread of complete faithlessness. All that torture in the name of faith and God had their effect on your world, this is clear now. But we're trying to make everyone understand that this was necessary, even if it had terrible effects on a lot of people.'

'Okay. How should we get started then? We realise what we should do by some source. What next?'

'Nothing. You just have to keep going and doing it. Following your feelings. If it is good, follow it; if not, don't. And this applies to all areas of life, Molly. If something doesn't feel good, if it no longer serves the purpose of your development, you need to let it go.'

'But there are things you cannot let go. It's not good, I'm borderline hating that it's there, but I can't shake it off, can't change it, because it sticks to me like a leech.'

'If it sticks, then it has to.'

'I don't get it.'

'These things have to stay. Or they simply stay until they teach you something. Possibly you gave the wrong answer to the given question. You can't proceed until you have the correct answer.'

'And what should one do in a case like this?'

'Ask for help.'

'Now… that's not fun. I don't like to do that, and others don't, either.'

'That's too bad.'

'We often pray to God for help. And what happens then? You'd expect things to turn better, but they do the opposite. Much, much worse. This is why we don't ask for anything even by accident, and why we accept what we have because it's still surely better what would come next. This is why you can see so many resigned and unhappy people on Earth. Everybody feels that this is okay, this is my share, I must deserve this, just let the days pass after each other so that this might finally be over, just without any change.'

'Yes, I know. That's what I call cowardice. And this is why you're here. Because we need to change this. This resignation, this "Let's get this finally over with" mentality, this lethargy that will cause the extinction of your race – if we do not change it in time. The problem is that you accept it on the surface, but somewhere deep down everybody feels that this is not okay, this is not right. Not individually, not globally. Habits and lives needs to be changed, because soon there will be nothing that you can change. And about that you asked for help and you didn't get what you hoped for... well... I'll try to be gentle with my wording.'

'Here comes the scolding.'

'Oh, yes, Molly, it does. You get your help in every occasion you ask for it. But it doesn't work like you ask for help, there comes a heavenly light, drags you out of your misery, and everything becomes suddenly magically beautiful. I know you'd like that, but it's not how it is. It works like this: there is something that makes you feel absolutely dreadful, and then you say, "Please, God, help me," and the help soon arrives in a manner that helps you get back on your path. You get the key to solving the given problem. And you respond to this with "I wish I didn't ask for anything." Because solving a problem often can only be done through pain, through giving up... or rather letting go of objects, people, habits, workplaces, and I could go on. I know that this is the hardest lesson. Letting go always causes pain, since you get used to things. But if you need to do

235

this, then it no longer serves your development, and you need to part ways. In your case the people are the problematic part. You cannot let them go, you want to protect them even though there is no need for it anymore. They want to leave, you should leave, too, but you say no and no. This is when they stay and the situation gets ugly, so you finally have to let go, having no other choice. But so that we don't always speak about you: everybody has to understand that the help comes, all you have to do is ask and, more importantly, accept it. If you do that, everything will be better.'

'And how do I know it will be better? Often it's as though something is bad, I get out of it, move on, start again and the same thing happens, repeating always. I don't even always notice it, only when I say, "Oh, it's this again…" again. How do I know that my life changes… I mean that I'm heading in the good direction?'

'Every change begins with a decision. If you feel that a situation happens to you over and over again, you possibly gave the wrong answer to the question. The worst case is if you saw that it happened every day. That is when the problem is the greatest. Think about what you might do wrong, repeatedly, every day. Then decide otherwise. If the situation repeats, you gave another wrong answer. If it doesn't, then the story will continue in another direction. In the correct direction. You can always know that it's the correct path if it makes you happy. Believe me, Molly, we always help you in everything, you just need to ask, and then accept our response. If you live keeping this in mind, paying attention to the small signs, then everything will be fine.'

'What signs?'

'There are countless ways of delivering information. For example, an article in a newspaper, or a discussion with someone who tells you about something that could move your life forward. Or you might see a play, a film, or a picture... There are countless ways of transferring information. This is like this because we cannot go to you, patting you on your shoulders and telling you "Hey, pay attention, you're doing this and that wrong." We cannot do this. I think most people would be scared to death if we'd did this, so currently this is the best way to let you know about things that you might need. Not only you, others too. Of course, there are exceptional people, like David, who doesn't need any mediator. We can tell him straight away if something's wrong.'

'I'm not sure they always appreciate this great gift.'

'They see your world from a different angle, Molly. In their lives, the ego does not play such a big role like it does in others' lives. Whether it's better or not, we don't know yet. This question is under processing. Based on what we've experienced so far, I can say that no, it's not any better. But this will not be decided in one or two days, or based on only one or two lives.'

'And while test is going on, they change the world.'

'Nice. Things must change, by those people that do this without any selfish reasons, to whom the collective progress means more. But we can only do this with souls who can remain clean, the souls whom the ego cannot and doesn't even want to take control, remaining in the position of sustaining life. These people keep the common goal in front of themselves. Of course, they too long for beautiful and nice things, for comfort, since they too live here. But they know that they'll have everything. They don't have to be prodded, saying, "Do it already, want it, believe it already that it will be good for you."

'Why do I always feel that you mean me when you say this?'

'Maybe because I do. You never believed that your life would change if you did what you had to. That you would get what you want.'

'No, because I never got it.'

'Hey, think about that for a second.'

'Well… erm…'

'Yes, erm… And I'll talk about your detours a bit, too.'

'Scolding again.'

'Something like that. But think about it as correcting a mistake, and there won't be a problem. So, I told you already: you have your path, that you have to walk on, this is fate; you have your tasks you have to complete, this is karma; and you have the free will that brings the little detours. Sometimes small, sometimes large ones. This all depends on the individual. You need to know that these detours don't serve your development, they are only like counter-examples in your life. They are needed because you want them.'

'I don't want anything bad for myself… not only me, others neither for themselves.'

'Sadly, you/they do.'

'I don't understand.'

239

'These things are your wishes, but ones that you don't need. If you think about it often, and pay attention only to this, you receive it so you might realise that you have no need for it. Actually, you draw in something that you shouldn't. I'll give you another nasty example, but it'll stick with you more. There is a person, who thinks about being diagnosed with cancer continuously. If anything hurts, they instantly think that they must have a tumour. Even though this sickness was not coded into their body at their birth, if they expect it this much, and nothing and no one can convince them otherwise, they will get it. So, they can know that they really didn't need it. I know, this is again an extreme example, but it proves the point. You often ask for things which you have no need of whatsoever. Of course, you think at your current level of development that that is the greatest gift possible, but it isn't. But if you long for it that much that it's the only thing in your mind, you'll get it. This is true for both positive and negative things.'

'But how can I avoid thinking about negative things?'

'You cannot. The ego relishes in this, it loves self-pity, because it makes it think that it's the centre of attention. It believes that it can overcome the spirit or soul this way, making itself more than them. Of course, this is not true, but it still tries sometime. All you can do in these cases, when a bad feeling like this comes, is think through how much basis does it have. If there is something you can learn from it, learn; if not, let it go, don't pay any more attention to it. It is crucial that you head in the correct direction, the one that makes you feel good, even if it's difficult, even if you don't see what's the point of it or why it's good for you.'

'Then what about the reward system? How does this whole thing work?'

'That you can get everything you wish for, anything, if you've completed your task. We don't just hand out goodness freely, since then your lives wouldn't progress. There are lot of films and books about this topic. Only one really important thing is left out: yes, the good comes; the dream house, car, vacations, partner – but you have to work for it. You won't get the good stuff just like that, for free. I told you, up until 30 is the period of learning and work. Until then even your partners are ones that you have some stuff do to with. It is important that this is just most of the cases, because we cannot draw a conclusion that is true for everyone, since not everyone brings tasks like this with themselves, and not everyone creates ones like that in their current lives. So yes, these things work, yes, you can have all you want, you just have to work for it. Do what you were born for and not what they want to force upon you. This differs with every person, but the point is that you have to do what you were entrusted with.'

'That's all?'

'Yes. But you too know that this is not that simple. If it were you wouldn't be here right now. This all sounds good in theory, but being in it and completing it is not that easy. Great things happen only through hard work, fight, and often pain and resignation, because only these will make you grasp their importance, so that you value them. Because you have to know, too, that this situation is not permanent. It's not as though once you achieved it, it'll remain with you for the rest of your life. There is always more. The most important thing is that no matter if you are top or bottom, or in between, you have to keep your faith, you always need to be able to be humble and grateful, and that you never forget where you came from and where you're going. If you can keep these rules your life will remain how you created it. If you can't, if you become arrogant or stuck-up, someone who doesn't respect their environment, their fellow humans, or their planet, someone who cannot be grateful for what they have got, you create extra karma for yourself. And this doesn't make your life easier; on the contrary, much worse.'

'Yes, knowledge and power often corrupt people. I often see that they don't use, but abuse it.'

'Not everyone. Those of pure heart don't. Those who don't let the ego overcome them, not letting it get too full of itself. Those who remain true to themselves, remembering where they came from and how they got to the place they are now – they won't be a problem. Sadly, this is rare, but there are examples.'

'I understand. I've got to be honest, I thought this reward system would be something larger, that we would talk a lot more about this.'

'I know. It's always like this, everyone thinks that there are various tricks in achieving the wanted good. But there's only one: DO YOUR JOB. If you're done, you'll get the fruit of your labours. People often answer "But I'm working" and "But I worked all my life," etc. Work is only for sustaining yourselves, that is completely different. You have to make a living, you have to eat, pay the bills, up until you get to the end of what you have to do, sure. There was a movie not long ago about this topic that caused a big uproar. I don't want to talk about the work of others, but I believe this to be important enough to mention. So, not long ago a film was made, that showed the reward system in detail, how this whole thing works, what is worth doing and how. A huge, worldwide uproar followed it, that this is all a lie, it doesn't work. Out came the second and third editions, but things didn't get any better. People wrote and said that it was all a big lie, but it wasn't; they just didn't pay proper attention. The core information was there, only most didn't notice it. Experienced people talked about how this reward system worked, what one needs to do, and even told their own examples. Only this core was overlooked. They had already done what they had to do. They did what they had to, worked off what they had to, what they undertook, and they were only enjoying the fruits of their labours. So it's not that you sit down in a room, imagining what you want and then you just suddenly get it. No. You have to work for it, doing your real job. If it's ready, good will come. And in addition, it doesn't work that I did half of the job, now get the reward. No. If you finished, you'll get your payment. Until that – fight. Even yourself. No. Especially with yourself. Why I tell you this now is that I know that there'll be occasions during writing that you'll grow uncertain, when you'll say that you can't do this, that this is all just bogus, not true, only a bad or a nice dream. Write, do it from your heart, put your soul and heart into it, and you'll get your reward.'

'I'll try to remember this, too.'

'If you don't, then I'll remind you.'

'Should I be happy for that or not?'

'Rather not. You have to know that the repeat system works here as well. At first all circumstances are given. I won't tell you it's easy, because if it was, you wouldn't appreciate it, you wouldn't learn the lesson – but it's not that hard either. We'll whisper, or send messages with others about what you should do. If you do that, fine; if you don't, we'll turn up the difficulty of your life a bit. Then harder and harder. It'll be so hard in the end that you'll be begging to do your job.'

'Noah, this sounds cruel!'

'Sounds like, and it is. But! Either you do it on the first or second try, or bear the consequences. It's the same with every task. If you give the wrong answer the first time, you'll get it again, in a way a bit more difficult. If you give a wrong answer again, you'll get the next and the next version made more and more difficult. You have to learn what you have to learn. Even through blood, sweat, and tears.'

'This is repetition.'

'Yes. You realise what's wrong because all you'll say is "This happened again." Listen to the first one, and think about what could be done otherwise, better, then try that way. If you get it back again, try another. If you are not sure about your answer being the correct one, ask for help. A simple "Help me, God" will be enough. An answer will come shortly. We'll always help you make the correct decision, and soon you'll realise that the given question or topic doesn't repeat any longer, but disappears from your life, since you've nothing else to do with it. You just have to be confident and not afraid of change, because it's not bad. Staying in the same place is much worse and scarier, you can believe my and especially your experiences.'

'It's strange hearing about these things like this.'

'I know it's not easy, but deep inside you must know that these things work the way I tell you, because you rarely argue with me, no matter what I say. What I advise you is that after your return just write it and try it after. Believe me, Molly, everything starts with a decision. Always make the correct decision, no matter how hard it seems. If you do it right you'll be happy; if not, you'll be sad. To whom does your sadness cause pain? To you. And me. Then? Why do you want to cause pain? I think it would be stupid. Hard? It is. But this is what's needed, like it or not. You just have to believe that you are brave enough and that you can do it. And most importantly, you have to know that you're never alone. I'm always here to protect you.'

'Thank you.'

'Well... I think we have talked quite enough about karma and the reward system. Let's move on to the relationship topic. You wanted to discuss that before.

8.

Relations and relationships. This is my favourite part. I dislike this topic almost as much as the ego topic, I would gladly skip it, but we can't. Because most people do it wrong.'

'I don't even dare to say a word.'

'You'd better, Molly. Your relationships are able to exceed every expectation. You can screw up relationships not in the way that it would be usual, you do it in a much grander way. I haven't seen anything like this. I don't know how you do it, but you exceed all expectations in this life of yours. We knew there'd be trouble, but this much…'

'I understand,' she said shamefully. 'Please don't say anymore.'

'I'm going to, because I have to. You have to learn to do it better, because there will be troubles. A proper relationship is nowhere near like what you imagine it to be. A karmic one is, because you have to work off a previous offence, but even that shouldn't last for years. You could solve the problem quickly by discussing it between you, both would tell what their problem is, what they'd like, how it would be better, then BOTH OF YOU would have to change that aspect because you'd like to live your every day in peace and tranquillity, and because you love each other. This is the theory. Practice gets nowhere close to this.'

'I'm thinking do we even need relationships? Because what is it that motivates people? Why are they together? Mostly it's sex. Sure, you need touch, the feeling of belonging to someone, of someone waiting for you in the evening. We need a person with whom we can discuss our problems and share our happiness, successes, and lives with…'

'So, you think that you need a relationship only because of sex and the feeling of safety?'

'Yes. Maybe. I don't know. I can't add anything to this topic, because I don't even want to think about it. I can't do this, so instead I leave this whole topic alone, pretending it doesn't exist.'

'And does that work for you? Is it good to be alone?'

'Better than suffering along with someone. Usually I have a lot to do; if not, I find something, so that the days pass faster. One after the other, so that I don't even notice that life slowly passed me by.'

'I can just ask the same question: does that work for you?'

'Yes… No… I don't know. I have no clue whether it's good or not. Maybe it isn't. I mean it's certain that it isn't, but that's it.'

'You are really certain… Let's do the following: you can give only one answer. And that can only be yes or no.'

'I don't know.'

'That wasn't a choice.'

'Noah! I don't care, I don't know whether this is good or not! After being left, this is the best. Some time passes, and it won't be best anymore, because I miss a partner, because it's horrible to be alone. And before you say that I'm never alone, since you're always with me and protect me… Yes, I know, I feel it and thank you, but believe me, this is something completely different. We need touch… physical touch, and sex, too. Those who say that we don't are liars, since the body needs the energies that are released during it. After good sex you feel relieved, you're lighter, because you let out all the negative energies from yourself, changing them to good ones.'

'Then what's the problem?'

'Everything.'

'Then think about this a bit more, Molly.'

250

'It would be easier if you were speaking now.'

'I know it would be easier. Now… Come, tell me how it needs to be properly.'

'As you can see, I have no idea.'

'You do.'

'It's the same always.'

'Do you even hear yourself???' Noah's question scared her.

'Good heavens!'

'Yes, that. Molly, you screwed up repeatedly, catastrophically. You, no one else. You got your first relationship as a task and as a debt. You should've learned to be…'

'Independent and self-sustaining.'

'You see, you can do this. You should have, but you didn't. But gave yourself up without a question or a request. Because it was easier, more comfortable, or better. Which is not true, of course. If you think about it, all of your relationships started the same way. You got to know each other. They fought for you, then earned your graces through great difficulties, and after that they couldn't recognise you. The woman whom they

251

grew to like, who had poise, whom they respected for her toughness, diligence, and perseverance was gone, and they got a maid instead. A bird locked in a cage, one that didn't want to fly even if they opened the door for her. They tried to get you out nicely at first, then in more and more aggressive ways later on, but all for nothing: the little bird clung to the cage she built for herself.'

'This sounds really bad.'

'Believe me, it was. We sent you the best, the most patient ones, but still, the end was the same: complete submission. Of course they treated you like a nobody afterwards, because you wanted it so. This is the basic law of life: the weak get trampled by the strong. And before you freak out at this, I would add: the only weak are those who believe themselves to be, and who let the others trample them.'

'Noah! I'm not freaking out, I am stunned. This is a disaster!'

'I know perfectly well, you don't have to tell me. You can't even imagine how many times I yelled at you so that you would stop and realise what you were doing. And, and this is the worst: you wasted many years of your life on this single task, and futilely, too. Because what was it you were always saying? That you need someone to be with you, someone who helps, who loves you, who you can cuddle up with in the evenings, someone who waits for you at home, someone with whom you can be free but not lonely with. Because if this was fulfilled, you could do your real task. We thought that if you'd get this, then maybe... You got it, and nothing happened, and you especially didn't do your job, because at first you were too much in love, then later because you were too much of a slave. When the actual man couldn't bear it anymore and ran away, you became a wreck, an undead. Whether you had someone or not, it was a problem for you. It just wasn't working, and you weren't progressing with writing. As a last desperate attempt, we brought you here. Molly, you need to understand that you have to write, no matter whether you believe in yourself or not, if you like it or not. You'll give something of value to the world, and to those who need it, those who are mature enough for your story – those people's lives might change. This could be 100, 1,000, or even 10,000 people. Or maybe just a single one. You'll see. Numbers doesn't actually matter as much as change itself. The point is: you write, and we'll handle the rest. That's enough about you, I think we have uplifted the lockdown inside you. I believe we can start the general analysis.'

'This was another great slap in the face. But I'm grateful.'

'You're welcome,' the angel smiled.' Slowly we'll remove all the blocks inside you, and this is one of the most important reasons you're here. Molly, there is a really important thing that you have to know! Everything happens because of you. Good and bad both. Don't ever look for the causes in others, don't blame anyone else but yourself. Your fate, your great task doesn't carry too much pain with itself, just enough so that you will remember it, so you can store it. But this is minuscule compared to those that you do as cause-effect or those you simply draw in to yourself. This is what you need to understand: for these things, YOU CAN ONLY THANK YOURSELF. Remember this, because this is really important. And now we can start discussing the relationship topic. Believe it or not, it's necessary. Naturally there are special examples, meaning exceptions, but they rarely last long.'

'Why is it necessary?'

'Mostly because of karma. This makes it easier to work off what you have to.'

'That's all?'

'Not really. No matter what anyone says, it's not good being alone. You can pretend on the outside how strong you are, how you don't need anyone, but inside you know you are wrong. But you keep telling yourself this because you think this will make you believe it. Or… you keep saying it to protect yourself from disappointments. Varies with everyone. But the fact is that every creature is a social one, this is how the world was created, and this is how it's perfect. Imagine a world where everyone was alone, and where there was no contact between people.'

'Okay, even I can see that's impossible. But what about relationships?'

'We don't want to get rid of them. They are good as they are.'

'Sorry for nagging, but I'd like to know why is that so. Why is it so necessary, since relationships ruin so many friendly or other relations? How many times I saw or experienced really good friendships ruined by the "intrusion" of a third person, because this person for some reason didn't like that friend; or new friendships were abandoned even before forming because the partner didn't like them, and, peace being the

255

better option, they didn't seek each other's company any longer.'

'Jealousy. Disgusting thing.'

'If it's disgusting then it's some ego-stuff.'

'Yes, it is. Jealousy is one of the motivators. Can cause a lot of problems.'

'I suspect that it is necessary, too.'

'Everything is needed, and everything happens for a reason, just like this. The ego is afraid of loss, because it doesn't see or understand what the spirit or the soul does. The ego's life is finite, and it believes that everything has a beginning and an end, and when it ends it has no idea; it doesn't understand what'll happen next. This makes it want to possess, in this case other people, because it believes that this way it can keep them. But it cannot. Sometimes it still possesses even when it has become cumbersome or unbearable for everyone. It doesn't understand that by letting go both of them would benefit – and not just them, many others as well. There are times when the joint road ends, when there is no longer "us," only "they and me," meaning that you reached an intersection where you shouldn't continue together, but separately. And if they can separate peacefully there, there is a good chance that the good relations will remain between them. This basically means that they continue together, but as long-time friends. But for this to happen they need to let each other go, no matter how hard it is. They have to understand that those who are bound to separate have to do so. Like it or not, even if it's hard. You can prolong this separation, but it's not worth it. The problem is that the ego doesn't know that for those who really love each other, this connection is permanent and untearable. It only feels as if they aren't there, and this hurts it. It doesn't understand that being close to or far from someone doesn't depend on their GPS coordinates. You can be in the next room to someone, and still be lightyears away from them, and you can be 2000 kilometres away, and still be really close to them. It all depends on what two or more people feel in their hearts. This is called love. And this not only applies to relationships, but to any other relation as well, but I'll talk about that later. Let's look at now what a good relationship is like. When two people get to know each other, both of them start with a clean slate. They cannot know what the other might give or bring with themselves. This is when that certain "seeing through rose-coloured spectacles" prevents people from seeing clearly.'

'Sorry for interrupting, but what's this good for? I mean love. What is it good for and why is it needed?'

'Love in itself doesn't even exist. It's just a chemical process, a necessary good/evil so that you might know that this person is needed for your progression in life. You have to learn something from them, something that you cannot learn from anybody else, only them. This lesson might be painful, or wonderful, or both. This only depends on you.'

'So, love is just the beginning of belonging together?'

'Yes. You feel something, something new, different than before, and you know that something must happen to you. If that feeling weren't there, how would you know who you should talk to in the street, who is it that you have to "accidentally" meet in a shop, a party, while travelling or going on a trip? You meet countless people in your day, you cannot and you don't want to remember all of them, because you don't need them. But those you need – you have to realise that somehow. This is when the first desire comes, then later love that lets you know that you have something to do together. And now... at that point when you meet, and you

258

receive that little spark that was needed for progress, you stand before each other with equal chances. Imagine it like the two sides of a scale. This is the beginning. Both of you start to load and unload on your sides. In the beginning, during getting to know each other, you only do that with little things, watching how the other reacts. If they don't respond, that little thing remains there. However, if they say "Hey, that won't be any good," you either quickly take it out or explain why it's needed or good. If after this the other agrees, it can stay, if they don't, it cannot. A good relationship is where you can maintain a good balance. Many ruin it at this early stage, saying, "I love them so much that I will let them do that. True, I don't like it, but I will let them because I love them." Of course, it's like this only in the beginning, because as the months or years pass by that thing they didn't like will create more and more arguments that might mean the end of the relationship. And by this I don't mean that you cannot allow the other to do what they'd like to do, because all relationships are based on compromise. Both sides have to allow certain things, equally. It is really important to understand that two different people have entered a relationship with two different temperaments and lifestyles, with different habits and attributes. You have to

259

harmonise the two, creating one from them, because this has happened for a reason. Unbelievably good things can come from these relationships. The two parties can take up each other's habits and attributes; they can become more than they were through the other, they can learn from each other, and can achieve great things together. They just have to want it and they have to maintain the balance. It's not an easy task, but it isn't impossible either. Now… this is theory. In practice it rarely goes this smoothly. You have to know that every relationship works in a way that one of the two takes up the role of a stronger person, meaning they'll become the leader. There are people whose nature is just like this and who need this leading position, and there are ones that only take this role because they have to, since it's for the sake of the relationship, especially in the beginning. And this is the crucial point: this should be only valid for the beginnings. The leader's main role should be to show the other that it will be better and easier if they do it together. They kind of raise the other, giving them confidence. Of course, the complete truth is that they have to remain in control for the whole of the relationship, but this should be very hard to notice. But… this needs 2 people. One who gives, one who accepts and embraces. The experience is that oftentimes the leader fulfils their role too much. They believe that they know everything better, that everything is correct only in the way they think it to be, and they stomp on their partner if they can. They reign, trying to force their will on the other with selfishness, arguments, threats, sometimes even with physical violence, because they think they can do anything. And sadly, they are mostly right, because the partner lets them do all this, meaning they can actually do it. Because there is the other one, the so-called recipient. I have seen it quite often that they are the ones completely giving themselves up. Like you did countless times. This can happen for a lot of reasons, but mostly it's because of a lack of confidence, cowardice, or laziness. This person is the one who says, "It's okay that the other wants to control, so be it, I'll just let my leg swing. The other will find out what's next, they'll fight for both of us, for me, for our family. They'll create and complete my task, not only theirs, while I rest." This works for a while, and both parties enjoy the benefits of this, and the drawbacks are swept under the carpet. But you cannot do this for eternity."

'I guess you don't let us.'

'You're right. We cannot let you, because this is not the order of life. Not that you bow and scrape before the other, that you let the other think nothing of you, or stomp on you. Not should you be controlling the other, stomping on them, just because this makes you feel greater or almighty. This won't create great things. Usually these relationships end when you cannot solve these oppositions. Or rather when the parties both are so fed up with the whole thing that they don't even want to fix their relationship. Because, you have to know this, everything can be turned around, everything can be changed, always, you just have to want it.'

'Maybe.'

'Certainly. Not once I have seen that those who let themselves be oppressed suddenly – in most cases because of some external impulse – shake themselves up and say okay, this is not good, this cannot go on any further. Then they start to change their lives. It is really difficult to bring a relationship back to balance where the controlling party took their role too far, but it's not impossible. Of course, we have to admit that sometimes it's not worth fighting. Sometimes the other one might just need the oppressed one to simply walk out the door. Those who control their partners this much are usually broken by this, since they never think that the other would dare to do this, since by this time they are convinced that their partners are nobodies. So, being left alone feels like a cold shower to their overgrown ego.'

'Like with Colum and Jessica?'

'Yes. You saw the fire in her eyes. You were surprised - not to mention her.'

'What happened to them?'

'Come, I'll show you.'

They went back to the house. Molly was surprised. The house was clean and tidy. They walked through the house, out into the yard. The kids were sitting on the ground, talking and laughing... with their mother and father. They were several years older, and Jessica looked much younger. Her face and especially her eyes were shining. Molly was shocked.

'Are we at the good place? What happened here?'

'The wife did what she should've done in the beginning, and stood up to him. When we left she stood up from the bed, straightened out, and said: "If you have nothing else to say, you might as well leave. I know your speech by heart now, I can recite it by word to you, and I don't want to hear it

263

any more. If there is something of importance that we need to discuss, I'll listen to you, but I'm no longer interested in these pointless matters.' Colum was so surprised by her cold and distant voice, her icy words, her poise, and most importantly by her resolve that he couldn't even answer. In his confusion he stood and left. For several weeks he didn't dare to come into the vicinity of his family, didn't dare to call them. He was thinking about what might have happened. Meanwhile, the woman cleaned the house, sought out a psychologist and family support, and tried to find out what they could do to bring back peace and harmony to their lives. Everybody suggested divorce - surprisingly, even her. She was afraid - no, she was terrified of solitude, but most importantly of how she would carry on, how she would manage on her own. She was afraid of moving on, but at those times she remembered the woman who she was when she had sent her husband away, and this gave her strength. Then the difficult parts came. First the threats, and then, when the husband saw that the woman was steadfast in her decision, came the wooing and compliments. When this failed, threats and blackmail, and then wooing again, but to no avail. She remained strong and firm. She stood up to her husband alone. At long last, they divorced. Colum did everything he could to prevent this, but he failed. In the end he was broken, but Jessica grew strong. She was confident, unafraid. She shined, looked younger, and started her own company, achieving success in short time, which increased her confidence even more. A few years later she started a foundation to help women and families who had suffered the same fate that she had. And the most interesting part: Colum became one of her greatest and most dedicated helpers in this great undertaking. He was really proud of the woman and what she had achieved and created.'

'The change is astonishing.'

'Molly, every change needs a decision, and that decision needs bravery, but more importantly, resolve. But if you want to reach what you feel that you should, you have to take such painful steps that you might not want to or dare to, either because you don't trust yourself enough or because you don't dare to be who you really are, or because you are afraid of change and responsibility. Your fate is inevitable, your path is set, like it or not. And since you're facing a challenge this big, here are a few things that might come in handy later on:

1. Every problem is just as big as you make it. If you view things this way, meaning what

happens to you, then you'll realise that there is no problem at all. There are only tasks that needs to be solved, and if you can solve them, it's good; if not, the solution might be that you have to let them go.

2. Everybody can do only as much to you as you allow them. I would like to add here that EVERY ruined relationship can be turned around. Of course, it's much simpler to draw the lines in the beginning than to fix things later on, but that's not impossible either.

3. Everything happens exactly the way it should happen. You can bide your time, fight against this, but if you have to experience it you'll receive it sooner or later. It only matters in what form.

4. The cause of your problems is you yourself. I told you already, that you cause everything to yourself, but we discussed this in the karma topic. You do something, which is the cause, and the answer comes, which is the effect. Your path might seem difficult at times, but – as I said before – you cause much more damage and pain with your little detours than you originally intended to. If you think about it… if you honestly think through your life, you'll admit that I'm right.

5. And another very important thing: if you are not ready for a certain task, you won't receive it. So don't say anything like you cannot do this, because it's not true. You can do it, since you prepared yourself exactly for this in your previous life. The ego cannot see this and shrieks that you cannot do this, that this is impossible. But that's not true. You can and you have to, because it's due time.'

'I got it.'

'Good then' Noah smiled. 'But you have to know that these rules apply to every relationship. If you don't break them, there won't be any problem.'

'And what if someone gives up on a relationship, then starts another, but that isn't any better? On the contrary, much worse.'

'This is when the person doesn't start a new one, but continues the last one, only with a different person. They don't make a different decision, so they just put another repetition in their lives. And the reason for it turning out even worse is that they have to learn and have to notice that this decision was not the correct one. If they still cannot do that, they'll get the next one, but in a much worse condition, and the next, then the next, and I could go on for days. You just have to pay attention to what I said before: you have to maintain the balance, no matter what role is yours. If you are controlling, you have to raise the other, if you are the one that is controlled you have to work on catching up to the other. I know that it sounds good in theory, and that in practice it's not that easy, that it's sometimes easier to say, "Okay, I'll do it," but believe me, you couldn't cause any bigger damage to your relationship than you do with this. You have to do it together, and if you cannot, you have to raise the other up, help them, never with force, but with love. This won't wake any bad feelings in them but increase their confidence, and make them feel that they are safe with you – and in the end, you'll be capable of doing great things together. This way it's easier to complete your personal task, then something together after that. The point is that you have to believe in each other and in yourselves. If you can be each other's support and help, then you can achieve anything. And this is the most important thing. And I'll add quickly what is usually the problem: doing something together doesn't mean that you give everything to the other, so that they "do it and I might help." This is not cooperation, this is help, but only the bad kind, because you hand out to others what you should be doing. And this doesn't even help you, because even if they do what you were supposed to do, it wasn't you who did it. It might be useful for you to see how you should proceed next time. You have to understand that a task is a task. The fate-related and the karmic ones especially, because you cannot give them to anybody. This is where you always messed up. You got special people, each one had the extra that made them special to you, they could've helped you or shown you the way, but you didn't want that. You didn't raise up beside them, but instead entrusted your issues to them. You said, "I'm here, I'll do anything, I'll be a maid, a slave, just do my task for me, because it's really difficult." Of course, they didn't do it, because it wasn't theirs. Their own was quite enough for them, why would they take up yours too? They wouldn't have progressed any further with that, but neither would you have. I know that I have said this quite a few times, but I think it's worth repeating, so it might stick with you, as it is really important: you should've noticed the repetition. You told me that everything repeated in your life: "It's the same every time." You should've thought about this instantly, but not like you did before, not pitying yourself – since now we know that if a question keeps repeating, we possibly didn't give the answer most fitting for our development. Those people who entered your life really saw something special in you, something that cannot be grasped, some great power... they saw you, your true nature. They fought for you, because you were unreachable and majestic. They looked up to you, adoring you. And when they got you, you instantly gave yourself up; suddenly you were not yourself, and they were shocked. You said that in the beginning everything was all right - movies, flowers, dinners - but slowly these were gone. This was because in the beginning they tried to get back the woman they got to know, whom they adored, but they gave up after a while. They more and more felt that you were not looking for a partner, a support, but for a problem and task-solver. A task that they had barely anything to do with, which was not theirs, but yours. The slap they gave you was their last desperate attempt, hoping it might wake you up. But no. So, you collapsed and they left. Molly, it is really important that you get that I don't want to hurt you with this, it's just that you have to understand that every coin has two sides. You experienced these in your way, they in a different one. You shouldn't be pitying yourself, instead, you should think it through, and you have to understand that what you've done is not good, not correct. You also have to understand that it is you who causes every trouble to yourself. Please, stop causing problems to yourself. I know that this was quite the wigging, but believe me, it was necessary. Take Jessica, for example. Not too long ago you were grumbling that hers was a counter-example. Take a look at her now. She decided, made a change, and now she is an example worth following for many people.'

'How do I know it's time for me to make a change?'

'Every day is a new beginning. Every day gives a chance... or a possibility to you so that you might change, or decide otherwise. If you feel that your life is not as you'd like it to be, that it needs change, then do that: change. Don't wait for the miracle, it won't happen just like that, you have to work for it. By the way, miracles do happen. Of course, not in a way you'd expect, not like "You did nothing for it, but here you go." No. A miracle is an opportunity that you get every day, so that it might change your life. And here pay attention to the "every day" part, because again, this is very important. Because the "You get it every day" part means that you still haven't given the correct answer to the given question/problem/task. If this happens, sit down in your favourite armchair, turn off your phone, your bell, put some music on and don't pay attention to anybody else, only to yourself and think through what you did wrong that day. What is that you should have paid more

271

attention to, where you should have decided differently? Where are the repetitions in your life? It is really important that you completely lock out self-pity during this, because it is a really bad adviser.'

'That's all I have to do?'

'Yes, that's all. Just think about what it might be that you're doing wrong, and decide otherwise. If you do this, believe me, your life will or will be able to change very soon. Just DO YOUR JOB!!! What's that, you ask? Pay attention to the signs, ask, ask for help, and you'll know soon enough. The answer comes in every instance, you just have to ask. You'll be shocked when you get it, and the things you believed to be of importance previously will turn out to be unimportant, and vice versa. It isn't a problem if you don't understand it yet. When the time comes everything will be clear to you.'

'Well… I thought before that in the life of a person the topic of relationships is not an easy one, but now that you told me all this I realised that it's much more complicated than I ever thought.'

'Not easy, but it's not impossible to do it properly. The most important thing is that you don't give up yourself and that you don't let your partner give up either. If this cannot happen for some reason, if you still separate in the end, you have to let the other go and strive for this balance in another relationship. Believe me, it's much less painful if you develop this in the beginning. What you have to understand at this time is that family life is in essence the same everywhere. You wake up in the morning, prepare for the day, clean up the house and yourselves, leave for work, shop in the afternoon, come back home in the evening, make dinner, shower, sleep, etc. You have to pay the bills, complete the daily routine. If you have a kid, then some more is added. If the relationship is not good, and you leave and start a new one, the family life will be the same, there will be no change, it will stay the same. This is a necessary repetition, since it's about your everyday lives, your sustenance. It's just important how you fulfil these. You can wake up every day with arguing from morning to evening, or you can do it properly, when you are glad for every minute spent together, waiting for the moment you can embrace each other. And this should be present not only in the beginning of the relationship. If you do it properly, it could last all through your lives, since your family relations are what you make them to be.'

'But what else can I do? Besides creating balance.'

'You should love and respect the other. Pay attention to them. You are the best partner if you let the other fly free. Believe me, if you give them the freedom to do whatever they love, they enjoy, if you don't grumble about every little thing, but instead you try to understand why that is good for them, they will be grateful to you, and happy and proud to have you as a partner. And if you start developing an interest in what they find important, they can tell you about it. And if you really find their hobby or passion interesting, your relationship can become even better. I'll tell you something better! If you can do it together, if you can be passionate about the same thing... there is no more uplifting feeling. But of course only if you both enjoy it. Oftentimes the interest from both sides is more than enough. It is really important to know that life is a big game. Your life together will be good if you don't play or live beside each other, but with each other, together.'

'But this is not that easy.'

'But not impossible either. There are problems everywhere, but these are rather tasks that need to be solved. Ones that you have to

274

complete together. It is really important that you shouldn't point fingers at each other, blaming each other, but instead quickly do what needs to be done, and then enjoy each other's company again.'

'And what about jealousy?'

'Jealousy is based on the lack of self-confidence, when you don't believe yourself to be good enough for your partner. It is you again who has to change. Do it... or you together should do things so that you are perfect for each other. If you can give everything to the other that you need emotionally – support, safety, base of life – in order to fly, believe me, none of you will want to find anyone else. Why would they? But here, too, just like everywhere else, balance and compromise are very important. You shouldn't force on the other something they don't want to do or are afraid of, or even disgusted by. But this rarely happens, since you don't really get a partner for a long time who does something that is unacceptable to you. Another important thing came to my mind, and after this I think we can wrap this topic up: I often see that couples fight for each other, but this dies down as time goes on, especially after having children. This is a problem. You have to fight for a relationship up until the last moment. You have to pay attention to the other, just like in the beginning.

You have to make the people beside you feel how important they are to you. Never take their presence for granted, because it isn't. Sometimes a dinner, a weekend spent together, a movie, or a play wouldn't hurt anyone. No matter what you do, just do it together, and pay attention to each other. A lot of people say "But the kid!" Nothing will happen to the kids at their grandparent's place for a few hours or a weekend. Even more so, it is much better for them to have their parents balanced and happy, rather than parents who argue all day long. Pay attention to each other, and everything will be all right.'

'That was a nice finishing thought.'

'Yes, I think so, too. Now, if you'd like to, we can rest a bit. Let's leave them. I'll take you to a nice place, if you'd like to.'

'If you want to rest, then sure, but we don't have to go because of me. We can continue.'

'Okay. Since we have nothing else to do here, I'll take you to somewhere. Give me your hand.'

9.

Molly did so, and suddenly they were at the edge of a really tall cliff. Beneath them the sea besieged the stone, like it wanted to push it further, but the stone resisted it. The sea pushed stronger and stronger against the wall, which still did not move an inch. The weather was lovely: sunny, a soft breeze played with the clouds swimming in the sky, slowly pushing them forward. The top of the cliff was covered with a carpet of green, in which small insects crawled along. The sky was filled with birds floating in the playful wind. This whole place was bursting with life. Molly admired the scenery with awe.

'This is beautiful,' she said finally, when she was able to speak again.

'I know that you like places like this. That's why I brought you here. Here you can recharge, and you can pay attention better after that.'

'There's no problem with that, Noah! I pay attention, make notes in myself, so when I get back I'll be able to write down everything that you showed me.'

'Would you like to go back?'

'No. Of course not. But I feel more and more that I have no choice. Even though it's nice here. Much better than down there.'

'Not better, only different. You need to learn to be able to discover the wonders on both sides, to be able to enjoy and value them.'

'Can we sit down on the edge? I always wanted to try what it feels like to hang my legs down into the abyss.'

'Sure, come, sit.' They sat down. Under their feet was nothing but the sea, and that too far-far down.

'This is good,' she smiled.

'I agree. But if you're ready, let's start the relations topic.'

'Sure, hit me. While you talk, I'll swing my feet.'

'Okay,' Noah grinned. 'Nice division of labour.'

'When I write we'll switch. I'll work and you'll rest. This is just.'

'Not exactly what's going to happen, but... something like that.'

'Now... speak to me!'

'Okay. So, just like relationships, relations can be tied to karma or fate, but these bonds are not that strong. Exceptions are family relations. They are probably the closest and most important ones, especially in the first 30 years, in the learning period. Let's talk about family first.'

'Okay.'

'As I said before, this is a really strong bond between people. You often say that you can choose friends but not family. You love them no matter what they're like, forgive their mistakes, since they're yours after all.'

'Not everyone's mistakes...'

'Yes, sure. There are special cases, but we'll discuss that too. As I said before, before your birth you and your helpers decide on the most suitable circumstances and family for your development, where you'll spend your childhood. Where and to whom you are born is crucial, since they shape you, they lead your way, especially in the earlier periods, but all in all they remain with you all throughout your life. They can be divided into two groups, too. There are those you have to work off a debt towards, and those you receive as a reward, as

279

a helper… or you receive each other as that. Here, too, feelings help in deciding who plays what role in your life. If you don't have very good relations with someone, if you don't like spending time with them, if you constantly fight – then there is something that you have to work off with each other. If there's someone you feel safe with, that they are an island of tranquillity – you have received them as a reward, as a helper. Or you received each other like that.'

'Like my grandma.'

'Yes, like your grandma. She could not be with you always, in every moment, because you had to fight your battles with your mother, but you knew that she was always there for you and that you could count on her. She loved you and protected you as well as she could, and she loves and protects you to this day to the fullest of her capabilities.'

'How many times does she fight with me?'

'Often. More than once a day. Like I do. What I have to tell you is that even though oftentimes she doesn't understand why you do to yourself what you do, she is still proud of you.'

'You just say this because you know how important this is to me. You know perfectly well that there is nothing about me to be proud of right now.'

'There is and there will be. You just needed a huge twist in your life, because the path you followed wasn't yours. That's all.'

'We'll change that,' she said.

'We'll have to,' Noah responded.

'You said that feelings show us why we get each person. I understand this. But how can you improve these relations? How can you work off your debts? It's different from the relationships, where we start out as equals, and we create the balance. How many times have I heard that you have to respect them because they are your father, mother, uncle, aunt, or just because they are older? But how if there's nothing to respect or love in them? I don't know things because they lived more than me. They lived longer because they were born sooner. So what?'

'Yes, a lot of people mess up at this point. They consider kids to be their properties. They possess them, but they shouldn't. Instead, they should help, love, and raise them. Every human is

281

an individual, with their own path, which might be different from what the parents have imagined for them. The worst case is when we see that the parents try to give their own tasks to their kids. No. Everyone will become what they have to. The parents' task is to give basic knowledge and information to their offspring, to provide a happy, joyful, and balanced childhood, so that they might become healthy and strong adults. And this is the second point people often get wrong. Nowadays people buy every bit of worthless junk for their kids, thinking that will make them happy. But this is not the key to happiness. For kids, time spent together is much more valuable than the half an hour they spend playing with a toy before throwing it into the corner, since they have no real need for it. Shopping fever is a huge problem in your lives. Buy, buy, buy. You hoard objects and things that you have absolutely no need for. This is some sort of supplementary action. Trying to fill in for something you miss. Obtaining a new object might result a temporary feeling of happiness, with which you want to make up for a lack of love, but you cannot do that. And as an addition, this is unhealthy for the future generations, because what do they see, how do they grow up? What is natural? Shop! The heaps of things become junk, and junk needs to be stored somewhere. You simply cannot continue this forever. Molly, I know that there is a huge responsibility pressing on the shoulders of your generations, since you are the ones who have to give up your ways of life and the learned norms, and change them for completely new ones. You have to start thinking differently than you did before, you have to raise your kids differently. You have to help them to be the people who they need to be.'

'What do we need to do for this?'

'Just love them, and spend time with them. Give them values and experiences, not junk.'

'But I already said: in family relations, things aren't like they are with relationships. It's not two equals binding together their lives. A little baby is simply unable to make its will manifest like an adult can. They are often forced to lied, to cheat, because the parent doesn't get that it's something really bad for them. They say something and the parents don't even listen.'

'Yes, I know. We're trying to help in this, too, but it's difficult. You cannot separate the parties in this case for quite long. It is really rarer when you can or have to move a child out of its circumstances. This can happen only in extreme cases, when there is really no other solution. Even then, it's not sure that it's the best for the kid. Molly, you have to learn to do it properly. You all have to understand that the basis of everything is love. You have to love, nurture, and help each other. And not just the parents helping the kids, but vice versa, too. Everyone has to understand that every person in the family is an individual, with their own free will and unique path. A closed community like this can work effectively if everyone respects the others' wishes and demands, if everyone helps and leads each other. It is the best when parents don't tell their kids what to do, but rather tell them about their own experiences and what they would do in a given situation. They have to prepare them for life, they should teach them, not command them. But kids, too, have to understand that parents are not their slaves, that the parents have tasks besides helping, leading, and taking care of them, and that children have to help and support their parents. It's not easy.'

'But then how can you do it properly?'

'There is a method. Called "complaint-day." A day when everyone sits down and talks about what they feel to be wrong, what they would like to change.'

'But this doesn't work everywhere.'

'Yes, because parents usually get offended… especially when it's their own children telling them about what they did wrong. But this is a mistake, since they have to live with them, so who else would tell them what's not working? They have to sit down, talk through what's wrong with whom, then change in a way so that it pleases everyone. This could work like this. It is really important that every member of the family understands that it's in everybody's greatest interest that they work together, since that would make everyone's lives easier. Parents need to understand that kids are not property, and kids need to understand that parents are not servants. The parents also have to understand that they don't always have to work, so they might have more money. It's not money that will love the children, but mother and father. Of course, it is necessary to sustain life, to complete tasks, to pay debts, since they are present in every part of our lives… it's just… they have to understand that there's more in life than work and money. Somehow you have to strive for balance in this, too. We have to pay attention to and respect our loved ones, because they need it very much. And vice-versa. Children the parents, parents the children.'

'Not easy.'

'No. It's not. And since we're at the not easy part, let's talk about relations a bit.'

'Another difficult topic.'

'Every topic is difficult, Molly. There are a lot of things in your lives that don't work as they should. The direction is wrong, but we'll try to correct it.'

'You think we might succeed?'

'We have to. And now: relations. Here, too, your karma or your fate decides with whom you'll get in contact throughout your life, only these people are those who are present as a sideline in your life, meaning you are not connected to them with such strong bonds as you are in the cases of a partner or family. They come, and if you have nothing more to do with each other, meaning you taught each other this and that, they leave. Separation is not that difficult in these cases, since no strong bonds form. All in all, it would result in a pleasant or unpleasant memory. It cannot be neutral, since every encounter happens for a reason, so it might help you on your path. This means that every encounter leaves some kind of impression in you. This could be an action, a sentence, a chat – the point is, that you receive help through these people. Even the unpleasant or bad encounters are helping, too, even if you don't feel it like that in the first or second moment. But if you think about it, you'll realise that you needed it, since you gained experience, meaning that you learned how or how not to react in a similar situation next time. Here, too, there are written and unwritten laws that are binding for everyone. These are usually norms created by society that you have to keep, since if you don't, you'll have to face repercussions. Just like karma. The difference is only that while the crimes committed against other people are not always punished by society, you cannot escape karma. You cannot make it right with another action, you'll get what is due in every scenario - meaning the consequences of your actions. They say, "God forgive me..." There is no problem with this, he doesn't have to forgive anything, since he's never angry at anyone. If you create a cause, then you'll get the answer. All you have to do is to accept it and understand that this is just a consequence. The consequence of your actions. Do more good, and you'll get more good responses. And it's not who deserves it or doesn't who you should be caring about, but how much you deserve. If your lives are bad, then you should really think about what are you doing wrong, even if this is the most difficult task. It is much easier to judge each other, since it is easier to see through things from the outside than if you had been living through them. I often see that when a person is suffering, the people in their surroundings, instead of stepping next to them and saying, "Come, I'll help", simply talk about them behind their backs, and rather spitefully.'

'But there are those you cannot help. There are those, to whom you say, "Look, I think you're doing this or that wrong, I think it might be better try it this way." And what happens? They get offended. They grumble and hiss for months, just because you tried to help. Then they graciously forgive you, but still mention the given situation for months and years. And all you tried to do was help. Their problem will remain, but they created another one for themselves.'

'The tone is really important in these cases. If someone has a sore spot in their lives, if they're stuck somewhere, and cannot see a way out, and if you'd like to help them, the way you tell them is more than crucial. If it feels like a lecture, no matter how much you'd like to help, things could go wrong, because the other could feel that even though they have problems galore, you still hurt them. If you help, do it with the utmost patience, even more than once. If you cannot, if they don't listen, let them go. Then they'll have to learn at their own expense. The smart learn what they have to from others' mistakes and teachings. Those, who don't... well, those will learn from the hard knocks of life. What is certain is that you cannot avoid your tasks. You have to learn what you have to. How big a price you pay for it depends only on you.'

'Not everyone likes others being nice, not everyone needs it.'

'True. You won't, either, when you go back. In order to be able to accept harsh criticism, meaning that you see the helping intention behind the harsh words, you have to reach a higher level of development, which is not too easy a process. It is really important that you don't accept this criticism from just anyone. You need to learn how to distinguish between good and bad intentions. Not everyone is trying to help or attack you that you'd think was doing so. I advise that you sift the given advice, and put it where it belongs. Either into the trash, because it's useless, or in useful places. And divide the useful into two groups. The first are those you can use in the current period, the second are those that you'll be able to use only later.'

'How will I know which is which?'

'You won't yet understand those that you'll need later. At these times it is useful to take notes, to put those aside. They'll come back around if you need them.'

'Yes, I know. The great coincidences.'

'There are no such things, everything has a reason. Finding your notes especially. Things come when you're ready for them, when they have to. If you want to rush things, trying to get them as soon as possible, all you have to do is to prepare yourself for them. Nothing else. If you growl and grumble, doubt and criticise, or will be disappointed and disenchanted – you'll not be helping your goals or dreams come true, but you'll just push yourself even further from them. The point is only that you should prepare yourself, be mature enough to accept things, meaning that you should do your job. You won't help yourself by sitting in your armchair and waiting. DO YOUR JOB! Uttering your wishes only once is enough. If they fit your path, you can even get them. All you have to do is say what it is, and ask what you can do to reach your goals or dreams. Believe me, the answer will come rather quickly, because we like it when someone wants to improve. Of course this, too, can happen only within reasonable boundaries. There are the so-called resting phases, when you can enjoy the fruits of your labours, and that will be really pleasing, because that's when you'll receive what you wished for. I know that I have told you many times, but I'll do it again: you have 3 really important tasks:

1. Do you job, your task;

2. Look for the signs,

3. If you're stuck, ask for help, and accept it, no matter where it comes from.

Because you have to know – and I think I spoke about this, too – that help never comes from where you'd expect it to come from, so don't expect it from anyone. Ask for it and if you need it, it'll come. Expectancies only create further problems, since it is not certain that a person who you'd expect it from would be able to actually help you. Often the problem is not that they don't want to, it's that they simply can't, because it is just over their limits, that part is no longer their task. Then someone new comes who can help you further down your road, all you have to do is accept them and let them into your life. Don't criticise, don't resist, don't cling to what or whom you shouldn't, because that will just drag you further from your goal, not move you forward. And I'm not saying that you should throw old relations away, like a used rag. No. Just learn how to treat them in their proper way. Believe me, it'll be much easier for everyone. Both them and you. And with this I feel we have got back to our original topic. I know that there are some little detours, but I think this is just so important – basically the foundation of your whole life – that it is important to revise, sometimes putting it in the middle, so you'll surely remember it.'

'Can I ask a question?'

'Sure.'

'Why don't you send someone the first time who can help you all the way? Why is this so fragmented?'

'Because you aren't ready for the final help. Development progresses gradually, you have to learn and experience. It is just like building a house. The workers don't start it by building the roof, but with laying the foundations. And for these, relations are perfect. Your fate binds you together, your task is to learn from, to give information and help to each other, and when you have nothing to do together, you simply part ways and your encounter remains only a memory. This goodbye doesn't really damage the parties. Of course, it's a bit strange at first that they aren't there, but that's just because you got used to it. You might send letters or call each other, even meet a few times in the future, but then you'll realise that you don't really have a common interest any more, there is nothing that you can talk about, since your paths are different now. So, finally you say goodbye, not looking for each other's company anymore.'

'Yes, I know this. Good old days,' Molly smiled.

'Yes. This is when the memories come that make you smile. And this is all the purpose of these people and these memories. And I think this is quite enough about relations.'

'That's it?'

'Why? What else do you want to hear?' Noah smiled with satisfaction.

'I don't know. Something's missing.'

'But what? I think we said everything that could be said.'

'That's not true. I feel it to be.'

'Then talk to me.'

'I know how you can do it properly. The point is that we shouldn't forfeit ourselves, and we shouldn't allow others to control us, just as we shouldn't control them. We need to understand that each one of us is an individual human, with our own plans, will, goals, and task. The point of relationships is to help us complete and fulfil these, nothing else. We should let our kids fly, too. We have to understand that they are not here with us so we that can possess them. They came to make us better people. You can often hear them say, "You're mine." And not only in relationships, I have heard it said to kids as well, these and similar words. But – and I just realised this – I'm only mine, everybody else is their own. Because if you give yourself to someone, they usually close you up and claim you. You can only remain free if you keep yourself to yourself. Of course, freedom doesn't mean that you should be lonely. Because you shouldn't be. Because freedom doesn't equal independence or loneliness. I know what I want to say, I am just struggling to word it properly, so you'll understand… Maybe this: you need someone to be with you, because you need to feel that you belong to somewhere, to someone. You need to feel safe, that it's necessary for there to be someone to protect you, to embrace you, but you shouldn't forfeit yourself for this, or your dreams, your goals, your plans. If there is balance, everything will be all right. I know too – but don't ask where from – that a lot of people serve as our mirror images. They show us our faults so that we might observe events unfolding as outsiders. We shouldn't be shocked by their actions, but learn from their mistakes, and not commit the same ones. Or, if we do, we have to learn how to fix them. I also know that everything always happens for a reason, so we shouldn't pass by something that catches our eye without thinking, because it's likely that we'll have something to do with that person or event now or later. I also know that the foundation for every relationship is mutual respect. A kind of give-take game. I mean by this that a relationship will be most rewarding - meaning that we will be able to work most efficiently together - if we can respect each other mutually. Therefore the best thing to do is to give to everyone what they would like to receive in return. So, if we want respect, we should show some.'

'Exactly,' Noah said proudly.

'Then what's missing?'

'Two important things. Firstly, we often hear when something is difficult that you say, "God doesn't love you." This is wrong. God loves everyone, no matter what you do. He doesn't give you the tasks to punish you, rather so you would actually do what you were born on Earth to do. You tend to choose another path, because it seems easier or simpler, or because you were raised to do so, as expected by you parents, relatives, friends, or teachers. You have to know that what others expect from you is often their own path, not yours. They should have completed or fulfilled it, not you. It's only that they believe that if the kid does it, then their karmic debts will be paid, or fate-tasks will be completed, since they have "hired" someone to do it. But it's not like that. It is theirs, and will remain so. You might be able to show them how they should or should have done it. Oftentimes they don't really have a clue that if they don't complete their task, they'll get it again either in their current or their next lives, but in a much more difficult version, just to make sure that the task will be completed. And this is when you say – I have heard it from you quite a few times – that God doesn't love you. This is not true. God loves. Always, everyone, unconditionally. And he shows exactly how much - you just have to do your job, even if it feels unbelievably difficult.

Secondly, the reason. You said that the reason for relations is giving help, nothing else. But there is another. Gaining information. Nowadays it's not a problem, since you just take out your phone, go on the internet, and you can access any information you want. You can get information about an event or reach out to someone on the other side of the globe without any difficulty.'

'Yes. I often see people walking around, looking at their phones. Not paying attention to the people, the landscape, only to their phones.'

'And do you believe it to be a problem?'

'Well… if you ask me like that… then I'm not sure. I would've answered instantly that yes, it is.'

'You would've been right and wrong.'

'What do you mean?'

'It's a problem, because personal relations will be neglected, which never was and is never going to be a good thing, since you can hurt the other person with this. But it is also good, because your society has reached a level where the whole world has opened up to you. A few clicks and you have all the information you need. This generation you've been born into can assimilate an unbelievably large amount of information. This is a sort of learning process, too.'

'Well, if the information is true.'

'This was the same before. Not every piece of news was true, not all covered the complete

297

truth. Many times, some things were left out for one reason or another. You too know that knowledge is power, and not everyone can handle this. There is a lot of misuse. Your task is to filter this information. Take out what you need from it, and leave the rest.'

'Now that I think about it, the whole thing is strange. Or is impossible, rather. A few hundred years ago... but even, a few decades ago we could only get information about our immediate surroundings. All we knew was what was going on around ourselves. We rarely got any information about anything that happened even only a few villages away. And now... we really can get to know anything, any time. Or, if we wanted to learn about something or understand something, we had to go to the library and get through tons of books to get the info we wanted. Now everything is available at any time.'

'And is this a bad thing?'

'Essentially, I don't think so. There is a greater chance of misuse, but it's not bad in its essence. And in addition, it makes it much easier for people living far away to keep contact, which is not a bad thing.'

'Now, is it good or not?' Noah asked again.

'It is progress.'

'Exactly. Progress sometimes demands sacrifices. But you can and you should harmonise the old with the new. This is how you can do it properly.'

'This information-flow is still a bit unbelievable to me.'

'And you still can't see the whole thing. I would like you to notice one really important thing.'

'What?'

'That in the end, who is in contact with whom? Who is affecting whose life, and who teaches whom?'

'I don't understand.'

'Yes, I can see that. I'll ask differently: what do you think, how many people are you in contact with? How many people's actions affect your life, your everyday life?'

'In what time period? In my whole life, or only in one year or what? I don't understand.'

'I see. Let's take one year for now. A lot of things can happen in that. What do you think, how many people's actions and lives will affect yours? How many people shape you?'

'One or two thousand. About.'

'Wrong. More. Consider the flow of information we talked about.'

'Okay. Then 10,000. But that sounds too much to me.'

'It's not.'

'Did I get it right?'

'No.'

'Then how many?'

'7 billion.'

'What?! 7 billion people?! But that's about the population of the Earth.'

'I know that.'

'Noah, isn't this exaggerating a bit?'

'No.'

'But why not?'

'Are you shocked?'

'Yes.'

'Then think about it for a bit. I'll help. I told you to include the flow of information in your guess.'

'But this is incredible. Even 10,000 was too much for me, even though I counted for a year.'

'Think about it. Just a simple thing. You wake up grumpy in the morning. You buy your breakfast in the small food store, but you don't smile as usual, God forbid you say something nasty to another customer or the shop assistant, or just bump into someone without saying sorry. With this you made that person's moment, 10 minutes, or half an hour unpleasant. In that half an hour that person talks to someone on the phone, or personally, or any way, and it's not certain that they react to the problem appearing there in the correct way, causing problems to someone, and this goes on… Just because you woke up grumpy you started a chain reaction, and by the evening you could have caused problems for a lot of people. And this was only your breakfast. I won't even talk about what happens in the workplace. And before you feel guilty for this happening – it's supposed to. Maybe you don't see the connection, maybe you don't understand what you started. To be more exact, you certainly don't. And it is not really you who started it, you were just a participant in this process. A step. And maybe by the end of the day this becomes insignificant for 100 people, but the 101st needed this chain reaction, so that they might learn something, or so their life might change. I know that this might be unbelievable at first, but on Earth every person is in contact with every other. They pass on information and messages to each other, and learn and develop this way. And this is the real reason.'

'Wow…'

'Is it shocking? It is. It really is.'

'And what if I'm not grumpy, but happy instead.'

'It works all the same, only in the positive direction. The flow of information is always in progress, it never stops. This is since the beginning of your existence. Of course, the underdeveloped technology a few hundred years ago didn't allow it to flow at such scale, the speed was not even close to this, meaning that the news took longer to get around, but at that time that was necessary, it was fitting. Now this is what you need.'

'Unbelievable. I'm shocked.'

'I see that,' Noah grinned. 'You really should pay attention to each other, but more importantly to yourself, your actions. I'm not saying that you should be saints and perfect. No. I… I mean we just ask you to pay more attention to your actions and their consequences. Think about others, not only yourselves. You might feel a decision to be the correct one in a given moment, but you should understand that it not necessarily is. Because what you give is what you'll receive. If you are selfish, others will be selfish with you. If you treat others with love or respect, then that. You could say that it's okay with you. But that's not true. Neither for you nor your environment, and as you could see, nor for the world. You always say that you are not enough to change the world, so you don't even start it, it's okay like this. But this isn't true. If you start doing things in order to make things better for your surroundings, if you do this with belief, you'll start a process. A simple action is enough. Like when you throw a stone into a lake. It's only a small stone, but the water starts to ripple, more and more, starting a chain-reaction. This is how life is, too. A small good deed always starts a process that can change the life of many others. And what does it need? Only a simple thing.'

'I think we'll need a lot more to solve the chaos reigning on Earth…'

'Exactly. This is why you have to write. This will be the first step, the first movement, the stone plunged into the lake.'

'Huge responsibility.'

'It is. I know it is. But believe me, it's worth it. You always ask who is going to read this? Who will be interested in your tale? Those who are supposed to. Not more, not fewer. Believe me, it will change the lives of those who read it, and with this change they'll start a chain-reaction, which will fulfil what is supposed to happen. Don't forget, everything happens for a reason, everything is like that because it's supposed to be. Even if you don't understand or see the connections. I know we ask a great thing from you, that you feel that this is an enormous, frightening responsibility, but trust me, you are ready, and you can do it. This is why we chose you. We prepared you for this moment in your previous lives, and you're ready now.'

'And how will I accomplish all this alone?'

'You'll never be alone. You'll always have helpers. Some of them you won't be able to see, maybe only feel, but there will be ones with you on the physical plane.'

'Noah, is this really necessary?'

'Yes. Come, I'll show you how much.'

'Can I retract my question?' Molly asked, frightened.

'No. Not this one. Come. Let's leave.'

'Okay. Where are we going?'

Noah stood up, then helped the girl up as well.

'Give me your hand.' Molly extended a shy hand towards Noah. She knew she would have to suffer through various horrors. She knew that she had to see them, but she also knew that it would hurt very much.

'Molly, if it hurts you, imagine how much it hurts your home, Earth. You haven't even seen what I wanted to show you, but you already know what's waiting for you. You have to see it so that you understand how much you need that change, how much that stone thrown into the pond is needed.'

'I understand.'

'Are you ready?'

'No.'

'Then come, let's go.'

305

10.

Molly took Noah's hand, closed her eyes, and let out a huge sigh. The man pulled her to him and embraced her like no one had ever done before.

'I'm here, don't worry. I'll protect you,' he whispered.

Molly felt that they are not in a nice place. She felt so much negative energy. She tried to imagine the place where they had been a moment ago, trying to hear the cawing of the seagulls, the rumble of the sea, but all she could picture was a dark, cold city filled with sad, almost undead people. Everyone was rushing about, seemingly doing their jobs, but as though they were robots. She felt no emotions in them. No joy running through their hearts, as though they didn't even have a heart, as though they had torn it out themselves, or as if they had been pushed so far so that they couldn't find it, so that they wouldn't feel anything even by accident. They were thinking. All day only two things circled in their minds: money and shopping. "Money, money, money, buy, buy, buy." It was almost a desperate cry. As though they had no other source of happiness in their lives but

307

shopping. The girl tried to further force the image of the sea into her mind, but to no avail. She only saw the city and its inhabitants in front of her. Even though she wanted to run away, even though see didn't want to see what she had to, she couldn't escape.

'Come on, Molly. You have to see. You have to see, so that you might pass your knowledge purely from your heart, with all your faith. I know it hurts, but believe me, this can all be fixed, you only have to believe in them, in yourself, and in the people whom you get to help you in all this.'

'Okay.'

Molly opened her eyes, and saw exactly what she had pictured.

'I hoped it would be a bit better.'

'It will be. Later. If you see something like this, always think about Jessica. What you experienced there.'

'Okay.' Molly let out an enormous sigh again, collected all her strength, straightened up, then said in a firm voice, 'Let's do this.'

'Yes. This is my queen,' he smiled.

'Let's go before I change my mind,' she muttered. Noah burst out laughing.

'Yes, now, that is my true queen.' He bowed, and extended a hand. 'Your Majesty, would you honour me with a walk? I would show you around the empire.'

'Thank you for your kindness,' she replied. And they went.

The empire was not in a good shape. Molly couldn't say a word. She just walked and shook her head. Sometimes she hemmed, or raised her eyebrows. All for the sake of protecting herself from the effects and pictures assailing her. Every moment hurt her tremendously. She saw and felt the numbness and sadness of the people. They were tired of life, disenchanted, and purposeless. They couldn't find the beauty and the good in anything; if they met someone, all they did was complain. They didn't say anything nice about others and had no honesty towards anyone. They flattered the others, but only while they were standing in front of them. When they separated, they grimaced at each other, and discussed everything confidential they had talked about with the next person they talked to. There was no exception, be it a friendly or a relatively confidential chat, it didn't matter. They just spoke and spoke, sometimes even added, so they might seem a bit better, to increase their importance. They knew, they knew what the others did wrong. Helping the others, stepping up to them and helping them find the proper way didn't even cross their minds. They didn't notice that their complaints were actually cries for help, not just another reason for gossip. They didn't realise that they shouldn't grumble, growl, or scowl at the other person, but instead help them to find a solution. They didn't understand that complaining was necessary not because they wanted to hurt someone, but because they were trying to explain what the cause of their problem was, what they could not find the solution to. And this is the general practice. Of course, there were exceptions. There were some who tried to help, but their words fell on deaf ears. People only got offended, and it resulted in lasting resentment. No matter what angle Molly viewed it from she saw this wasn't any good. Even if she found a person with a pure heart, they, too, were filled with this. No matter how hard they tried to escape, somehow, they still got sucked into this circle; no matter how hard they tried to resist this whole thing inside, somehow they couldn't. So, in the end, nobody was happy. People were looking for the source of their problems, what they could do in order to achieve happiness, but the problem was that they looked for it on the outside, not inside themselves. They blamed their spouses, their kids, the neighbours, the colleagues, the boss, the parties, the state and their leaders, the neighbouring countries, the continent, the inhabitants of Earth, God... They blamed everybody but themselves. Everybody else was stupid, only dead weight, only they were perfect, the innocent, the victims. They always said, "But on the contrary, me" or "But me." It was easier to blame the others than admitting to their own weaknesses and sins. Again, John came to her mind. Their chats. Maybe he was the only person she could turn to with absolute trust and honesty if she couldn't find the solution. During these chats she felt embraced, rocked, and all the while she got the casual and rational rocket. Maybe this was why she was never offended, but instead hung on every word of her helper. John never scolded or hurt anyone. Neither Molly nor the source of the current problem. He only focused on the solution, so that he could help her. Somehow she still got here. Maybe they were both too busy. Maybe they didn't pay enough attention to each other. Maybe she complained too much... Molly remembered a sentence uttered not too long ago: "Everything happens for a reason." But what could be the reason for this? Maybe that she had to find her inner strength? That she had to learn to complete things by herself, that she had to learn to find the solutions alone, since she could not always depend on John in every living moment, because it would be like giving him her task, which she could not do. Yes. That's what she should've learned, but she had run away instead. She had run away into a really bad illness. Somehow, she wanted to attract attention subconsciously: COME HELP ME, BECAUSE I'M IN TROUBLE. COME, PROTECT ME, LOVE ME, BECAUSE I CANNOT DO IT WITHOUT YOU. Isn't this blackmailing?! Her sickness - even the panic disorder in itself was a subconscious blackmail: "Don't let me go, because I cannot do this alone. Don't let me go, not even if this is bad for both of us, when we no longer have a common path. Don't leave. Hold my hand, because without you I'm scared. Hold it even when it is no longer the task. I'm standing at the edge of the chasm, and I should jump because I should learn how to fly, but I don't dare to. I know you don't have wings, but jump with me, like it or not. Or don't. I'm not hurting you by forcing you to jump. Since that is no longer your job. Let's just stay here, neither of us jumping. Let's stay at the edge of the chasm and look at it. Wait, maybe it will change. Maybe there will be another path, a bridge, so we don't have to jump." And so they stayed. This wasn't good for any of them, both of them suffered from the other. One of them would leave, but they didn't dare, because they were afraid of letting the other go, since they were ill, and have attacks. They could not help them, deep down didn't even want to anymore, but how could they let go of an ill person? They could not do that, even though somebody else was waiting for them. And the ill person saw that this worked. Somehow, subconsciously they made themselves even more ill so that the other wouldn't leave, even if it was bad for both of them. After all they should be flying by now.

'Oh my God!' she cried, frightened.

'Yes, Molly. Panic disorder is a nasty illness. One of the great inventions of the ego. It doesn't sicken the body, since it doesn't have any rights to do so. It only produces the symptoms, letting its environment know this way that it's in trouble and is afraid. The worst thing in all this is that the ego doesn't stop these symptoms, not even when it's conscious that this is not good either for them or the body, because it's them who suffer most from this whole thing. It hurts them, it's bad for them, it's unpleasant for them – all in all, it causes the biggest problem to itself in its everyday life. But you know this perfectly well, you have experienced it yourself. You couldn't stop or bridle the attacks, they just came, until you became calm again. All this is caused by the complete lack of self-confidence and faith in people. Everything would be much easier if you could understand that you shouldn't be afraid of change and the future, since only better things await you there; and that you shouldn't get stuck in the past or the present instead of looking forward; if you learn to trust yourselves and us; if you can understand and accept that everything happens for a reason, that every hit that life deals you serves your development, and if you can be grateful for it, standing up without anger, growling, or threatening, truly acknowledging the reasons INSIDE YOU why you got what you did. All you have to do is believe. That's it. Believe in what you cannot see, don't be afraid of the future, and don't cling to what you shouldn't. You cannot cling to others, waiting for others to solve your problems, since that might not be their task. On the contrary, it surely isn't. Yes, letting go hurts, since oftentimes you are not letting the person go, but the feeling of safety that their vicinity provided. Often it is the feeling you cling to, not the person. If you notice this in time, not letting the relation between you go toxic – you might not even have to let them go. You might stay together, only approaching things from a different angle, viewing them from a different perspective, from where it will be better for both of you, since you'll find the support and the help in each other, but in a way that would make both of you happy. I know that it is really hard to fix something that's broken, but it's not impossible. All you have to do is let the other go. You need to let them fly on their own path, over their own chasm. Maybe not like they were before, but they will find their way back if it is needed. If they were your partner, they might return only as a friend. I know that this is hard to accept, but it's not impossible. You need to let go of past grievances and everything will work out.'

'Well, it's not that simple.'

'I know. It is really hard to admit you made a mistake. Maybe the hardest thing. But if you think through what I have said, honestly and without self-pity, you'll realise it's true. From here you have two options:

1. You'll be brave, change, and heal.

2. Not.

The choice is yours. You can say that you are not brave enough, you don't dare, you cannot do it alone… These are all just excuses, because you're brave enough and you are never alone. Ask for help, it always comes. You just have to ask, then accept. But don't forget, help often is just a direction, never a takeover of your task, because no one will heal you, since they cannot; you will heal yourself, since this is your fight with yourself. Help is ONLY good for and is ONLY needed for showing you what you need to do to make your life better and to conquer your fears. The point is that you have to want it and do it. If you don't want to – not a problem. You'll become a counter-example. That's all.'

'I understand.'

'Good. I'm glad that you do. Life will demonstrate how much exactly. We'll see how much you'll be able to use what you learned here.'

'Noah, we'll soon finish.'

'I'm aware.'

'And after?'

'You'll see.'

'I'll miss you.'

'I'll always be with you.'

'And what if I want to talk to you? What if I get stuck?'

'Then write. You'll always find the answer in writing. That way we can discuss everything.'

'I'll miss you.'

'I'll always be with you, don't forget that.'

'Will we pull it off?'

'No questions about that.'

'And what will happen to you when you don't have to entertain me all day long anymore?'

'I'll have to. Believe me, I will. Though not in this form as I do right now. But it's not yet time for goodbyes. Come, Little Girl, we've got work left to do.'

'I love you. You know that, right?'

'I do not know it... I feel it. Huge difference.'

'And what if I mess up again? If I get lazy or give up again?'

'That won't happen. You now know what you have to do. But if you really get stuck, I'll make you read your own tale!'

'Don't punish me! Anything but my story!'

'Ha-ha. Really funny, Little Girl.'

'I know. You love me because of my bad jokes, too.'

'I love you in every scenario. But don't think about losing me, because you won't. I'll always be with you. Just think about what an enormous task and work awaits you. You can also see that the crisis on Earth is getting bigger and bigger. The time for sorting things out has come.'

'You're the boss. You say it, I do it.'

'Oh, if only you knew how wrong you are. But you'll understand when you need to, my Queen.'

Molly just dismissed this with a wave of her hand, smiling, thinking: this is just another crazy guy. They went on, surveying the decay of the kingdom. Her smile faded pretty soon. She could not find a truly happy person anywhere. She saw the city being grey and unhappy. She tried to find colours, but she couldn't. People rushed about busily, not caring about each other – or themselves for that matter. A great part of the populace was ill. They didn't (always) complain, but their bodies showed signs of unhealthiness.

'Why is this the way it is?' she asked. She knew that she didn't have to explain what she meant, since her guardian angel would feel her every thought.

'What you see is a world created by the ego.'

'But this is all wrong.'

'I know. But let's continue. Let in all the information.'

Unlike he did usually, Noah didn't explain it further. He let Molly experience and evaluate. They walked on. The sight was disheartening. Grime and filth everywhere. Piles of junk thrown about the street. Cans, candy wrappers, tissues, chewing gums, pieces of clothing... basically anything that could be imagined was lying about the street. Often right next to the trash bins.

'I don't get it. It's a single motion to throw away the things we have used up, so why aren't they using the designated containers for it? Why do they throw things next to it? This is the top level of carelessness,' she grumbled. Noah remained silent. Walking on, not saying anything. They reached the bank of a river. She was shocked.

'Look! The water, the most important element of the human body, which should be protected like our greatest treasure, is full to the brim with junk. What is this good for? Why do we have to throw tyres or metal signs or pour oil into it? Look at it: black, dirty, and worn-out. It's almost dying. This cannot be true, the human race being like this! Where are the fish? Where is the flora and fauna of the water?' Her questions sounded almost like a scream. Noah still didn't say a word, just walked on silently. In the distance, factory chimneys bellowed smoke to the air.

'The air!' she screamed. 'The water and the air! What will become of us like this? Noah! Say something! This is horrible. What will happen? Humanity is killing itself by killing nature, air, and water! We can't be this mindless!'

They went on. They found a huge shopping mall by the river, filled with all sorts of shops. It was also filled with people, each pushing carts in front of them, shopping. The girl listened and looked at them and at the products they put in their carts. They were full of junk and unnecessary things. Here and there were some things useful to the human body, for example meat, dairy products, vegetables, or fruit, but only a few. Everything else was junk. They followed two women who were happily talking about their husbands and kids while they were shopping. They were nicely dressed and looked pretty. It was obvious that they cared about themselves, that their health and bodies are important to them. Molly thought that maybe they would show how to do things properly. She followed them, watching where and what would they eat. And she was shocked. The women cared about themselves, but not about their families. They packed their carts full with sugary drinks and candies, all the while laughing and saying that at least the kids will stay silent while they eat and drink these. They bought everything healthy for themselves, since health was a priority, but they didn't care that much about their families. Junk and more junk. Molly didn't back off. She still hoped that maybe, maybe they would still be able to show the correct way. The two women reached the clothes section. They were almost shining with happiness. It was obvious what a pleasure buying a piece of clothing caused them. They were sorting through and putting pieces aside, one after the other. In the end their carts were so full that they were barely able to push them to the cashier. Meanwhile, they discussed that this or that might not even be their sizes, that they didn't really like it, that they might not be able to wear it anywhere, but it didn't really matter, because it only cost this or that much, and that is not too much. And anyway, their wardrobes were already full of clothes that they didn't wear once. They'll have to throw them out when they had time for it. Or not. When they thoroughly discussed this topic, not having anything else they could talk about, they turned their attention to the people around them. They made fun of them, laughing at their fellow humans, just because they didn't dress according to the latest fashion, or because of their perfect shape… how they or their kids looked… Okay, theirs are sometimes like that, too, but still… This is where Molly had had enough, she left them. She didn't pay any more attention to the people, but instead turned to the product range on the shelves of the shop. She looked for good, useful things. She found a few items, but their number was minuscule. She found the sports equipment far away, in a corner of the shop, almost hidden. However, candy, soft drinks, and other useless things could be found on every shelf.

'They don't even give people a chance to lead a healthy life,' she said. Or thought loudly, rather, because she knew her escort wouldn't say anything. 'Only the junk. They fill shelves with it. And they wonder why there are so many obese and unhealthy people.'

'Come, let me take you somewhere. Give me your hand.'

'A good place?' she asked while extending her hand.

'Look around, what a nice place I brought you to,' Noah said. Molly didn't understand.

'Yes, this is really nice. Where are we?'

'Where we were already once during our adventures... Tell me what you see.'

'Nature. I want to run around in the grass, play with that group of gorillas resting over there. I want to jump into this river. I see the fish swimming, the frogs hopping around, the bugs flying about, the small rodents and insect bustling about in the fallen leaves. Everything is so beautiful, it's almost enchanting.'

'And what keeps you? Do what you want,' the angel smiled.

'But we're talking... or learning. I can't, I need to pay attention.'

'Who said that?'

'Nobody.'

'Them go. Enjoy it, since you are quite enthusiastic about it,' Noah smiled.

And Molly went. Something disturbed her, but it felt good to rest a bit after the previous experiences. She enjoyed nature and the closeness of animals. She was happy, but this happiness was not unclouded. Something was off – a strange feeling took over her. She sat down next to an animal in the grass, touched it gently. The animal winced for a moment, but didn't move or run away, it just lay there. Molly didn't feel the warmth of its skin, but tried to imagine it. She remembered what Noah had told her not long ago: you could imagine the feel of touching something, but it wasn't the same. She never valued it before, taking it for granted, an unimportant aspect. She had it and she didn't care about it, didn't realise its value. It was then that she finally grasped what it really meant that we don't know how much something or someone means to us until we lose them. This was true. And sadly, we could not realise their value until the trouble happens.

'But let's look at the bright side. How many people can tell that they petted a gorilla?' she asked the animal lying on the ground. 'Do you agree, little guy?'

The animal raised its head a bit, then put it back down instantly. It seemed like it gave her a tiny nod. Molly just smiled. She felt everything to be perfect. She became one with the landscape, with nature, she became a part of it. She didn't feel a visitor now. Quiet, peace, calm and safety. Harmony manifest.

'Feels good, doesn't it?'

'Why don't you come and play with me?' she asked.

'I can't now. And it would be better if you'd joined me.'

Molly didn't understand what was going to happen, but she knew she had to go. She stood up, walked to the man, who extended his hand towards her. When the girl took it he pulled her close, and whispered: 'I'm here.' Suddenly, three hunters appeared out of nowhere, disrupting the previous peace. They struck at the herd, murdering them. Molly felt the unimaginable hate and contempt inside them. They didn't look at anything, only wanting to kill. They ravaged and tore up their victims, without paying attention to age or sex. The girl knew that this was just a massacre, a bloody sport. No motivation except the lust for destruction in them. They felt proud and superior. The fact that they could destroy made them feel almighty.

'Do something, this is horrible,' she whispered.

'I can't,' Noah answered, then hugged the girl even more strongly. They watched helplessly as the panicked animals tried to defend, to fight for their lives, but it didn't matter. There was no escaping the three killers. Screams and death throes filled the landscape. Molly felt the fear of the animals, their begging for help, for someone to help them, or for this to be over already. Maybe their attackers felt this too, because they slowed down. The previous quick, remorseless attacks bringing quick deaths were replaced by playful murders. They let their victims to lie in pain for longer, they didn't kill instantly. Chased and shoved the animals around. Those who tried to escape were further ravaged, those who gave up and didn't move were left on the ground to die.

Molly tried to get out of Noah's arms. She couldn't watch the animals suffering passively any longer, but the man didn't let her go.

'This is how it has to be. You cannot do anything,' he said in a calm voice. 'I know that it's terrible to watch, but you have to see this.'

Tears were streaming from her eyes. She was powerless. The animal she was resting with so peacefully just a minute ago was lying in the ground, dead, its blood soaking the ground. The land slowly grew quiet. The killers had finished, no one had survived from the group. They collected their trophies – they cut off the heads and extremities of the animals, skinned them, and then left their bare bodies there, then left, laughing. As they were walking away, one of them turned around and there was an especially disgusting grin on its face. He felt unbelievably strong and cunning. He was perfectly content with their 'work'.

Molly was sobbing. What she saw had hurt her immensely.

'These were peaceful animals. They didn't hurt anyone,' she screamed in pain. 'What was this good for? Why did they do this?'

'They didn't kill because they were hungry. Just because they liked it. Because they could do it, because they had the strength and the skills to do so. The human race – no one knows why – thinks that they can exterminate herds, groups, or complete species just for fun. Come, I'll show you something else.'

As he said this they were on a ship, where people were cutting off the fins of a huge shark, throwing back the still living, bleeding animal back to the sea, shouting 'Take that, killer.' Molly felt immense pain. She wanted to scream, but no sound came out her throat.

'Come,' Noah said. They found themselves at the scene of another senseless massacre. Here people were killing, decapitating, and skinning lions, elephants, dolphins, and whales. They just watched the countless majestic animals die for no good reason. They saw and felt the fear of the animals, felt their begging for help, for a miracle.

'Come,' the man whispered. They were in a rainforest. They watched as those huge trees were cut down. They weren't picky, they destroyed huge areas. Then the girl and the angel were back at sea, on board another fishing ship. An immense amount of fish was caught and then transferred to the nearby market, then to the factories from there. Without being picky, or keeping things in moderation. They watched as the huge factories bellowed toxic gases, as the pipes poured toxic waste into rivers and seas, as carcasses of animals floated on the surface of the oily water, in the middle of islands of trash…

'Noah, enough!' she cried, sobbing. 'Enough, I can't take it anymore! The destruction the human race does each day... it is horrible! I had enough!'

'Yes. This is what we said, too, Molly. Enough,' the angel said. His voice was low and sad, but firm. The girl cried.

'Noah, seeing all this, I'm not sure that there is a need to do anything or that I want to do anything with this place. The human race destroying their own lives and habitat, not thinking about what will come next. You cannot see anything but senseless destruction and killing. Why do they need that many fish? They don't use half of them, so they goes to waste! Humans kill more than they need to sustain life. Why do they need to kill animals whose flesh they don't even eat? The bodies just lay on the ground, they just needed them as trophies, showing off how great a people they are, disposing of an innocent animal that was not capable of defending itself against guns and knives. What did these animals do? Nothing. They called the shark a killer. What killer?! Who is the killer? And those gorillas...'

Molly fell silent. She couldn't say a word. She just stood around silent. Noah hugged her again.

'I saw that before…' she mumbled. 'Same place, same thing.'

'Yes, you're right,' the angel said.

'No,' said Molly, determined. 'I'm not doing anything. They don't… we don't deserve it. We didn't learn from the mistakes of the past. Humanity deserves extinction. They deserve all the pain for the crimes they have committed.' Her voice was stern and determined.

'Now think that through once more.'

'There is nothing to think through,' she said even sterner. 'You saw what's going on. You know perfectly well that there is no point, that we just destroy, not caring about how much damage we do to ourselves with that. Slowly we are driving ourselves to extinction.'

'Then come with me now.'

'I'm not going anywhere. I'll stay here and die with them. Look at the water. Look at the carcasses, Noah! Look at the oil stain and the pollution. Earth is dying! And I'm dying with it. My decision is final.'

Molly sat down at the riverbank and cried. She felt that she could not go on. She could not handle it anymore. Noah sat down next to her, pulled her close and just hugged her. They sat like that for a long time, in silence. The things she had seen flashed before Molly's eyes. She relived again and again what she had seen and felt. Every detail flashed back to her again and again. What she experienced hurt her tremendously. She didn't want it to, but it kept repeating and repeating. She cried in agony: 'NOOOOOOOOO!'

She tore away from his embrace and jumped up, standing before the man.

'Tell me what to do,' she said determined, with feigned calmness.

'Come with me.'

She didn't object, but raised her hand immediately. They were again at the edge of the cliff from where they set off.

'Let's rest a bit.'

'I can't,' she said. 'I want to do something. Tell me what, and I'll do it.'

'Okay. Then rest for a while.'

'Noah!' she raised her voice.

'Molly!' he said calmly, but firmly. 'You said that I should tell you what you need to do. You need to rest.'

'No time for that. We cannot waste time.'

'You won't. Firstly, as I have already said to you, and what you have experienced first-hand: there is no time here. Time is only needed on the physical plane so that you can sort and store the experiences and what you have learned inside yourselves. You don't have that here. You can be anywhere and anytime. You can be at 100 places in the same moment, since you can jump around in space and time as you wish. Secondly: you need to calm down. You cannot let the information in if you're so upset. I know what you saw was almost too much. Believe me, I wouldn't have subjected you to these monstrosities if it wasn't absolutely necessary. But it was. You had to see everything that was going on on Earth, around you, because you were ignorant towards them until now. You acted like they didn't even exist. Not long ago I told you something that went like, "When you receive the answer, things you believed to be important become irrelevant, and vice versa. It's not a problem if you don't understand it yet. When the time comes everything will be clear." I'm not sure I quoted myself with perfect accuracy, but that is not the point. The emphasis is not on the words, but on what they carry in themselves. Think about it: what were you looking for?'

'Happiness, love, a dream life.'

'And?'

'And they're irrelevant now.'

'They are still important, but they're no longer priority. Because soon there will be no place in which to make these come true. But come, sit. Let's discuss what we saw.'

'I can't sit now.'

'Then come, let's take a walk on the beach.'

She automatically gave her hand. He didn't need to ask anymore, it was instinctive. She imagined that they were on a beach with clear blue water and a sandy shore, with palm trees in the distance… she imagined a beautiful landscape, and suddenly they were there.

'What happened?'

'You are waking up,' Noah smiled.

'This was strange.'

He didn't say anything, only smiled. The girl started to ease up, but was still tense a bit.

'Once I strolled on a beach, a long time ago,' she began. 'I was really desperate back then, too. I thought that I had no idea what to do next, because it was really hard alone, and I cried. A white feather flew by me, right into the sea. The high tide was coming, and the waves came with it. But the feather flew against the tide, submerging under a wave from time to time, but it went on unstoppably, it didn't give up, it didn't let the sea wash it back ashore. And this was a strengthening experience for me. Okay, it is really difficult, but I cannot give up, and the obstacles are there to make me stronger. The feather didn't give up, and so neither can I. It was interesting, but good at the same time! It helped a lot back then, and from that time on if I felt something was too difficult or I didn't know how to proceed, what happened back then comes back to my mind, giving me strength. But I realised what truly happened back then only now. You have to go on, continue, and never give up, no matter how hard it is. If the path is that you have to fly against the tide, then that's what you have to do. There'll always be help, like that little, fragile, weak-looking feather was helped by the breeze. It was there for it and helped it to go on, empowering it.'

'Then really don't forget that. Ever,' Noah said. 'How do you feel? Are you ready for the explanation?'

'Sure.'

'Then let's do this. What you or we saw was a world created by the ego. It can only create one like this for itself.'

'Why did you let it? Why did you let things escalate to this point?'

'Counter-example. Hell needs to be created and experienced so you might realise the value of heaven. I told you, you are at a crossroads. There are two ways. One is the continuation of the current one, and you saw what was at the end of that.'

'Complete cleaning.'

'Yes, exactly. The other is different path, leading to a better life, but it is not easy. You have to forfeit, change a lot of things, and you have to do a lot of things differently and better. On that road you cannot let the ego control, you have to give the control to the spirit and the soul. I know perfectly well how hard this is. I know perfectly well that the ego will shriek and shout, will throw a tantrum, because it's no longer getting what it wants. It will be afraid; oftentimes it's not going to want to fly freely, because of the "but what if" show of its. You know what was the result of these three words in your life. You got ill, you made yourself ill, then you died. If we view the life of Earth through your counter-example, then you can see what end awaits you. The illness is already there. People and Earth are both ill. What did you see? The ego feels that this is not right, that something is not how it should be, but has no clue about what that exactly is. It rushes, fights time, and extorts the body. Wants more and more. More money, a bigger house, greater wealth, more expensive cars, clothes – since it believes that these are the key to the happiness it longs for. But somehow that eludes it. It repeats "Money money money," and "Buy buy buy," inside, and extorts the body to its limits, and the body obeys it. Well, there is a temporary happiness that it gets through these – but that cannot be long-lasting, maybe only for a few hours, then it's gone. But it wants more, more, and more. This is what you saw in the shopping mall. You saw that the shelves in the shops were stacked with unhealthy things. Yes, I know. But just because this is the demand. This is the invention of the ego, as well. It feeds itself. It sends the body a message to eat more trash, because that'll make you happy. Yes, sure, it causes a momentary happiness, since chocolate and other sweets create endorphins, but that also goes away after a short time. This way it feeds the body again and again so it can experience it more times. Just as a side note: the body creates endorphins while doing sport or dancing. But for that you need to move, for which the ego is too lazy. It is more comfortable to eat chocolate while sitting. Everything is just an effect: the pollution, not caring about others, killing the world, animals, and environment around them, everything. The cause, the reason is the search for happiness with the ways imagined by the ego.'

'Then people are ill because they cannot find this secret?'

'Yes. Every sickness or illness is caused by over-extortion. Every illness is a call for attention, that there is a problem. The soul and the spirit send this message to the ego: "Change, because there is trouble, you might even die." When the ego notices this, it starts to make rash decisions instantly. Rushes to one doctor to another, getting poked and cut, trying to solve the effect. It doesn't always understand that it should solve the cause, the reason. Or even if it does, it doesn't want to understand, since then it would have to admit its own failure and mistakes. Because making a change is hard and scary.'

'I see now what the basis of eastern medicine is, what its core is. Solve the cause, not the effect.'

'Exactly. The body, like everything else in the world, is an energy field. You see it as a body, but really it isn't. It's a field of energy and information. Think about it. You look at someone, and you gain a lot of information about their lives and habits. How they live, how much money they have, how much they eat or drink, do sport or don't, happy or unhappy… and I could go on. And this information is just at first glance. But if you get to know the person, if you talk to them, you can get more information than you could use in your own life. Oftentimes a single, well-placed and timed sentence is enough to change your life.'

'Yes, I have experienced that.'

'I see you relaxed. I'm glad for that,' Noah said. 'You have to learn not to freak out from anything you see, ever, no matter the consequences. I know it was painful, and it will be for a long while, but this is all just effect. Be wise like the ancient healers were, and always look for the reason, the cause, and not only the effect. Think with the guidance of the spirit and the soul, and never with the ego's. The ego will yell and throw a tantrum, the soul and the spirit will never. They always know that what is visible to the eye is just a result of mistakes made in the past.'

'And what do we have to do to change?'

'Change. Leave bad habits, follow your feelings, no matter how scary they are. Do you job, no matter how unbelievable or impossible it seems. You can do anything if you want it hard enough. Of course, by this I don't mean that you should abandon everything, that you shouldn't work, or only following your feelings. No. That's not the solution. You need to work, since that also forms and shapes you. Through your jobs you work off what you have to, the causes and debts from the past. The other very simple reason is that until you do what you have to, what really is your job, your task, until you receive your due rewards, so-called payments – you have to sustain yourselves somehow. Oh, how there are many examples for this, too. Very famous people... mostly musicians, actors, or sportsmen, talking about how they started out from nothing, being waiters, shop assistants, and about how they worked hard. But while other people went home after work to lie down to sleep, they fought for their dreams, what they felt they had to achieve. And when they did, they received the awaited good. Since then they live in better conditions, like they wanted to. They still work, since they still have tasks, but they have easier lives, since their passion sustains their lives. Believe me, it's worth working for the "Big Boss." Those who do that, meaning that they do what they feel they have to, can lead a much easier, happier and fearless life. Just research these people. Take a look at where they came from, what they achieved and who they are. You will be surprised. And in what aspect were they more? Better than the others? Only that they dared to overcome their fears, that they believed in themselves and their dreams, even when everybody else told them that they were impossible or crazy. They were bold and brave, and if needed, they went against the world. They have shown that yes, it can be done. It can be done. They are the examples. Those should not be envied, but looked up to and followed. What does the ego say to this? "Oooh, this is impossible, I can't do this, what if they laugh or make fun of me, I'd rather not, and anyway I'm too tired for this, and it's easier and better to lie around all day than moving and actually doing something…" Essentially, everyone has the right to do this. This is free will. But you'll have to endure the consequences, the hits dealt by life, since we'll allow laziness only on the surface. The goal for you is to complete your task. In order for this to happen, you'll receive more and more difficult tasks, so that you understand that you'll come out better if you stay on your path, not just always resting. You'll rest when it's time.'

'And what happens when I start what I feel to be the good choice? Will life be easier?'

'No. This is why it's important when you start. But that depends on you, too. You can do it when it's easy, or when it's really difficult. Just so that you can imagine: you can collect firewood in a light breeze, but in a storm as well. The point is the same, you want warmth in your home, and you need wood for it, but it is your choice when you do that. You have to know that the storm won't stop just because you started collecting firewood. Because with that, you neither want or have to stop the storm, you only want warmth. So, if life is really hard already, and you start doing your job, the circumstances won't change just because you started. Things will remain like that, so that you might learn that it's not worth waiting and doubting, and that you have to do what you feel that you have to do, when you feel that you have to do it, and everything will be all right. Is that clear?'

'Yes. Thank you.'

'Good.'

'And what now? What do we have to do so we might cure the cause?'

'You little impatient girl. Everything in its time. I told you that the individual life is much shorter, changing it is much easier, and we have a shorter time for it. On a global scale you'll have to get through a longer, bigger road. That won't be two days. First, write your book. Then the rest will come. Don't be impatient. Have faith, believe in yourself, and in your helpers later on. You'll get people that can and will help a lot. Always keep it in mind, they are helpers, meaning that the task is not theirs. If you want to give someone your task, they'll leave you sooner or later. With these decisions you could lose valuable helpers, so it's better if you don't do this. Second thing: always pay attention to who you surround yourself with. Get to know them before trusting them with anything. We won't always send people that should or can help you. Often you'll receive counter-examples, too, so you can know that not everybody is suitable for the role of helping you. There will be a method that will help you

342

distinguish between them. You have a bad habit of taking yourself as a basic example. Don't. Ever.'

'Understood. But why are we talking about only me?'

'Because I have tunnel vision and can see only you,' Noah grinned.

'Ha-ha,' Molly said, mockingly.

'I was only half joking. Write your tale, send it to people. This will be another step towards change. You are not the only one creating things promoting and urging a better way of thinking and change. There will be a continuous flow of blockbusters and books that will all be about change and making the world a better place. These works will show that it can be done, that everything can be maxed out, you just have to want it. Many will be about strengthening confidence and overcoming fears. And as you have experienced, more and more urgently, because time is running out, the state of Earth is deteriorating, you cannot wait for the trouble to come, you need to act before the catastrophe happens, so it won't be that painful.'

'I told you: I'll do everything I can. I cannot promise anything else.'

'You don't have to, that's enough for me. Then I will know that everything will be fine.'

'I would do it just to see what will come out of all this. I'm curious what can we make out all of this and how people will react. Dare they change? Can they?'

'Change is in everyone's interest. Now it's really your lives… more correctly, the existence of your species is at stake. I know that this is a huge responsibility, and that it's difficult, but it isn't impossible either. You can change right now without too much pain. You just have to WANT IT! That's the point.'

'Can I ask what'll happen if we won't change?'

'A lot of movies have been made around this topic. Now you receive "smaller" warnings. Tsunami, volcanic activity, earthquakes, other disasters. If nothing changes, drought, absence of water, mass destruction. If still no change, complete destruction. But luckily these are still far away, and if you're smart, all can be avoided. You need to be able to learn from the warnings, you have to change before the greater problems arrive, while it is not too painful.'

'And what happens if I write the book and those that have to read it and ask me what they can do, what is their task? They read my book, they want to help, but they don't know what and how... What can I tell them? How can I help them? Since I don't know either what can be done, so that things will become better. Yes, I understand, I have to write and publish... but I perfectly know that that won't be the end of the story. I perfectly know that I cannot lean back, making myself comfortable, saying, "I did what I had to do, everything is fine, the rest will be done by others..."'

'That won't be in the near future.'

'I know. But you also know that questions will come. How do I know all this, what if? etc. But most importantly: yes, I read your tale, I can see, too, that something needs to be done. But what? And how? And with whom?'

'Molly, the answer is really simple. You know it too... you have to, it's just three words. Or more like ten.'

'Do your job, what you feel you have to do?'

'Then don't ask, say it.'

'Do your job, what you feel you have to do.'

'That's all. You'll see that the shopping fever and overeating will disappear. People won't eat that much junk and will pay more attention to themselves. There will be fewer alcoholics, drug addicts, or sick people. Because this is all just compensation. They can't find their places, they're afraid, looking for something that they don't have but they know they should have. You cannot just take these unhealthy obsessions and compensations from these people. That is not the solution. Until they find themselves, their places, their tasks, they are needed. It is a false thought that these things will be completely gone. No. They won't because they don't have to. In small portions every harmful-looking thing is needed, and can be even healthy. You just have to know where the limits are.'

'Drugs, too?'

'Drugs are painkillers, helping really ill people endure pain, meaning they are needed to fight past mistakes, the consequences.'

'What do you mean?'

'Molly, illnesses are only consequences, effects. But I already told you that. When someone is born ill, that is the consequence of an action committed in one of their past lives. With their

346

illness, they have to work off something towards their family or circumstances that they were born into, and they have to learn something from their state. Cause-effect; you cannot escape this, neither can you escape the flow of information. You shouldn't judge anyone based on their weight, bodily handicaps, skin colour, gender identity, etc. Those are their individual paths. They have to make the most of them and learn what they have to from what they have received. And this is true for everyone. If you do it properly, if you're smart, you can learn from other people's mistakes, but it's really important that you never judge anybody. Because yes, you might do one thing properly, but you might make a mistake in another. You hurt each other, starting out a chain-reaction, which will never end. Learn, help, and accept help. That's the most important thing.'

'Noah, you told me that in reality every person on Earth is in connection with all others, that we shape and teach each other with our actions. But I don't think that is accurate. I believe that on Earth, and later in the whole world, every living creature is in connection with each other, we shape and form each other, including the smallest blade of grass.'

'Nice,' Noah smiled. 'That is exactly right. None can exist without the other. That is why you should protect each other. Take only as much as you need. Respect and value each other. You should respect the rules of the great circle of life, which is just basically a give-take game. If you could do that, the order would be restored on your planet. The second thing that you should understand is that your current way of thinking is not right. Because now you have divided yourself into countries. You compete, trying to take territories or natural resources from each other with force. You, too, know that this is what wars are about. Scrounging, just to gain more power. This worked until now, because you were - you thought you were - the only intelligent species both in the world and the universe. Sure, those who think with at least a little bit of reason will realise that this is wrong, but never mind. This thought can remain common for a while, but not for long. So, you divided yourself into countries and compete with each other. This was a perfect rehearsal, you practised what you should be doing later on. Because – and you need to start practising for this – there will be no division by countries, but by planets, and Earth and its populace will be a race, a country, which will have to protect its interests from other nations. And like now, here on

Earth, there will be poorer, less developed nations, but more developed ones, too. Luckily the more developed ones are mostly over scrounging, but not all of them. In essence, you'll realise that what you think to be great right now is actually insignificant. Or - I hope you'll be able to realise - this is your future, Molly, not what you live in right now. You just need a small step for everything to change, and for that you need a huge amount of bravery. But believe me, it's worth it. Believe me, if everyone will do their jobs everything will be sorted out and will be a perfect whole. Because these small-looking tasks create a complete whole when they connect. Just like a chain. And maybe this way you can understand what I explained. Together you form a perfect whole. And I think this is the end of the tale.'

'You left out a few things.'

'What?'

'For example, the neutral and good feelings. The soul and the spirit. Because all you talked about is the ego.'

'Then let's talk about them, just for the sake of completeness. Neutral feelings: basically, the things and events that don't trigger an emotional response, with which you have nothing to do. You will be happy if something good happens to you or in your vicinity, sad if bad. But if an event doesn't concern you, then it won't trigger any emotion in you, because you have nothing to do with it. Usually what you say when these happen is "Okay," and you forget the whole thing immediately. That's it. Good feelings: you know these. Or you heard about them, know them in theory, and I hope you'll experience them first-hand. But I'll mention some, since I have listed the bad ones too. So, the good feelings are the following: happiness, gratitude, joy, love, humbleness, humility, patience, calmness, a reasonable-level of self-confidence, fervour, gladness, tolerance, contentedness, and I could go on. These are the feelings that make your day and simply your mood better. If you strive to experience these as many times as possible during your days, you'll be much happier. You cannot let the bad feelings overtake you or take over the shaping of your days. Sure, I know that sometimes really unpleasant things happen, but those are only there for you to learn something, or to warn you about something; they are never there so that you can grumble about them the whole day, poisoning your life and the lives of the people around you.'

'But what can I do to make it better?'

'Easy: create a rule for yourself.'

'What?'

'Make the rule that for every bad thing you may grumble about it for only one day, tops. That maximum one day should be the absolute limit, so you only have a day for extremely bad things. And if it's possible, let go of everything grumble-worthy before sleeping.'

'So it might be better if I wasn't anxious about anything.'

'That is not good either, because it cannot happen. With expressing your displeasure, you release negative energies from yourself, meaning the feelings that the given event triggered in you. If you don't they will continue to eat you up. You can say that they don't bother you.... but they will. Even if for only a moment, but they will, because how will you know if they're bad, if you don't notice them? How will you know that you have to learn from them? Yes, bad feelings are needed, too, because they teach and shape. What is more interesting is how you treat and how long you store these for. The best method is: something happens, if it gives you a bad emotion, you know that you have to do something with it, you immediately start to look for the causes, for something to learn, and for the solution. You can grumble if it pleases you, just pay attention that no one sees or hears it, because you can accidentally hurt others, creating further karma.'

'Then it really is better not to do it.'

'Better and not. The best is if you can find something… a word, a sentence, that can release your tension while not hurting anyone. With that you can release what you have to, letting it go while you focus on the solution. This is hard, because the ego loves to be angry, but it's not impossible. The whole thing is just a question of habit. It's like an everyday routine. You wake up, get dressed, clean your face, have breakfast, go to work, have lunch, sport in the afternoon, have dinner, sleep…. just add "Not going to be angry for more than a day" to this list. If you keep this rule for a while, not allowing any exceptions – you'll get used to it after a while. How much time? That depends only on you, on how conscious you are, and how much good or bad you want for yourself. Believe me, it can be done – like everything else – you just have to want it. All you need is determination, belief, and bravery to overcome your fears. A lot of people will say that sure, it's easy for you. No. It's not easy for anyone, it's hard work understanding this, too, but it isn't

352

impossible. It's worth a shot trying it out, the results will come. That's all. What's left?'

'Soul, spirit.'

'Come, I'll show you those,' Noah smiled.

'Where are we going?'

'Surprise.'

Molly extended a vary hand.

'Will you tell me where are we going?' she asked.

'We're only making a quick visit at a nice place. We won't be for long, don't worry.'

'I don't.'

'Can we leave then?'

'Yes,' she said uncertainly, then extended her hand.

'Don't worry, Molly. This'll be nice.'

11.

They found themselves in a huge corridor of a building. It was like the thinking room in some aspects and yet it wasn't. There were colours here, but only smooth, soft ones. The whole place emanated a special vibe. It was as though it embraced and rocked you. The floor was marble and the white walls were filled with pictures. Their themes varied: landscapes, families, human and non-human figures. Molly wanted to study and admire them, but she couldn't, as she had to keep Noah's pace. She stopped from time to time, but the man just went on, not hurrying, but not slowing either. Molly noticed a strange thing. It was as though the pictures were organised by time periods and themes. All were centred around a female shape, and the others were around her. As though these all were memories. And the woman... she was really familiar. As though Molly had seen her somewhere before. It was strange. She wasn't sure that it was the same woman in every picture, because they weren't perfectly the same, but the shape and features were the same.

'Noah, where are we?' she asked.

'At home,' he replied.

'Who is this woman then? She's everywhere. She's so familiar...'

'Who do you think it is?'

'I don't know, because we're rushing so much that I cannot take a proper look.'

'You don't have to look properly. Just take one look and tell me who she is. Don't think, don't doubt, just say it.'

'Me?'

'Don't ask. Say it with confidence. Who is that woman, Molly?'

'It's me.'

Noah stopped before a picture, not hurrying anymore.

'Then let's repeat the last lesson. You saw the pictures, and the figures on them. The lady is you, the others are your loved ones who usually accompany you on your journey. They love and protect you; you protect each other during your learning process. I say usually, because it is not accomplishable in every occasion, since your individual developments must be taken into account, and that cannot always be synchronised with the others' development. But usually it is possible. So, if you travel, you usually travel together. You guard and help each other, like a big family. Who has to do what in the current process differs. One is the mother, at other times something

355

else. Sometimes this one is the grandma or the kid, the friend or the love, sometimes the other. It all depends on who has to learn what. When you are born down you could not know who was what – but you didn't even have to. Your fates, your lives will shape accordingly, so you will meet when you have to. You will always know that you belong together, because there will be such a strong bond between you, a love rooted so deep that you cannot tear it out of your heart, no matter how hard you want to. It's really hard for you to let go if one of you reaches the end of their paths, and this is exactly why; because you know you belong together.'

'Like me and my grandma?'

'Yes, Molly. Exactly like that. I know that her absence is really painful, since you two had a really close relationship. But don't think that she died and with that she left you. She didn't. She protects you, it's just that you cannot see, but should feel. Think about it like this: She is resting now – she earned it -, but you'll meet again soon.'

'What I wouldn't give for a hug. I can see her in front of me, smell her scent, hear her talk... I miss her.'

'I know, Molly. And because you worked so hard, I have a present for you.'

'What?'

'Rather "Who?"'

'Who?'

'Well, me,' said a familiar voice behind her. Molly's hands and legs shook - even her heart. As she turned around, she faced the most amazing woman and human in her opinion who had ever existed.

'Grandma!'

Tears streamed from Molly's eyes. They hugged and held each other as though they haven't met in a thousand years. They had so much to talk about, yet none of them could say a word. Molly thought that this was the most wonderful present she ever received. She felt that this meeting was worth all the suffering, everything she had experienced and learned so far. She felt that this hug was worth all the treasures in the world - no, this was way more than that. We cannot know how long this moment lasted, but it's not important either. They just enjoyed being together. Finally, Molly's grandma broke the silence.

'Hello, darling.'

'Hello, Grandma. I am so very glad to see you. I missed you so much!'

'I'm glad, too. But you know that this is not where you should be. As it turned out like this, I requested that we meet, but you know that this is not good like this. Come, let's talk a bit. There's a bench, let's sit down. Of course, only if Noah has no objections.'

'No, nothing of the sort. I have something to do. I'll be back shortly,' he replied, and was gone in an instant.

The girl looked at where he had been. Separation was strange and painful. But she didn't care about that. Her happiness was much greater, since she had her Grandmother with her. They walked to the bench and sat down. Just like in the old times. Molly drew up her legs and snuggled into Grandma's guarding embrace. She even got a kiss on her forehead…

'I miss this the most.'

'I know, love. I miss it, too. But you know I had to come. I didn't leave you, it's just that my body was really worn out, and I couldn't live a proper life with that.'

'I know. I might've been selfish – or still am - but I still miss you nevertheless, even though I know and understand the reasons.'

'That is just natural. Especially with a relationship like the one we had. But you need to learn to let go of your loved ones, sweetie. No matter how hard and painful it is. Because the goodbye is just temporary. You see, we are here together again, I can hug you again, and you can snuggle again, even if it's only for a short time now. If our time comes we can be together for much longer. I'll be here waiting for you. This will be your reward for the work you have to do.'

'Do you think I can do it?'

'Molly, you can do anything, you can achieve anything if you want it hard enough. You stood your ground in the greatest storm, against the strongest wind for your loved ones. Think about Earth and humans as your loved ones. Yes, sometimes they do stupid stuff, sometimes they don't do their jobs properly, but love them unceasingly, protect them, like you did with your immediate family. Let them do their jobs properly or badly. Try to help. If you don't accept what you give them, just let them, the given situation, or the problem go – they will learn their lesson from their own mistakes. You cannot help those who don't listen to you, because they don't embrace what you give – you don't have to help those. Then that, too, belongs to their personal paths.'

'Okay, Grandma. I was thinking about what you said to me when we were walking between those houses for a long time. I can see everything in front of me, smell the scents; I can see you, and I know that you said something, I just can't remember what.'

'Because you were really paying attention.' Molly got another kiss on her forehead. 'I said, "Learn to map out your time better." And I told you how I do it.'

'I remembered something like that, I just wasn't sure. But for some reason it was important, because I was thinking about it for months.'

'Yes, it was. You are over 30, and you still don't know how to do it properly. Think about how I did things, what example I set for you, and you'll be able to do it.'

'Yes. You are my idol. I want to be as strong as you.'

'No, sweetie. You should be much stronger. Great things await you, and I'm already really proud of you, like I always was, because I always saw the great strength and fervour in you that is necessary to achieve great things. You only have to believe in yourself. Not like you do now. Much more than this. And you have to learn to let go. You need these two things; everything else will be a walk in the park. You can believe me: you can do it. And if everything is done, when you have done your job, I'll be waiting for you here.'

'Promise?'

'Promise.'

'I would like to apologise that you couldn't be there at my university graduation ceremony. I promised, and I didn't fulfil it. I'm really ashamed.'

'I'll be with you, sweetie. When the time comes I'll be there and I'll be the proudest and happiest grandma in the world, like I already am. Because you're my little granddaughter.'

Tears streamed from Molly's eyes. She was happy and enjoyed the moment, because she knew that they would soon have to part - they could not stay like this forever.

'I'm sorry,' Noah said softly. 'We've got to go.'

Before she could say anything, her grandma kissed her forehead softly and whispered only this: 'Learn to let go, even if the parting is painful. We'll meet soon. Do your best. I'll be waiting here when the time comes.'

Molly couldn't say a word. They got up from the bench, gave each other a long hug, enjoying every single moment they had spent together.

'I love you so much, you know that?' she asked.

'I feel it. Huge difference. I love you too, sweetie.'

They let go. Molly's grandma left. She turned around once more.

'I love you, sweetie,' she whispered, then disappeared. Tears streamed from Molly's eyes. She would have preferred to run after her, but she knew she couldn't. 'You need to learn to let go' - she heard her words. So she stood silently, staring into the empty corridor.

'What's left?' she asked finally.

'The soul and the spirit,' Noah replied. 'After that I'll show you something, and then another. Or two. We'll see.'

'Okay.'

'So, the spirit is what is forever. The unit. The one. And the soul is a little vessel, with which the spirit collects and transfers information. Do you understand?'

'Of course not.'

'The point is that the soul is a little container located between the spirit and the ego. It is a sort of mediator. Takes a bit from both sides. It is necessary to note about the soul that its contract is not only for one life. It carries information through many lives. As it has experience, it knows that it's better to listen to the spirit, following its orders, but tries to pay attention to both sides, trying to pick up things from both sides. Sadly, often useless things, too. I take most of those from you. You must feel - or I hope that you feel - that you are lighter and lighter. This is because whilst we chat, whilst you learn, I'm continuously cleaning out the unnecessary things from you, those that hinder your development.'

'But why does the soul collect junk?'

'Imagine it like a game of tug-of-war. The soul is in the middle, the ego and the spirit are the contenders. A single life is a match. Yes, it is an unfair one, like a kid versus an adult... but yes. This is basically what happens. Sometimes the adult lets the rope go towards the kid a bit, letting it experience, loosens it, but not much, since rules are rules, tasks are tasks, you need to keep those, no excuses. Since the soul is somewhere in the middle, since it is only just that way, when the spirit lets the rope slide towards the kid, the soul moves that way, too. Now... there is where it collects the useless stuff. These are the things the ego experiences as the greatest of pains – since it doesn't know, doesn't understand the reason for them, only focuses on the pain - and the soul thinks that this information should be stored no matter what, that it has to learn it for a life or two. Of course, it later realises that that was stupid, but that will be too late – the information will get stuck in the soul. This is why I told you that you should never look at the consequences. Rather search for the cause, and what you have to learn from it.'

'And isn't there some sort of a soul-cleaning system?'

'There is. After your death there is a cleaning so that you won't poison your further lives with the junk, but still, you suffer through your current life with something on your back which you shouldn't have carried. I think this is enough of this topic. If you have any questions, let's hear them.'

'Actually, I don't. I get the gist of it. The ego and the body is a single use, the soul multiple, and the spirit the eternal traveller, the one, the whole.'

'Exactly,' Noah smiled. 'Now I'm going to show you two things, since when someone comes here these are that they're curious about.'

'I guess they're Hell and Heaven.'

'That's right. If you want I can show them to you.'

'Sure, why not. Is this really what people are most interested in?'

'Yes. Which one first?'

'Hell.'

'Thought so,' Noah continued, grinning. 'Come, give me your hand, and please don't let go this time. No matter what you see, or feel, don't let go of my hand under any circumstances.'

'But why? Could I get stuck there?'

'No. You don't belong there, it would eject you either way. It's just that it's not a pleasant sight. The damned souls reside there. Those who took up too much from the side of the ego.'

'So essentially Hell is the purging process?'

'That's right. You can get out of there, but only at the end of the purification process. Not a moment sooner, because we cannot trust tasks to a certain soul until it's completely clean.'

'Yes, I heard about the cleaning fire before. Does this process take a long time?'

'The duration depends on how they decide. Everyone can decide when they let the needless stuff go. The smart ones do so in their earthly lives.'

'And how do you do that?'

'You need to think through what you learned from any given situation; you have to regret and let go.'

'Forgiveness…'

'Something like that, similar principle, but still not the same. Because you cannot buy this. Nobody can release you, only you can release yourself, with an honest and pure heart. Of course, you'll receive the consequences of your actions either way, but you won't necessary get to where I'm now going to show you around. I need to say this before we go there: this will be shocking, you cannot see it for long, and you cannot let go. Or rather I won't let you go. I'm not asking if you're ready, because you cannot prepare for this sight. Come, I'll show you.'

Noah took her hand and they found themselves in front of a huge black metal door. It was rigid and cold. Even standing before it felt bad and depressing.

'Now… come, let's do this.' The door opened, and Molly instantly wanted to get away. She wanted to run, to escape. So much pain, despair, anger in that place… she could barely endure it. She had never felt such pain in her chest before. 'This is Hell, Molly. This is where the souls in need of purging go.'

'Then why don't you do so?'

'Because, as I already told you, they have to clean themselves. We can only help them, but only if they accept it.'

The souls were in a horrible state. It was dark as night everywhere, and there was mud all about. That is where the damned souls lay. A

367

horrible, barely endurable stench filled the air. Some of the souls noticed their arrival. They cursed, swore, blaming them and others for their mistakes and wrongdoings.

'Who are here?' she asked.

'Everyone who did something wrong and didn't regret their sins, or didn't learn from their committed mistakes. Thieves, burglars, murderers, those who commit suicide...'

'I thought that drug use, alcoholism, chain-smoking, and overeating or obesity was just another form of suicide. Do they also come here?'

'Yes, they do. There is no problem with these substances in small portions, only in great ones. You need to keep a limit. But this is where every harmful habit belongs; for example, shopping addiction, but the chronic kind. Basically everything belongs here that can harm you or your environment.'

'Why the shopping addiction?'

'Because you damage Earth with that. The "Buy buy buy" thing gives more work to big factories, which causes more pollution, then in the end you buy some junk that you won't even use, and when you throw it out it becomes just another piece of trash. That is why. These are not such big sins, you can "get rid of them" easily.'

'But why don't you tell them what they have to do? Maybe they would regret their sins then...'

Molly tried to approach one of the souls to help it, but Noah stopped her at the last second. A huge ball of mud flew towards her, accompanied by various insults that she should leave it alone, what did she even think? She was assaulted with hatred of such magnitude that it left her shocked.

'That's what I told you, Molly. You can only help someone if they let you.'

'And where is the cleansing fire? I cannot see it anywhere.'

'Inside. That's where you have to look for it.'

The girl tried to tear her hand away from Noah's. She couldn't just watch these souls suffering, she wanted to help them no matter what, but he didn't let her.

'Molly, don't,' he said, his voice deep as the ocean. 'This is just another form of letting go. You have to understand that you cannot help those that don't let you.'

'But at least we should try to tell them what should be done.'

'Believe me, we do tell them. They know. They just don't care. Come, let's leave this place.'

Molly didn't want to, but she knew she had to leave. She knew Noah was right, it was just that everything was so painful here, everything was so bad here that she would have done anything to help.

'You can help,' he started when they were back in the corridor. 'Now you know what the world created by the ego is like and you also know its consequences. You can save countless souls if you write, and show the way with your stories. If only a few people's lives change because of your book, if only a few people understand what they should do, they will be saved. If nothing changes… you saw where they'll get.'

'Can Earth turn into this if we don't change?'

'Yes. Sadly, it can.'

'Then we have to change.'

'That's right.'

'You know, it's interesting that harmful habits are another form of suicide.'

'They are, because you shorten your life with them. Suicide might seem an easier way, but it's not. On the contrary: you'll receive the same task in your next life, only made more difficult... and you saw where you go until your earthly life is over, since until then you have nothing to do in heaven. Regret is useless then, no matter how hard you want to make it right; you don't have a chance, not until you have served your time and you are allowed to start again.'

'I would rather not experience that.'

'I don't think so either. While you are on Earth you have the time and the possibility to change. You just need to be brave and determined. If you get stuck, because you don't see what you're doing wrong or what the correct way or solution is, just ask for help. True, your task cannot be solved, but you'll get directions from somewhere. But never forget: the task is yours, nobody else's. You cannot transfer it, but you can always ask for help, and if it's necessary you can get it too.'

'I get it.'

371

'Good.'

'And now?'

'Come, I'll show you something.'

Molly automatically raised her hand. Noah smiled.

'We walk now,' he said. 'But before that you get a picture. Think about it, imagine it.'

Molly saw herself in a beautiful, long, white dress. The top half of the dress was snug, the waist was slimmer, the bottom stretched out. It had a long tail, its sleeves were like wings. The silk material was covered by a lace topside. Molly felt like a princess in that dress.

'Where are we going? To a wedding? Who's going to be the groom?' she asked, surprised. Noah just laughed.

'Just think about it,' he said finally. 'Just imagine it.'

She did what he asked. She imagined the dress on her, and suddenly she was wearing it.

'I want this,' she said.

'You have it. This is called "attracting." This is the reward for a task completed. If you are done, you imagine what you want, and it will appear. You'll get it.'

'Really?'

'This is what I've been talking about, Molly,' Noah laughed. 'Do your job, and if you're ready, you can get everything that you want, if it is in accordance with your path. It works like this: you imagine it, you get it. Essentially, you attract it.'

'I just have to complete my real task?'

'That's correct.'

'Isn't it enough to start it, or complete half of it?'

'Half the work, half the reward.'

'How do I look?' she asked.

'You are gorgeous,' he replied.

'Wait… I'll imagine a nice hairdo and makeup for myself, too. I can't go there with unkempt hair, no matter where we go.'

'Woman…' Noah replied.

'Man!' she retorted, then imagined a long, beautiful and wavy brown hair with a moderate makeup, and they appeared instantly. 'Now… is it better like this?'

'Yes. You're beautiful. I think we should go if you are ready.'

'I don't know whether I'm ready or not because I don't know where we are headed, but I trust you, so we can go.'

Noah bowed, and extended an arm towards her.

'Your Majesty, please allow me to escort you home.'

Molly accepted the arm, took his arm, and they strolled along the corridor like a royal couple. Then they stopped before a huge door.

'Everything will be fine, don't worry,' Noah whispered.

'I feel it,' Molly replied, then quickly added: 'Huge difference.'

Noah smiled as the doors opened before them. They stepped into an enormous room. Everything was white, the walls, columns, the marble floor, the carpet under their feet – but not the blinding sort, rather the calming one. Everywhere she looked Molly saw angels, who bowed as they approached them, showing their respects. Molly felt that this whole thing was familiar, that she had seen this before, that this whole thing was completely natural to her, even though it surprised her at first.

'Welcome home, your majesty,' they said together.

'Thank you,' she said, then looked at Noah. 'I hope that wasn't meant for you,' she said. 'If yes, I thanked instead of you.'

Noah didn't answer, only smiled.

They walked on until they reached the thrones. They stopped in front of them. Noah turned to Molly.

'Welcome home, Your Majesty,' he said. 'Please take the place that is yours, even if only for a brief time.'

'Noah, stop playing games with me, please. What's this all about?'

'Your home, your place.'

'Mine?'

'Yes, yours. You have to feel it, even if you don't believe it. Thirty years ago, you decided that you would go down to Earth to clean up the mess. Now sit down, please.'

'Is this for real?'

'Yes, it is. Everything is here for you to know who you are, what a huge task awaits you, what an enormous responsibility it is, and that you can do it.'

'This is shocking.'

'I know. But let's do this now.'

Molly looked at the thrones, then sat down in one of them.

'Whose is the other one?' she asked.

'You'll know when it's time,' she got the answer.

The angels cheered and applauded her. They danced, and the celebration began, since their queen had returned, even if only for a short time. Molly accepted the celebration graciously. Noah was really proud of her, because she did so without the faintest feeling of arrogance. Others could feel this too: 'She's the same as she was, she hasn't changed a bit,' they whispered to each other. Everyone was happy, so Molly was, too.

It is uncertain how long the celebration lasted, but that wasn't really important. Molly and Noah enjoyed their well-deserved rest, since the recent period had been trying for both of them. When finally they were alone in the throne room, the man looked at her queen. Their eyes were filled with sadness. They didn't try to conceal it, knowing it would be useless. They just looked at each other, since they knew it was time to say goodbye.

'Let's go then,' she said finally.

'You are stronger than me,' Noah said.

'You know that isn't true. There's just no point in waiting any longer. Let's discuss what will come next, what I have to know. Will I remember everything we have experienced here?'

'You'll remember everything. The first step for you is to write, then comes the rest. Everything in its due time.'

'I understand. And now? Did we discuss everything, or did we leave something out?'

'I don't know. I think not.'

'I don't think anybody thought that I would have such a big task ahead of me. Not me, that's for sure. Me, the silent, introverted country girl...'

'You'll notice that the weakest-looking are the strongest, because those who seem weak can fight, while the strong only boast, more bark than bite. You'll notice that the ones with a loud voice will get along for a while, will be able to attract those who want things, and they will want to stomp on the smaller ones, just to prove their own greatness – but this doesn't last forever. The little ones break out, but not because they find their loud voice. No. They do their jobs with faith, pure heart, and with perseverance, even against the strongest headwind. This is why they become the greatest. And the best part is that they won't forget where they came from or who they were when they reach the top. They can stay the same people they were. Humble and kind.'

'I'll try to remain that.'

'You don't have to try. I know perfectly well that you can stay the same you were and are.'

'I promise. You know what came to my mind? The swan couple and their cygnets. You told me there that nature is a great teacher. I'm starting to understand what you meant back there.'

'Yes. When you arrived here, you were the little cygnet, an uncut diamond, who became majestic by the end. You had the potential back then, too, you just didn't believe in yourself enough.'

'You may be right.'

'I am.'

Then they just stared at each other again. They tried to postpone the departure, but they both knew they couldn't.

'We need to go, Noah,' Molly said finally.

'Yes, I know.'

Noah bowed and extended his arm toward Molly.

'My Queen, I'd like to escort you back.'

'The pleasure is mine,' came the reply. She got up from her throne and took his hand. She tried to stay strong, but her eyes were full of tears. She knew this was going to be their last trip together for a long time.

'Now you do it,' Noah whispered.

She closed her eyes and thought about her body lying on the hospital bed, and at that moment they appeared there. Molly saw herself, machines plugged into her, she saw John sitting on the side of the bad, praying, making promises about what he would do if he got her back. Molly was touched.

'He really loves you,' Noah said. 'You see and feel how much. Never rush him. Give him time so that he can deal with his own issues, to think about what he wants. You just do your job. He will be with you, even when you feel that he isn't. Just like I will. Never forget: you're never alone. You need to have faith in yourself and in us. Do your job, let everything new in, don't doubt, don't criticise. Everything always happens exactly the way and exactly when it should happen. If you don't doubt and criticise, if you keep going, no matter how hard it is, without little detours, then you'll achieve great things with your helpers. Follow the signs; if you get stuck, ask for help.'

'Sure thing.'

Molly tried to fight back her tears, but she couldn't. Noah pulled her to himself and they closed in a tight embrace.

'I can't tell how much I love you. You know, right?' he asked.

'I feel it. Huge difference,' she said.

Molly felt strange. Her body was heavy, she felt pain and stinging in her arms. She tried to open her eyes but for some reason she couldn't. Even though she felt it, it didn't happen.

'Don't feel, but want it,' she heard somewhere. An inner voice whispered to her. She wanted and she could.

'Molly!' John's voice was trembling, even though he tried to hide it. 'Finally, you're back. You scared me so much, Little Girl! Don't ever do this again. Promise me that you won't do this again!'

'I promise,' she whispered. She could barely make a sound.

'This was the longest two hours of my life. I thought I was going to lose you.'

'You won't, don't worry, you're not that lucky.'

'Stop messing with me, woman. You scare me to death, fall into a coma, you wake up and then joke around?'

'Yes.'

At this time an army of doctors and nurses came into the room. They examined and questioned the girl to check if everything was all right, or if her brain had suffered any kind permanent damage because of the heart failure. They found everything to be okay.

'Everything's going to be fine now. It's over,' John said when they were finally alone.

'You're wrong,' she answered. 'It's just beginning.'

Printed in Poland
by Amazon Fulfillment
Poland Sp. z o.o., Wrocław

58105907R00228